"You have a way with the polka, Reeve."

He dipped her backward, sideways, and quick-stepped her about to the tinkling tune. At times, his broad hand slid up her back. Once and again he drew her forward so that her apron's bodice grazed his plaid shirt.

Still, the most intimate step of the promenade was when he held her at arm's length and simply gazed into her eyes.

A meeting of bodies was tantalizing, but a meeting of souls...well, that was spellbinding.

Was she a fool to be drawn in when there was no future for them?

* * *

Outlaw Hunter

Harlequin® Historical #1211—December 2014

Author Note

When I typed 'The End' on *Rebel Outlaw* I kissed the characters goodbye and sent them off to my editor. Story over. To my surprise, there was one character who kept tapping me on the shoulder because her story, she assured me, had only begun. Kidnapped bride, Hattie Travers (now known as Melody Dawson), had a good bit to say about her future...and not hers alone, but also that of Reeve Prentis, the US marshal who had agreed to escort her and her children home after the outlaw ranch where they lived was burned to the ground. Hattie wanted her happily-ever-after, and she wanted it with Reeve. It was a pleasure to be able to give her that. I hope you enjoy Hattie and Reeve's tale, where love heals mistakes of the past and anchors the foundation for the joyful future that Hattie requested.

Best wishes and happy reading.

CAROL ARENS

OUTLAW HUNTER

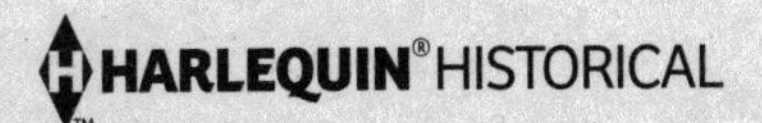

ISBN-13: 978-0-373-29811-2

Outlaw Hunter

This edition published by arrangement with Harlequin Books S.A.

For questions and comments about the quality of this book, please contact us at CustomerService@Harlequin.com.

HARLEQUIN®
www.Harlequin.com

Printed in U.S.A.

Available from Harlequin® Historical and CAROL ARENS

CAROL ARENS

Scandal at the Cahill Saloon #1071
Renegade Most Wanted #1095
Rebel with a Cause #1119
Christmas Cowboy Kisses #1155
"A Christmas Miracle"
Rebel with a Heart #1160
***Rebel Outlaw* #1191
***Outlaw Hunter* #1211

*Part of the Cahill Cowboys continuity
**linked by character

To my sister, Nancy.
Of all the special gifts Mom and Dad had to give,
I cherish you the most.

CAROL ARENS

While in the third grade, Carol Arens had a teacher who noted that she ought to spend less time daydreaming and looking out the window and more time on her sums. Today, Carol spends as little time on sums as possible. Daydreaming about plots and characters is still far more interesting to her.

As a young girl, she read books by the dozen. She dreamed that one day she would write a book of her own. A few years later, Carol set her sights on a new dream. She wanted to be the mother of four children. She was blessed with a son, then three daughters. While raising them she never forgot her goal of becoming a writer. When her last child went to high school she purchased a big old clunky word processor and began to type out a story.

She joined Romance Writers of America, where she met generous authors who taught her the craft of writing a romance novel. With the knowledge she gained, she sold her first book and saw her lifelong dream come true.

Carol lives with her real-life hero husband, Rick, in Southern California, where she was born and raised. She feels blessed to be doing what she loves, with all her children and a growing number of perfect and delightful grandchildren living only a few miles from her front door.

When she is not writing, reading or playing with her grandchildren, Carol loves making trips to the local nursery. She delights in scanning the rows of flowers, envisaging which pretty plants will best brighten her garden.

She enjoys hearing from readers and invites you to contact her at carolsarens@yahoo.com.

Chapter One

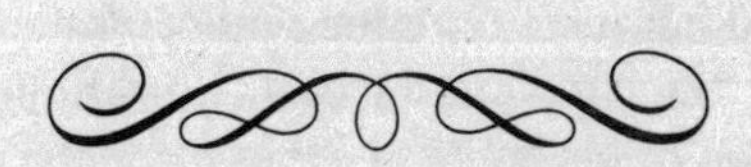

The Badlands, Nebraska

Hattie Travers had dreamed of her husband again last night. The fact that he had been dead for eight months didn't make her any less fearful of him.

Even in the cold light of morning, with the children safe in the buckboard with her, his ghost had the power to put her into a cold sweat.

"Go away," she whispered to the wicked-eyed vision haunting her mind.

She focused her attention on the US marshal sitting tall on his rum-colored horse, leading her, her children and the ranch orphans away from the cindered ruins of the Broken Brand Ranch.

The marshal's carriage was straight, his shoulders broad and, from what she had seen so far, his honor incorruptible.

She owed him a great deal…her life, really, and more than that, her children's lives.

If only she could take a deep cleansing breath and

purge the stench of the outlaw ranch from her soul. If she could just relax and trust the marshal, but she had been wrong about a man before.

The marshal turned his head, peering out from under his Stetson at the flat, dry land, scanning it from horizon to horizon. His eyes were the only bit of green that she had seen in nearly three years.

He held her gaze for a long moment then nodded and set his face toward the east…toward home. The regular clop of his horse's hooves made the fringe on his buckskin shirt dance and sway.

"You reckon he's looking for stray Traverses?" Beside her, thirteen-year-old Joe Landon gripped the team's reins in his fists. He sat tall, imitating the lawman's erect posture.

Joe had to be cold but he didn't shiver. The marshal didn't, so he wouldn't, either. It was chilly, though, even with the sun coming up over the ragged land.

"You shouldn't worry, Joe." She held her baby tighter, trying to follow her own advice. "Marshal Prentis will have us well away from here before any of them show up. The ranch is gone forever. Colt Wesson saw to that when he burned it down."

Joe touched something in the pocket of his pants, tracing its shape with his thumb.

"There's only Uncle Jack and Cousin Dwayne to worry about," fifteen-year-old Libby said, clutching her little sister, Pansy, close for the warmth. She glanced toward the back of the wagon then suddenly lunged. "Come back here, you little wild man!"

Libby latched on to Flynn's collar and hauled the toddler back from the edge of the buckboard.

"Noooo!" Flynn went limp-boned then kicked his heels. "Mama!"

"I'll trade you my sweet baby Seth for my wild thing, Libby."

"Are you sure your folks are going to welcome us?" Libby asked, taking the infant from Hattie.

Flynn rushed to fill his little brother's place. Hattie hugged him close and kissed his cold, red nose.

Sometimes she wished she had never met Ram Travers. He had ruined her life. Without him, though, she would not have had her sweet babies. It was a trade she would make again in a heartbeat.

"With open arms and a big, hearty meal," she answered Libby. "My folks have a huge old house and too many empty rooms."

The one thing she knew for certain in this world was that her parents would welcome her home. They would weep for joy over their new grandsons and would take in Joe, Libby and Pansy as if they had been waiting for them all their lives.

Mama and Papa had always longed for more children, but after she was born, they hadn't been blessed again.

"You sure you remember the way back?" Joe asked. "Uncle Ram kidnapped you to the ranch a long time ago."

"There's something about the road home that stays etched in your heart," she said, ruffling Flynn's hair.

"The Broken Brand won't stay etched in my heart." Joe's fingers turned white, his grip around the reins tight with tension. "I'm never looking back, not even giving it a minute of my thoughts."

"It's a lucky thing for Pansy that Colt Wesson and the marshal rescued us in time that she won't remember the place," Libby said.

"Colt gave me something. It was when he was here to bury Pappy Travers. Reckon he sensed I didn't hanker to be an outlaw like the rest of them. He asked if I wanted to leave with him. Couldn't, though; there was more than myself to consider. So he gave me this." Joe reached into his pocket and withdrew a small, sheathed knife. It was a pretty thing for a weapon, with an ornate handle bearing the initials CWT.

He held it in his hand for a moment, balancing the weight, then he put it back in his pocket.

"Thank you for staying, Joe," she said with a lump swelling in her throat. "I'm certain that the marshal is competent, but you never can tell when another man might be needed."

For all that Joe wanted to be a man, to keep everyone safe, he was still a boy. She wasn't surprised to see relief wash through his posture, believing that she trusted Marshal Prentis.

Hattie took baby Seth back from Libby, who hugged the lapels of a deputy's coat tight around her chest. Last night, before the deputies had begun the journey to take the captured Travers gang to jail, the marshal had strongly urged each of his men to donate their coats to the children.

Not one of them objected with so much as a frown. Apparently, Marshal Prentis's word was law.

She lifted her gaze from her son's soft, sand-colored curls to look, once again, at their leader. As big as he was, he ought to have been frightening, but somehow, he wasn't. She felt safe in his presence, which was disturbing because there had been a time when Ram made her feel the same way.

Whether she fully trusted Marshal Prentis, or not, their fates were in his hands for the time being.

With the outlaw ranch a heap of smoking embers, she had been offered the choice of going with Colt Travers and his lady, Holly Jane, to begin a new life in some friendly place, or going home to her parents.

There had been no choice, really. She had longed for home ever since she'd run away from it. She had wept for her mother's soothing embrace on more nights than she could count. A sun hadn't set that she hadn't watched for her father to come riding over the hill, even though he had no idea where she had gone—or why.

So, with the burden of five children's safety on her shoulders, she had, once again, chosen to trust a man she didn't know, to let him lead her across land so rough that, left on her own, it would eat her alive—her and the young ones with her.

One thing was certain, they could not be worse off than they had been at the Broken Brand, where food was scarce and degenerates plentiful.

The big lawman riding ahead of the wagon peered out from under his hat, scanning the land for danger. He didn't seem like a degenerate.

Indeed, he was a United States marshal, appointed by the president himself.

Ram had been a false charmer, appointed to bring home a bride by no one but his own twisted kin.

For all of their sakes, she hoped that the president's judgment was sound.

* * *

Reeve had pushed the widow hard, leading her and the children over inhospitable ground. The sooner they were away from this snake-infested, bone-dry land, the safer they would be.

He couldn't recall ever seeing a place so barren, and he'd traveled over some of the sorriest country there was. It was no wonder the Travers gang had gotten away with their crimes for so long. The local law was more than a few days' ride from the Broken Brand. They weren't likely to leave their towns undefended for the time it would take to travel here.

Reeve had only heard of the outlaw family when one of their own turned on them.

Had it not been for Colt Travers wanting to rescue his woman, whom they had kidnapped, the gang would still be committing crimes.

Colt had demanded his conditions, though, for turning on his own. He wanted to be the one to burn the place to the ground, and he wanted to do it before the arrests were made.

That wasn't the way Reeve liked to do things. There was an order to be followed, first the arrest then the justice.

It rankled to let Travers do it his way, but Reeve wanted those criminals. There had been no choice but to play Travers's game.

It had been plain good luck that a man armed only with a long knife had been able to best that nest of vipers. The only reason Reeve had agreed to hold back until he saw the smoke was because the outlaws were Travers's kin.

In spite of his misgivings, things had worked out. The outlaws were on their way to prison and the innocent on their way home.

He'd pushed his charges hard because the farther east of here he got them, the safer they would be.

The woman, especially. She looked worn to the bone...bone that he could nearly see through the thin cotton of her dress.

He figured she wasn't as old as she looked, but he couldn't be sure. With water out here as scarce as anything green, he doubted that she'd bathed in some time. Dirt coated her lank hair and dusted her face as it did the ground.

Even her expression seemed defeated.

Watching her sitting on the wagon bench with her wriggling son Flynn clutched in one arm while trying to soothe her infant in the other, he wished they could stop for an hour, to let the young ones stretch and play.

Six rattlers and several scorpions creeping over the ground, and all within the last mile, convinced him to press on to safer territory.

He couldn't help but admire Hattie Travers, though. As haggard as she appeared, the woman had backbone. They'd been in the wagon for nine hours and he'd yet to hear her complain or speak harshly to the children.

What had she been like, he wondered, before she had become the unwilling bride of Ram Travers?

Her eyes might have sparkled instead of looking lined and defeated, as they did now. They might have been fire-warmed amber instead of muddy brown.

What Ram Travers had done to her was a crime. Reeve was half-sorry that the man had already faced the Ultimate Judge. It would have given him a good deal of pleasure to haul that lawbreaker before an earthly judge and have his sorry ass slammed into jail.

At least that miserable family wouldn't continue their practice of kidnapping brides. By now the deputies would have the criminals halfway to their jail cells to await trial. In a few more days the men would begin rounding up the two who hadn't been at home when Colt Travers served up his justice.

He escorted the wagon east for another hour before Hattie Travers called his name.

He turned in his saddle. "Yes, ma'am?"

"The children need a break from the travel." With Flynn climbing her shoulder as if his mother was a ladder, Hattie looked small, frailer even than when they had begun the journey this morning.

"Give me a few minutes to check the area." He didn't like making the stop, but he could see that it was necessary. "We'll take ten minutes."

"Thank you, Marshal," she said, and he watched the relief roll through her in a wave.

It took twenty minutes to make sure the ground was free of snakes and other creeping dangers. When he was assured that it was clear for a hundred feet all around, he waved his arm, a signal that all was safe.

Joe leaped from the wagon with a whoop, and Hattie climbed down with a suppressed groan.

The ladies led Pansy and Flynn several yards away to take care of their needs. He and Joe walked in the opposite direction to do the same. Since there was no privacy to be had, he kept his eyes averted from the women and he reckoned they did the same.

A few moments later, Hattie strode toward him, her back bent with hours of holding her infant.

She could only be five feet three inches to his six foot four, so she had to look up and shade her eyes from the sun's glare in order to see his face.

He reckoned he looked as shaggy as an old bear, having been on the trail for a month or more. He'd lost count of the days.

"I haven't had time to thank you, Marshal Prentis, for bringing us home. I'm grateful as can be." She shifted the baby in her arms. "I'm sure you have more pressing things to do."

"No need for thanks, ma'am." He reached for the infant. "Do you mind?"

She hesitated, but not overlong. He snuggled tiny Seth in the crook of one arm and watched while his mother worked the aches out of her back. She twisted from side to side, then front to back. He couldn't recall seeing her without one child or another in her arms since he met her yesterday morning.

"You reckon Flynn would like to ride with me for a while when we start up?"

She smiled up at him. Under her cracked, dry lips, her teeth were straight and white. He was just noticing a spark of animation in her eyes when Libby screamed.

"Mad dog!" the girl shouted, shrill and panicked. "Mad dog!"

It wasn't a dog, but a coyote and as mad as they came. Its wild eyes settled on Flynn. Bandy-legged, it wobbled toward the boy, the foam coating its muzzle a sure sign of disease.

* * *

"Flynn!" Hattie screeched. She locked her knees so that panic wouldn't knock her to the ground.

The marshal shoved Seth into her arms, then ran, eating up the ground in long powerful strides.

She raced behind. The breath wheezed in and out of her lungs. Her side cramped, but she was too frightened to care.

Somewhere along the way she shoved Seth at Libby. She shut out every thought but grabbing her son away from the coyote, who was one deadly leap away from him.

Dimly, she registered that the wagon horses pranced, nervous in the confinement of their tack. The marshal's horse stood still, his ears pointed toward the danger but his training keeping him in place.

She wouldn't make it in time. Not even the marshal, with a thirty-foot lead, would make it.

The beast, ravaged and skinny, hunched his legs for the jump.

She stopped and snatched up a rock. She wouldn't be able to halt the animal, but maybe she could distract his attention for the seconds Marshal Prentis needed to reach Flynn.

She pitched the rock. Joe saw her and did the same, firing stone after stone in the coyote's direction.

They might as well have been hurling feathers. The beast's full attention was riveted on Flynn.

"Mama!" Flynn cried. He backed up, then he turned to run.

The coyote lunged. She screamed.

Marshal Prentis dove. Midair, he drew his gun. He snagged Flynn about the waist.

A shot exploded.

Dust clouded the ground where the marshal rolled with her son tucked close to his belly.

The coyote was propelled backward by the blast. It crumpled to the earth, a lifeless mound of filthy fur. A few feet away the marshal hovered over Flynn, clearly offering himself as a shield in case the shot had missed.

Hysteria and relief gripped her at the same time. She wanted to collapse where she stood, to cover her face with her hands and sob. Her little wild man had come within inches of death.

Even though the danger had passed, fear pumped her heart hard.

What if Libby had spotted the coyote a few seconds later? What if the marshal hadn't been a quick runner? What if his shot had missed? What if he hadn't been willing to shield Flynn with his own body?

She wasn't sure she would ever purge this nightmare from her heart.

As much as she needed a moment to give in to her emotions, she couldn't.

Flynn sobbed, "Mama! Mama!" Even the big solid hand of Marshal Prentis stroking his back could not calm him.

It did calm her, though, enough that her knees didn't give out as she dashed forward. She plucked Flynn from the strong hands reassuring him, then pressed his small head to her breast.

She cooed over him for a moment, until his sobs turned to hiccups.

When she finally looked up, she saw Libby standing in the buckboard, hugging Seth to her chest and clutching Pansy's hand tight.

Joe bent over the coyote, the marshal beside him.

"Got him straight between the eyes!" Joe said.

"Poor beast." Marshal Prentis put his hand on Joe's shoulder.

Hattie heard him talking to the boy while they returned to the wagon. "We'll need to be on our way, and in a hurry. Coyotes stay in their packs even when they're mad. Could be more of them."

"Yes, sir. I'll do the driving so Hattie can tend to the little ones."

Joe scrambled into the wagon.

Marshal Prentis slipped his wide hand under her elbow to help her up.

"We'll need to travel late, get as far clear of here as we can," he told her. Behind his back the sun had begun to set. "It'll be rough travel for a while. We'll have to sleep in the wagon tonight."

That suited her fine. She was not about to allow any of the children on the ground until they were far away from this horrible, barren of anything gentle, land.

The marshal turned toward his horse. She tapped the shoulder of his buckskin shirt, halting him. He looked back, and up. For the first time she noticed how handsome he was, with a bold, square jaw dimpled with a slight cleft.

He clutched his hat in his hand, showing off hair that was very dark. Nearly but not quite black, it grew in close-cropped waves about his face.

In another lifetime she would have flirted with him.

The young woman she had been before Ram would be dreaming of his kiss.

It was just as well that Ram had laid that girl to rest. She was a mother of two now…a guardian for three more. There was scarcely enough time to breathe, let alone go soft over a handsome face.

Hattie had been asleep in the wagon bed for only an hour when she woke suddenly. She tried to stifle her gasp but it escaped before she could call it back.

She willed her heartbeat to still. By breathing slowly, she pushed back the panic.

The jab to her back had been inadvertent, only someone's knee. Sudden movements in the night still terrified her. How long, she wondered, would it take before she could truly put her memories behind her?

Fortunately, her outburst hadn't wakened the children. Carefully, she moved Flynn away from where he had curled his small self against her bosom. She sat up slowly, dislodging Libby's knee from her spine.

She groaned under her breath, stretching and easing the aches from her muscles. Sleeping on the hard wagon bed without enough room to turn was difficult.

But it was a difficulty she blessed with every heartbeat.

Anyplace, no matter how barren or dangerous, was preferable to the Broken Brand.

"Mrs. Travers, is something wrong?"

The marshal appeared at the side of the wagon, a frown creasing his brow and his breath puffing white in the cold. She couldn't see lower than his chest, but from the position of his right arm, she guessed that he had his hand on his gun.

It alarmed her that he slept wearing his weapon. Perhaps he expected another mad animal to appear out of the dark. If so, he should not be sleeping on the ground under the wagon.

"I just need to get up and walk for a few minutes."

"I'd advise against it, ma'am."

So would she, but just the same she stood, careful not to wake anyone with her stiff-jointed maneuvers.

The marshal helped her down from the wagon with one hand under her elbow and another at her waist. She forced herself not to cringe.

A man's touch was not something that she welcomed. Sadly, that was one more thing that Ram had ruined for her.

Perhaps with time that aversion would ease. She prayed that her dead husband had not cursed her soul forever.

He let go of her as soon as her feet were solid on the ground, and she took a quick step away.

She looked up at him. He hadn't been sleeping with his hat on. The moon shone full on his face.

As handsome as it was, it made her nervous to make eye contact. It was just the two of them with the night so dark and still…and he was such a large man.

She walked in a circle about the wagon, stretching and breathing deeply. Her footsteps crunched soil and broke dried twigs. The marshal walked beside her with one hand at his waist.

As much as he tried to disguise his stance, he was ready to reach for his gun at the slightest sign of danger. It was kind of him not to want to frighten her by touching the weapon directly.

Kindness in a man was not something she was used to. She wished she could relax and trust that a man of the law would behave with honor.

He had certainly given her no reason to believe that he would not. He had saved her son's life at the risk of his own. What further proof did she need of his high standards?

Unfortunately, what she believed and what she felt were not in alignment.

Curse you, Ram, she thought, but then, no… She cursed herself for allowing him into her life.

"Are you hungry?" Marshal Prentis asked. "I've got a bit of jerky in my saddle."

Yes, she was! Hungry for food and hungry for a new life.

"No, but thank you. I'll do." The last thing she would do is take food that the children might eat.

"Come with me, but walk close, Mrs. Travers."

Because he touched his gun while staring into the shadows, she did. Danger lay beyond the wagon.

Safety, she reminded herself, lay with the marshal.

He led her to where the horses were tethered. His saddle packs lay on the ground beside them. He lifted a leather flap, drew something out.

He escorted her back to the wagon, then with a nod of his head he indicated that she should sit under it. Because she was not ready to climb back into the cramped confines of the wagon bed, she did.

After a long, hard look at the surrounding area, the

marshal crawled under and sat down across from her, his feet crossed at the ankle and his knees spread.

The fringe on the arms of his buckskin shirt swayed in the wind that shot up suddenly from the south.

"You need to eat," he stated and pressed a slice of dried meat into her hand.

To satisfy him she took a bite. It was tough but surprisingly tasty.

"I'll save the rest for the children."

"No need…I'll hunt some game in the morning." In the dark shadow under the wagon he frowned. "I won't let the young ones go hungry. Trust me, Mrs. Travers."

And didn't she want to? If ever she'd met someone who deserved trust, it was this man.

Perhaps her hungry days were over. Because of the marshal, she was going home. Once she got there she would never be hungry again…and neither would anyone who belonged to her.

She chewed on another bite of the jerky. The marshal sat silently watching her.

Strangely, she didn't mind.

On the morning of the third day, Hattie spotted a tree in the distance. It grew alone on the top of a hill, its bare branches reaching toward the bright blue sky.

She had always loved trees, and it had been three years since she had seen one. It didn't matter that this one's leaves had gone for the winter. They would come back in the spring, green and full of life.

Maybe, she would do the same.

Just now, her spirit felt a hundred years old, but once she was back home, in the circle of her parents' love, spring might come again for her. The dismal pall that Ram had cast over her life would lift.

"You always told us that trees were green and shady, Hattie." Sitting beside her on the wagon bench, Joe frowned at the tree on the hill. "That looks like a bunch of sticks."

"Didn't you read the books that Great-Aunt Tillie told you to?" Libby asked. "Some were all about trees. They go dormant in the winter."

"Well, except for the evergreens." Joe turned to glance at Libby sitting in the back of the wagon. "I miss Aunt Tillie and Granny Rose. Things got worse at the Broken Brand when they went away."

"They were better off with Colt Wesson," Hattie reminded them, but Joe was right. Aunt Tillie had kept everyone in line, as much as was possible, with her firm spirit and her cane. She'd taught the ranch children to read even though their parents considered it a waste of time.

Hattie had cried for days when Colt Wesson had come home the first time, to bury Pappy Travers and bring the old ladies to their new home.

Maybe she ought to have asked to go with them, but Colt was a stranger to her, and she had been full-term with Seth.

Well, the past was the past. She would do her best to put it behind her. Ram was dead…and Mama and Papa were getting closer each day.

Soon their comforting arms would fold her up.

"I want to see me a leaf…grass, too." Joe watched Marshal Prentis sitting tall in the saddle, trotting toward the wagon. "Do your folks really have shade all over the place?"

"Shade and a creek nearby."

"I reckon I'll need to learn to swim."

A memory flashed in her mind and she nearly wept with the joy of it. Daddy, years ago when she wasn't much older than Flynn, carrying her into the water and showing her how to waggle her arms and legs so that she wouldn't sink.

It must have grieved him terribly when she ran off without a word. She would die of a broken heart if one of her boys grew up and did the same to her.

Her parents would forgive her—she knew it without a doubt—but how would she ever make it up to them?

Filling their home with children would be a start. At least she was coming home with more than her own sinful self.

"Come summer, you'll all learn to swim."

Imagining it, picturing the children in her mind while they splashed and laughed, made her smile.

Joy tickled her heart. She hadn't felt that optimistic spirit in a good long while. "My daddy will enjoy showing you how."

"If he takes to an outlaw's brat." Joe chewed his bottom lip, staring down at his knees. "He might toss me out."

"Look at me, Joe." She tipped his face up, his chin tucked between her fingers. Cold sunshine illuminated a dusting of blond fuzz on his upper lip. "What your daddy was or wasn't has nothing to do with you. You are a good boy and someday you'll be a fine man. My daddy will recognize that and be proud to have you in his home."

Thank the Good Lord that Marshal Prentis had come along before the Travers men had turned Joe into an outlaw. At thirteen years old, he had already become proficient at shooting a gun. Next month he would have been included in a holdup or a bank robbery.

The marshal reached the wagon, then turned his horse to trot beside it.

"There's a place I'd like you and the children to see. It's a few hours out of the way but worth it. We'll stop there for the night. If the weather's not too cold we won't have to sleep in the wagon."

His voice sounded deep and smooth. It made her think of fertile soil, tilled and ready for gardening, or a hearth fire banked low but still sending warmth into the night.

Somehow, with all that had happened over the past few days, she hadn't noticed the rich timbre of his voice.

She noticed it now because it stirred something in her. A little finger of hope tickled her insides, faintly, as though wondering if it was safe to come out.

When she thought about it, it had not been days, but years since she had felt joy over common things, like a bare tree or a deep, masculine voice.

There had been joy over her babies, of course, along with a great deal of worry about their futures. Loving them, and the fact that they needed her, was what had kept her going during the dismal days at the ranch. For their sakes she had kept on, singing when she wanted to weep and smiling when there was only anxiety behind it.

"I know I've said it before, Marshal, but it deserves repeating…I thank you…we all do."

The marshal didn't seem to be a man who filled empty space with words. When he said something, though, folks listened.

She listened now, hoping that he wouldn't answer with only a dip of his hat. Now that she was aware of the husky, virile tone of his voice, she wanted to hear it again.

"No need for thanks, Mrs. Travers."

Mrs. Travers. She wanted to spit.

Even when spoken in his wonderful voice and delivered with a slightly lopsided, completely handsome smile, she hated that name.

Curse it, if her boys would carry it.

Steam curled into the frosty night air. After seven hours of camping near the hot spring, Hattie still could not believe that heated water bubbled right out of the earth.

It was as close to a natural miracle as she could imagine.

And all around it, there were woods! Sitting beside the campfire, she peered up through the bare branches, watching the show of stars creep slowly across the sky.

Even though it was cold on the ground, it was a relief to be out of the wagon, where nights had been spent dodging elbows and pushing away invading knees.

The Broken Brand was a world away from this magical place. If only she could bathe in the spring, let the hot water cleanse away the dust clinging to her, she might be able to put the past to rest.

Of course, there hadn't been time for bathing, or the proper privacy. Truly, she couldn't possibly strip down to her skin with the marshal close by.

While there was no doubt that he was brave and self-sacrificing, he was still a man. From her own pitiful experience, she had discovered that men took what they wanted. A woman's body was his to do with as he pleased, especially when the woman was his wife.

Oh, but the simmering water of the spring did call to her.

She glanced over to the far side of the campfire. Libby, wrapped up in a coat with Pansy, slept deep and sound. A foot away, Joe slumbered with his face toward the sky as though he had fallen asleep gazing at the branches scratching against each other in the breeze. Flynn slept in the wagon to insure he wouldn't wander during the night.

Marshal Prentis sat with his back propped against a tree and his rifle across his lap. She couldn't see his eyes because his Stetson was tugged over them. Judging by the slow even pace of his breathing, he was asleep, too.

She stood up quietly, tucking the coat around Seth and making sure the pocket of warm air surrounding him didn't leak out.

After a brief peek into the buckboard to make sure Flynn was covered, she made her way toward the spring.

Fifty feet away from the campfire, she sat down on a large rock beside the water, listening to the peace of the night.

The surface of the water moved with the warm current, the breeze shuffled through the tree branches and the fire crackled. Someone began to snore. She thought it was Joe.

Now was the time to shed her filthy gown, step through the warm mist and slide down into the water. She couldn't, of course, not with Seth nuzzling his warm little head on her breast.

That didn't keep her from imagining how it would be, though. First the warmth would kiss her toes, then it would ease the chill out of her calves.

She would sigh at the pleasure of it.

"Go ahead, Mrs. Travers." She heard the marshal's footsteps crunching the dirt close behind her. "I'll hold the baby while you soak for a bit."

It wouldn't be proper, undressing in front of him and sinking blissfully into the water. She shouldn't even consider it. Putting aside propriety was what had landed her at the Broken Brand in the first place, a prisoner of Ram.

"I thank you for the offer, but…" She shrugged and shook her head, wishing with all her heart that she could say yes.

"I won't drop him." She might, though, if he came any closer with that smooth-sounding voice. "I have three younger sisters, and nieces, too, if that puts you at ease."

"It's not that. Mercy, you wedged yourself between Flynn and that mad coyote. I'm sure you won't drop Seth."

"Like I said, I have three younger sisters. I'll turn my back."

"I don't think—"

"Keep him wrapped in the coat when you take it

off so he doesn't get chilled." He reached out his arms, waiting for her to hand over Seth. Moonlight caught the glow of his badge where it formed a circle over his heart. "I'll turn my back while you decide what to do."

It wouldn't hurt to do that much. She could pretend to consider the offer for a moment then carry Seth back to the fire.

Wriggling out of the coat, she handed him the baby. He turned around. Behind her, she swore she heard the bubbling water call her name. There would be nothing wrong with taking off her boots and her stockings. That could be modestly done beneath her skirt.

At least her feet would be clean.

"Where does your family live?" she asked to make polite conversation.

"Indiana."

She sat on the rock, dangling her feet into the pool. Warmth caressed her toes. It hugged her ankles. Wouldn't it be pure heaven to feel it all over her body?

She turned to glance behind at the marshal. His back was still to her. So far he had kept his word. His broad, leather-clad shoulders tipped side to side, rocking her baby.

Ram had never rocked Flynn.

"How old are your sisters?" she asked, staring regretfully at the water.

All she had to do was unbutton her dress, step out of her underclothes and slip down into the warmth. It would take ten seconds.

"Sarah's twenty-five and filling her house up with babies. Next there's Delilah—she's twenty-three and a schoolteacher. Last is Mildred—she's only seventeen and full of the dickens."

She flicked the water with her toes. The spray caught a glimmer of the full moon before it drifted back into the pool.

"They must have adored their big brother."

She would have, had she had one.

"Bedeviled is more like it. Go in the spring, Mrs. Travers, I'll keep watch over the young ones."

She stared at the water for another moment, watching the churning surface reflect the silver globe of the moon, which shone directly overhead.

"Thank you, Marshal," she said, then stripped off the filthy rags that passed for clothes.

She glided off the rock slowly, submerging her knees then savoring the tickle of the warm water where it kissed away the cold air pebbling her thighs. Her nipples puckered with the chill but she didn't hurry.

This was a moment to savor. Inch by inch she slipped under, the warm water touching her like a pair of tender hands. It slid over her bottom and up her hips; it rushed up her ribs and washed over her back. She felt the tingle in her breasts, which meant that her milk was letting down. She pressed her forearms across her chest to stop it, then went down, down and down, until every last strand of her hair went under.

She held her breath, feeling the grime lift from her skin. She rubbed her arms and her belly before she broke the surface of the water for air.

Her toes touched the smooth stones at the bottom of the pool. She lifted her legs then floated for a moment, nearly euphoric at the sense of weightlessness.

She filled her lungs and ducked under again.

This time she swished her hair and rubbed her scalp, watching while the strands floated back and forth before her face in the moonlit water.

She pushed up for another breath then sank down until her bottom rested on the warm stones. Water pulsed against her gently, wiping away all traces of the Broken Brand.

In her mind she imagined every place that Ram had handled her. The water erased the residue of his touch…washed him from her body and her mind.

Her husband was dead. He had no power over her.

She pushed up slowly, feeling energy pulse through her thighs. Hattie Travers was gone, left at the bottom of the pool to dissolve along with Ram.

She broke the surface, grinning.

Marshal Prentis didn't pivot, even though he must have heard the water. The sway of his hips and his shoulders rocking Seth didn't falter.

Perhaps she shouldn't compare all men to her dead husband. It seemed that, maybe, Marshal Prentis was a man to be trusted.

It wasn't his fault that her judging ability was faulty where the male species was concerned.

As soon as the warmth of the pool faded from her skin she began to shiver.

This was a predicament. She couldn't put on her dress until she dried off.

All of a sudden the marshal flung out his arm. A blanket hung from his fist. Still, he held true to his word and didn't turn, even though he knew she stood only feet behind him, wet, naked and utterly vulnerable.

"Dry off with this, Mrs. Travers."

She took the blanket, wiped off then hurried into her underclothes and her dress. She hated to put the rags back on, but for now, she would have to.

Even though he wasn't looking, he must have been listening. As soon as she slipped the last button of her bodice into place he turned and handed Seth to her.

His eyes blinked wide, almost as though he were startled.

She knew she looked different. She could feel that she did, from the inside out. New hope coursed through her and it had to show.

The spring had cleansed her, washed away the ugliness of the outlaw ranch.

Home was only days away. For the first time in three years she looked forward to the future.

Only time would tell what it would be, but whatever it was, it would be what she chose.

She took Seth from the marshal's arms, glancing up at his face as she did.

He smiled and she returned the gesture. It had been a long time since she felt her heart light up, but she felt it now, as fragile as a candle flame.

"My name is Melody, Marshal Prentis…Melody Irene Dawson."

Chapter Two

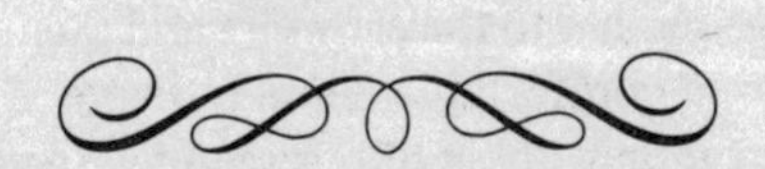

A pair of lovely, amber-colored eyes gazed up at him in the moonlight. He felt as dumb as a tree stump, with no more knowledge of how to respond than a dried-out piece of wood.

A helpless sparrow of a woman had gone into the water, but someone else had stepped out.

She even had another name.

"Pleased to make your acquaintance, Miss Dawson." He reckoned *Miss* was the right way to address her. Chances are she had gone back to her maiden name.

And a good thing, too, in his estimation. The lady taking her child from his arms had a smile prettier than the bright full moon. She resembled a "Hattie" as much a songbird resembled a mud hen.

"Won't you call me Melody?"

It would change things, being on a first-name basis. As it stood now, bringing her home was a part of his job, his obligation as a US marshal.

Ordinarily, he transported criminals whose first names he didn't care to know. His only duty was to see them safely to trial and then a jail cell.

Miss Dawson was offering friendship. It would make the trip more pleasant, no denying that. But once he delivered her to Cottonwood Grove, he'd never see her or the children again.

Keeping an emotional distance would be proper.

"I'm Reeve," he said, and by the blazes, he was smiling when he said it.

He followed her to the campfire and then sat down beside her, a comfortable enough distance to allow for conversation without things seeming too intimate.

The evening was cold but with no sign of snow. It felt good to have a fire burning from the branches he'd found scattered among the trees. Nothing was better than a true wood fire. It glowed hot enough so that the part of one's body presented to the flames grew toasty and made it easier to ignore the chilly side facing the dark.

While he considered how to bring up the Broken Brand without discouraging the new confidence brewing in her, she settled the baby on her lap then drew her wet hair over her shoulders. She fanned it through her fingers.

Even damp, her hair wasn't the dull brown color he had assumed it was. Far from dull, it caught the warmth of the flames and reflected shots of honey gold.

He knew he shouldn't, but he looked forward to seeing dawn sunshine glinting in those long silky strands.

Too bad they couldn't have an easy fireside chat about nothing of great importance, but there were some things he needed to know. Things that would keep the Travers family in jail for a very long time.

"I don't like to bring it up," he said, deciding that

the only way to approach the subject was straight on. "But I need to know what went on at the ranch. Colt's lady, Holly Jane, told me that you had been kidnapped."

"That's true. It's what they called The Travers Way. It was required of a man to go out and pluck a bride out from under her family's nose. It was a little different in my case, though."

"How was it different? I wouldn't ask, but I don't want some fancy lawyer twisting the truth and setting those—" he cleared his throat of the cussword he had been ready to blurt out "—those criminals free."

"I understand," she answered.

Her smile faded, but the defeated expression she used to have did not come back. In fact, she squared her shoulders and looked directly at him. The dusky beauty of her dark-lashed eyes nearly made him forget what he had been talking about.

"I don't regret anything, mind you, because of my babies, but the day I saw Ramsey Travers walk into the Cottonwood Grove General Store was the worst day of my life." She shrugged her shoulders and cast a glance at the wagon, where Flynn slept. "I didn't know it was, at the time...I thought it was the best. That day, watching Ram from across the street, I told my friends that I had fallen in love. They said I was silly—I couldn't know that with just one glance. Well...until that point in my life I had been a cherished only child... What I knew about the world outside of Cottonwood Grove wouldn't fill a thimble."

She turned Seth around on her lap, facing the other side of his blanket toward the flames.

This close to winter, the woods were bare and silent. Still, there was a symphony in the air, with the crackle of the flames, the bubble of the spring and the branches overhead rustling against each other. And there was Joe, already snoring like a full-grown man.

"I left my friends and crossed the street, pretending to need something—a ribbon or a gewgaw—I can't recall, but it was something frivolous. Quite truthfully, Reeve, I was a frivolous girl. I flirted with Ram and he promised me the moon if only I'd sneak away with him. He filled my head with romance. He told me I was the first girl he'd ever kissed and the last one he ever wanted to. Fool I was to believe him."

"You were young. Besides, I'm the last person to judge youthful foolishness. I only want to see those folks stay where they belong."

"That would suit me fine."

The baby began to fuss. Seth turned his head toward his mother's breast and gnawed at the blanket where it covered his cheek.

"Looks like he wants a feeding."

Reeve got up and walked over to his saddle. He took a blanket out of his pack then carried it back and settled it over Melody's shoulders.

"Let me know when he's settled." He walked to the other side of the fire to check on the sleeping children. The deputy's large coat had slipped from Pansy's shoulder where it covered her and her sister like a blanket. He tugged it over the curve of her round, pink cheek.

"You seem to know a thing about babies, Reeve."

His name sounded nice, the way she said it. It was hard to recall when someone had uttered it quite that way.

"I have nieces. I know when it's time to hand one back to her mother."

"Seth is settled in. Sit beside me so I can get this sorry tale over with."

He sat down a few inches closer than he had been before, but somehow it seemed the right distance.

"We were to be married, be gone for only a day, he'd promised. We were to return and spring the grand and romantic news on my parents. I was so full of the dreams he'd spun I didn't give anyone else's feelings a thought. I left my folks without a word or a kiss, only a note that I later found among Ram's things.

"I was wretched to them when all they had ever been to me was devoted. Until Ram, the three of us had been each other's world."

"Girls do grow up." Way too fast. He thought about the little ones who hugged his thighs whenever he visited his sister. His heart twisted.

"Most not so thoughtlessly," she answered, staring at the flames. "I've told the children my folks will welcome me back, and them, as well. I only hope that's true."

"Would you welcome Flynn or Seth in the same situation?"

"I see your point, Reeve, but for all I know they might think I'm dead."

Reeve. Every time she said his name it sounded special. He gave himself a mental shake. It was time to wrangle his thoughts back to business.

"They'll be that much more relieved to see you, then. So, are you saying you weren't kidnapped?"

"Oh, I was…" She looked away from the fire and

straight at him. "Half a day out of Cottonwood Grove we rode right past the Justice of the Peace where we were to be married. I told Ram that I'd changed my mind. I wanted to go home, to be married with my parents by my side. That gave him a good laugh and me a good cry.

"We kept on riding, avoiding towns so I couldn't tell anyone that he was taking me against my will, because by then he was. I tried to escape once and he tied me to the saddle until we got to the Badlands, where I wouldn't dare try to run. Once we reached the Broken Brand, Pappy Travers married us. I had to say *I do.* They were going to punish Libby if I didn't."

"I wonder if your marriage was legal?"

"I signed a license that looked real. They say Pappy Travers became ordained, just so he could perform weddings at the ranch."

Another crime came to mind. One he had to ask about, but damn, he didn't want to.

"I'm asking this as a lawman, because I have to." He took a breath. Questioning a criminal was a hell of a lot easier than questioning a witness. "Before you got to the Broken Brand, did Trav—"

"No." Silence stretched for a moment, broken by Seth's contented sighs. "It wasn't allowed. Pappy Travers had decreed—and what Pappy Travers decreed was law—that the men had to wait until the vows were spoken and the paper signed. They broke every other kind of law. I don't know why they drew the line at rape.

"After Pappy pronounced a marriage binding, that was another thing. It didn't matter if the bride was unwilling, she was now her husband's property, to be treated as he saw fit."

He nodded, clasped his hands around his knees and tried very hard not to erupt into anger. There were two more things he needed to ask, one much harder than the other.

"Were there others like you?"

She was silent for a long moment, and then she nodded.

"I've heard the stories of how some adapted, became no better than their husbands. Some didn't. Joe's mother died giving birth to him. His daddy is in jail—no one remembers where, though. Libby and Pansy's mother went crazy. She walked away one day. That happened the year before I came, and Pansy was an infant. Libby said they looked for her, but not for long."

"It's hard to accept that they got away with it as long as they did."

"The ranch is remote…and not all of the Traverses got away. Some got caught, some shot. Ram and his brother were both killed robbing a bank. They were buried where they committed their crime." She looked at him straight on again, her eyes welling with moisture. "I'd like to say that I grieved the loss, but when word came…well, my tears weren't sorrowful ones. All I could think of was that he wouldn't be a poisonous influence on Flynn or the coming baby."

As much as he'd told her that his questions were not personal, only what he was required to ask, her answers cut him to the quick. The few Traverses out there walking free wouldn't be for long.

This brought him to the final question, the one he dreaded asking more than the others.

"Will you testify against the ones we have in custody when it comes to the trial?"

She bowed her head, closed her eyes. He thought she was not going to answer, but she nodded her head.

"Yes, Reeve," she whispered. "As long as you'll be there."

"I'll be there."

It was his job to be there. Even if it weren't, he'd be there. Somewhere during this conversation, he had changed from lawman to friend.

Where Melody Dawson was concerned, things were no longer strictly business.

"I can't believe it," Reeve heard Libby exclaim while she and Melody sat on the back of the buckboard with their legs dangling over the edge. "Your name is really Melody Irene? Why did you tell us it was Hattie?"

Reeve drove the wagon team while Joe took turns giving Pansy and Flynn rides on his horse. He didn't worry about his mount. The horse was good with children, having been exposed to his sister's brood.

"I just… I guess I wanted to keep that bit of me for myself." Melody's voice drifted toward him on the wood seat. "Ram took everything I loved away… I didn't want to give him my name."

"How is it he didn't learn your name that first day, when you met him in front of the general store?"

"Libby, I hope you are never as foolish as I was. Meeting Ram began as a romantic lark. I thought it would be fun to pretend I was someone else."

"You aren't foolish. You are the best person I know. I can't think of how we would have gotten by without you."

"Still, I was very foolish."

For a moment, the only noise was the sound of the wheels crunching over the road and the creak of the leather tack.

"I only hope that bringing you all home will help heal my folks' grief."

Reeve turned his head to look back. Libby slipped her arms around Melody's waist, and Melody put her arm over Libby's shoulders. They leaned together, blond head meeting red head.

"I hope they take to us," Libby said, the worry in her voice apparent all the way to the front of the wagon. "We look like riffraff that the cat dragged in."

Their clothing did look ragged, and that was a fact. It would be important for them to make a respectable impression. Melody's folks might be happy enough that they wouldn't notice what their daughter or the others had on but other folks in town would be looking, and looking hard.

Adjusting to town ways would not be easy on the children, especially Joe and Libby. They'd have a stigma to overcome, having been raised by outlaws.

Looking their best might make a difference.

"We'll be coming to a town tomorrow." Reeve looked over his shoulder again.

Melody and Libby glanced up at him at the same time. Libby would grow to be a beauty, once she got some food in her and her blue eyes lost their slightly haunted look.

"It's the last one before we reach Cottonwood Grove.

We'll do some shopping. We could all use something clean to wear."

Melody let go of Libby then crawled across the back of the wagon, pausing for an instant to check on Seth, asleep in a wood crate. She climbed over the seat back, then settled beside him.

"We might just as well go around the town," she whispered. "What we have on will do."

It wouldn't do. Neither would the flush of embarrassment tinting her face. He should have realized that they didn't have any money before he spoke up.

"There's a fund. A victims' fund." There wasn't, but he hoped that she believed him. "The government sets aside money for people in situations like yours. Just to see that you get off to a fair start."

Melody frowned down at her worn skirt. She grabbed a fistful of fabric in her lap. When she glanced up, there was moisture warming her dark amber eyes.

"I've hated this thing for a very long time. I'll pay the government back every cent. For what it spends on the children, too."

He believed that she would.

There were women in the world who would not have made it through the kidnapping and the captivity. Like Libby and Pansy's mother, they would have simply walked away. He admired the fact that life's struggles had made Melody stronger rather than weaker.

He'd seen her strength from the first moment, but ever since she emerged from the hot spring, she had taken on a new radiance.

Not only was he impressed with her poise and her

grit, but her sunny beauty, as well, even though she was a mite thin.

Just now, he wanted to kiss her, to pull her tight against him and taste her. He wanted it more than he'd wanted anything in a long time.

Chances were this warm feeling for Melody Dawson would stay with him for a long time after he left her safely in Cottonwood Grove.

It was hard to believe that she was walking down the boardwalk of a real town—a town less than a day's ride from home.

Melody recalled coming here with her parents once, but the memories were dim.

To her right was a bakery with its door open to the cloudy afternoon. Out of it trailed the scents of vanilla and cinnamon.

The aroma went straight to her heart. It felt as if she had landed in Heaven instead of Tawberry, Texas.

Next door to the bakery was a milliner. Hats with pretty ribbons and bows decorated the window. The whirl of textures and colors made her want to weep out loud. Life had been dull for so long.

It was the next establishment, though, that made her gasp and Libby spin about in alarm. The name on the frosted glass door read E. M. Probst, MD.

Each night of her captivity she had gone to sleep thanking the Good Lord that her children remained healthy for another day. Way out on the Broken Brand, illness could be a death sentence. There were several small graves on that cursed land.

Somehow, she managed to regain her composure

by the time they reached their destination, Henry's General Store.

A splat of moisture hit her bare head, cold and stinging as though it couldn't decide whether it wanted to be rain or snow.

She hugged Seth tight to her chest. Beside her, Libby shivered. Tonight she would offer thanks that they would be sleeping in the hotel, that the children would not catch a chill by staying out in the elements.

Government money would pay for the cost, Reeve had assured her—just like the cost of the new clothes they were about to purchase.

She didn't believe that, not for a moment. If she had to work all hours of the day and night she would pay Reeve Prentis back.

But Libby was right. They did look like riffraff that the cat had dragged in. Well, not all of them.

Reeve looked perfectly wonderful, walking ahead of her on the boardwalk. He carried Flynn in one arm and Pansy in the other.

He had left his gun belt in his saddle pack so that it would be safer to tote her little wild man about.

The marshal strode straight and tall. Even without the weapon he had the bearing of a man of authority. Yes, he spoke to the children and made them laugh, but all the while he glanced about, scanning dim alleys and watching folks as they passed by.

It must be habit for him, looking out for trouble.

Once again, emotion pressed tears to the backs of her eyes. Because of Reeve, she felt safe for the first time in a long while.

He carried Flynn and Pansy into the store. Joe followed.

Needing a moment and a deep breath to once again compose herself, Melody stood outside while Libby went in before her.

Libby screeched.

Melody rushed inside to see the girl frozen in place with one hand over her mouth and her finger wagging at the counter where a display of jars containing hard candy shimmered in a rainbow of colors.

The store clerk, very clearly, did not share her joy. His eyes narrowed. He swung his head back and forth, taking in each person's disreputable appearance.

"Is there something I can help you with?" he asked with an arrogant arch of his brows.

"That's candy!" Joe exclaimed.

He and Libby approached the counter, shoulder to shoulder, their eyes as wide as their grins.

"Those are peppermint sticks," Joe said. "I recall one time that Uncle Cyrus brought some home from a raid."

"He didn't share them," Libby said. "But they sure smelled good."

On the right side of the counter was a basket of hair ribbons. Libby turned, reaching toward the ribbons. Her fingers stroked the air over them.

"I reckon the shiny ones are satin," she said in an almost-reverent tone. "And those others, are they velvet, Melody?"

"Don't you touch those, young woman," the counter man ordered. "And you, boy, keep those dirty fingers off the candy jars."

Poor Libby, her cheeks flamed.

"I wouldn't take one, I swear," she said.

Reeve set Flynn and Pansy on the floor. He approached the basket, patted Libby's shoulder then scooped up all the ribbons in his big fist.

"I'll take these and whatever else the young lady wants." Reeve shrugged off his coat, exposing his badge. "Give me all the peppermint in the jar and the licorice, to go with it."

The skinny man gulped, sending his Adam's apple sliding up and down his throat.

"Yes, sir, Marshal."

"Mind your manners, mister, and help these good folks with whatever they need. If you don't have it, find someone who does and have it brought here. Be sure to pack everything up in nice, neat packages and have them delivered to the hotel."

The counter clerk bobbed his half-bald head.

"I'll be back to settle up in half an hour."

"Yes, sir, Marshal." The man blinked pale green eyes that were a size too large for his face. "It'll be just as you say."

"See that it is."

Reeve turned to Melody, then took her by the elbow and led her to stand by the big potbellied stove that heated the store.

"Buy whatever you need. The government's got more money in the fund than it knows what to do with. I've got to pay a visit to the town marshal, but I'll be back shortly. We can all walk over to the hotel together."

He took a step toward the front door, but she touched

his arm, halting him. The supple leather of his shirt felt warm and his muscles firm under her fingertips.

"This is the first time any of the children have been inside a store. Thank you for not allowing the clerk to disrespect them."

He answered with a nod, then went out the door, closing it on an increasingly angry-looking storm.

She went to the window and pulled aside the curtain to watch him dash across the earthen street. He was a big man walking in long powerful strides. His shoulders, hunched against a sudden downpour, looked as if they could carry the world.

Chapter Three

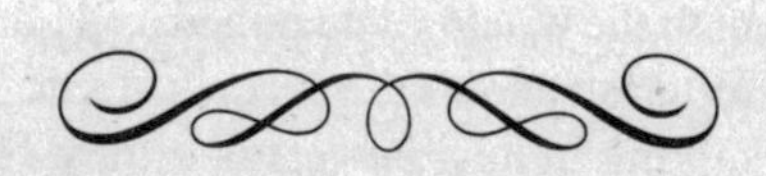

Melody stood in the center of the hotel room wearing her clean, new shift. She clenched her toes against the smooth wood floor, listening to the storm that howled under the eaves.

Unlike Libby, Pansy and Flynn, curled in a cozy tangle in one of the beds, she could not sleep. Even a simple doze was beyond her reach tonight.

Sleet hit the window with a quiet splat. She checked on Seth tucked into his crate. With his little belly full, he ought to be asleep for a few hours.

Quiet breathing, heavy in sleep, sighed through the room. There would be none of that for her tonight.

Nothing, it seemed, could ease the anxiety she felt over finally going home tomorrow. She wanted it, as much as her next heartbeat, but she dreaded it, too.

How would her parents receive her? And not only her parents, what about the rest of the town? Some might see her as a victim, but others might believe that as an outlaw's wife, she was tainted.

Perhaps she was. She was certainly not the carefree girl who had run away with Ram, her hopes and dreams as fresh as sunrise.

Life had hardened her, and yet motherhood had made her more compassionate.

She hated to think it, but her parents might not even recognize their little girl. They would love her, still. She knew that. Maybe once she fell into their embrace, something of that carefree girl would return.

In the end, all of the hoping in the world was not going to allow her to sleep. Nerves jittered inside her until all she could do was pace from the window to the door, from the door to the window.

It was late, eleven o'clock. The clerk downstairs had told her that they kept a fire going in the lobby all night for restless guests and folks coming in at odd hours.

She paused in front of the hook on the wall where her new dress hung. She took it down and put it on. It smelled fresh. She doubted the day would come when fresh-smelling clothes would go unappreciated.

Not feeling like making a fuss over her hair, she combed her fingers through it and let it fall loose about her shoulders. She put on her new shoes then bent over Seth's crate to make sure his breathing remained deep and slow.

Good, it would be safe to go downstairs for a short time.

She closed the door behind her with a quiet click then walked down the hall to the stair landing.

From where she stood she could see most of the lobby. The scene was cozy with stuffed chairs placed in a half circle about the fireplace. Lamps on side tables were turned low for the night. They cast the parlor in a pretty amber glow.

She heard the ticktock of a grandfather clock but couldn't see it.

At the foot of the stairs, she paused, faced with a pleasant decision. Should she pass these quiet moments in front of the fire, or sit beside the window and watch the storm blow by?

It had been an age since she felt this secure.

It occurred to her that she didn't have to make a choice. She could do both.

She would start with the window.

All of a sudden the front door opened, blowing in a gust of sleet and Reeve Prentis.

"Evening, Melody." He removed his slush-dampened hat and coat then hung them on the hall tree beside the door. "I wondered if you'd get any sleep tonight."

Lamplight and fire glow certainly flattered Reeve. The warm light cast his eyes a deeper shade of green. A shadow brushed the cleft in his chin and highlighted the curve of his smile.

If she were a different person, at a different place in her life, she would reach out and touch his cold, ruddy-looking cheek.

"I tried but…" She shrugged. "What are you doing out so late and in this weather?"

"Town marshal's down with a fever. I told him I'd make his rounds."

"That was kind of you."

"Just part of the job."

"That was dedicated of you, then."

The smile he flashed gave her heart a skip. That

would not do. Last time her heart gave a skip… Well, she did have her boys.

"Would you care to sit for a while?" he asked.

"By the fire or the window?"

"Window. We can enjoy the storm and keep warm at the same time."

He enjoyed storms? So did she. There was something so snug about sheltering inside while everything raged outside.

"Would you like some tea, Reeve? Maybe I can find some in the kitchen."

"I'd be grateful."

Those long fingers of his looked as if they needed to be wrapped around something warm. For an instant, she imagined being that something.

What, she wondered, would those big calloused fingers feel like, touching the curve of her…? That was a thought she would not indulge in. Someday she might be able to think of a man that way, but not yet.

She hurried away, hoping that he hadn't noticed the blush heating her face.

After ten minutes, Melody walked into the parlor carrying two cups of fragrant, steaming tea. Reeve was almost sorry that the blush had faded from her cheeks. She looked pretty with that high coloring.

He took the cup Melody offered. She sat down on the chair across from him.

A mixture of rain and snow dripped down the window. Wind whistled and moaned.

"I wonder if the weather will keep us from leaving the hotel in the morning," she said with a sidelong glance outside.

"Would you want it to?" He studied the delicate pucker of her brow, wondering about the troubles that had to be churning her mind. It would only be natural for her to worry about what would happen tomorrow.

"No!" She looked out the window again. "Well, maybe..."

"Things might not go easy at first."

"I'm used to hard, Reeve." She snapped her gaze back to him. "I can handle that for myself. But my babies, and the other children... I want things to go easy for them. Libby and Joe have only known hard."

"I reckon your folks will need some time to adjust. That's only reasonable, but they'll come around."

"I hope so." Her mouth firmed into a look of conviction. "I believe so."

"So do I." He took a gulp of his tea then smiled at her. "Thanks for this."

"You don't need to thank me for anything, Reeve." She reached over and squeezed his hand. Something in her eyes told him that the gesture did not come easily. "I can never pay you back for all you've done for me. And don't tell me it's just your job. I won't hear it."

"You're welcome, Melody. You and the children have been refreshing traveling companions. It's criminals that I normally escort."

Not one single person that he'd escorted had ever touched his hand in friendship.

"It must be lonely, spending so much time away from your kin."

Lonely and necessary.

"I see them when I can…holidays and such."

"That doesn't seem like enough. You speak so fondly of your nieces."

Being away so much wasn't right. He knew it. But he had a living to earn for his mother and his youngest sister—and a sin to atone for while he did it.

"You're right. It isn't enough."

"Surely you could take more time off."

Did he want to confide in her about his past? The night seemed right for private talk, with the storm wailing like a forlorn ghost and the two of them safe behind the glass. So late at night, it seemed that they were the only people alive with just the tick of the clock and their voices to fill up the night.

What had happened, what he had done to his family, was no secret, but he rarely spoke of it and they never did.

After tomorrow, it was unlikely that he would ever see Melody Dawson again. Sometimes, it was easier to talk to someone just passing through your life than it was to your own kin. At this time of year the guilt gnawed at him hard.

"I can't take the time off for a pair of reasons." He set down his tea, leaned back then folded his arms across his chest. If anyone could understand his sin, it would be Melody. "I'm the sole support of my crippled mother and my youngest sister. The reason that I am is that I trusted someone and it ended up getting my father killed. It put my mother in a wheelchair."

If she was revolted by his confession, it didn't show. Her gaze softened and she set down her tea. She leaned forward in her chair, resting her elbows on her knees and her chin on her folded hands.

Melody Dawson was an exceptionally becoming woman, with her golden-blond hair falling softly over her shoulders and her warm, caring eyes looking at him with understanding.

"I'm so sorry, Reeve. Would you like to talk about it?"

He didn't want to talk, but somehow he needed to unburden himself. Given her own past mistakes, she might be the one person to understand.

"Growing up, I was the oldest. I told you about my three sisters. The girls were always up to mischief. Ma and Pa were busy making a living. My folks were jewelers and had a shop in town so they were gone much of the time. It fell to me to keep the girls in line.

"But I was eighteen and didn't want to stay in line, myself. One day I met a couple of fellows who were my age and full of the dickens. I admired them because they were free to do the things I could not."

She nodded her head but did not comment.

"They took me in, acted like I was one of them. I wanted their respect so badly that one day I began to boast. How could it hurt if I confided a secret? So I bragged and told them there was a safe full of money in the store. I realized later that the only reason they befriended me was to get at the safe. It was December tenth. Our family was supposed to go to a Christmas music recital that night, but Ma and Pa stopped by the store first while I went on with my sisters."

Melody bit her lip. She gave a slight shake of her head, probably guessing where the story was going.

"Pa went after the intruders with a gun. My bravado cost my father his life and my mother her legs.

"The criminals disappeared and my family was broken."

There was her touch on his hand again, hesitant at first but gaining courage as her fingers warmed his skin.

He couldn't help but wonder what she had gone through to make a simple touch so difficult. For all that she flinched at the contact, her touch was powerful in its emotion. It gave him the strength to finish his story.

"I worked odd jobs to see Ma and the girls fed and sheltered, but those were hard times. When I came of age I became a lawman, in part so I could find those men."

"And did you?"

"Within that first year. The two of them will spend the rest of their days behind bars."

"I'm not so sure I wouldn't have just shot them. Maybe the Traverses got to me more than I know."

"I wanted to…almost did. The gun shook in my fist, I wanted to do it so badly."

"What stopped you?"

"It would have been one more betrayal to my folks. They had tried to raise me to be law-abiding and honorable. Those fellows lured me from that path once. I wasn't going to let them do it again.

"Besides, over time I've found that justice lasts longer than revenge."

She nodded, then turned her face to watch the sleet slide down the window. It was a moment before she spoke.

"Have you been able to forgive yourself, Reeve? I'm not sure that I can, for what I did."

"I don't know that I've forgiven myself. But I have learned to get on with my life and live it in a way that honors my parents. Whenever I lock up a criminal, I'm doing that. It's a hard life, on the move. I don't think I'll ever have the comfort of settling down in one place, but I reckon that's my penance."

"Someday, Reeve, I'm certain that one of my boys will act in a way I wouldn't choose. But I'd be sick at heart if he paid for that by sacrificing his own happiness."

"Serving up justice makes me happy." It did. It filled the crater that his transgression had carved in his soul. As long as he could do that and provide for his mother and his sister, he would be content with his life.

His nieces would stand in for his own children. And as far as never having someone of his own—a wife? Well, that was also part of his penance.

Cottonwood Grove had not changed in three years. Melody stood in the wagon bed gazing down upon it from the hilltop north of town.

From up here, one could see that the town was designed like a wheel. Grove Circle, the business district, formed the hub of the wheel and the center of town. Radiating out from it, like spokes on a wheel, was the residential area.

Come spring, the whole town would be shaded by huge leafy trees. The open land spreading away from town consisted of miles of lush grassy hills cut by three creeks lined with cottonwoods.

Cottonwood Grove was a world away from the Broken Brand.

This late in the afternoon, smoke rose from chimneys all over town as folks got ready to settle in for the evening. The familiar scent of burning wood floated up the knoll.

Melody's heart squeezed so tight she thought she might bawl out loud. The sights and sounds of home made her want to leap from the wagon, run down the hill and hug the first person she saw, stranger or not.

Did the boardwalk in front of Miller's Dry Goods still squeak? She spotted Mary Weller coming out of her bakeshop. Did she still bake the most delicious cinnamon muffins in the county? A hammer striking an anvil told her that the blacksmith was working late, as had always been his custom.

And there, the last house on the spoke of town leading due west, was the home she had grown up in. Its three stories gleamed white in the late-afternoon sunshine.

It was odd that no smoke rose from the chimney. Mama loved nothing better than a cozy fire, and Papa loved nothing more than pleasing Mama.

"Are you ready?" Reeve's voice snapped her away from a dozen memories that crowded her all at once.

She glanced toward the side of the wagon. He sat tall on his big horse, peering at her under the brim of his Stetson. She was going to miss Reeve once he went on his way.

She'd had many friends growing up, most of them she'd known all her life. But she had never taken to one as quickly as she had Reeve.

Was it foolish to trust him so quickly? Possibly, but he was everything a man ought to be and not like Ram in any way at all.

She could not deny that with Reeve, it was almost as though they were kindred spirits with the common bond of a guilty past. He was struggling to make amends, and she would be in just a few minutes.

She watched him move ahead of the wagon, riding tall with his broad shoulders and narrow hips rocking with the horse's gait. He was a rare man, and she would be a long time forgetting him.

"As ready as I'm going to be," she whispered under her breath.

"I'm worried, too," Joe said, then jiggled the reins and clicked to the team. "It won't be a secret that we're outlaws' kin."

"These are good folks." She clutched the back of the wagon seat, too nervous to sit down. "We might be a surprise to them at first, but they'll come around."

"Can we attend school?" Libby knelt behind her, close to her knee.

"Mama will insist upon it."

"I think I'm going to like your mama."

"And she is going to adore you."

"'Dore me, too, Meldy?" Pansy asked, hugging tight to her sister's arm.

"Especially you, little flower." Melody turned about and ruffled the little girl's curly hair.

Then, all of a sudden, she was home. The large white house came into view. A sob tore from her throat.

She couldn't help it. She leaped from the wagon, picked up the hem of her skirt and ran.

"Mama!" she cried, opening the gate of the faded picket fence.

That was odd. Papa never let paint fade.

She ran up the walk. Tears streamed down her face but she didn't care. She was home. She was safe. "Mama!"

She tried the doorknob. It was locked. She pounded on the door. Paint chipped against her fist. She pounded some more.

"What do you think you are doing?" a shrill voice called from the other side of the road.

She spun about to see a woman charging forward from the house across the street. She was not the round and cheerful Mrs. Cherry whom Melody had known all of her life.

This woman was tall, lean and pinch-faced. Her eyes snapped with indignation, as though Melody were an intruder.

The woman wore a dress that looked as if it had come from Paris, France. She had rouge on her cheeks and even a dash of kohl around her eyes.

"Who are you?" the woman barked, snapping her skirt as she stomped up the walk.

"Melody Irene?" Thank the Lord! Her father's voice came from the right, near the corner of the house. She spun toward it.

"Papa?" she gasped.

He took a step toward her and she dashed into his arms.

"Papa!" She sobbed and hung on to his neck. He seemed shorter than he had, thinner, too, but she hugged him as if he was her lifeline.

"Is it really you?" He cupped the back of her head, holding her close. "My little girl?"

"It's me." Relief flooded her. She was home and Papa held her in his arms. Everything would be all right now.

"We gave up hope." She felt his chest heave then cave.

"I'm sorry, Papa. I can't tell you how sorry."

They hung on to each other for a long moment, hugging and weeping.

"Mama!" Flynn called.

At last she pulled away. "Papa, there's someone I want you and Mama to meet."

She gazed into eyes that didn't seem like her father's. They used to be snapping blue, his expression always on the verge of a laugh. Now they were clouded… It was all her fault.

"I'm sorry, baby…truly, truly sorry, but your mama… she passed on two years ago."

Papa turned her about by the shoulders. Her heart had stopped. Surely it had. Through a dizzy haze she faced the neighbor who looked as though steam might spout from her ears.

"And this is your stepmama, Dixie."

Chapter Four

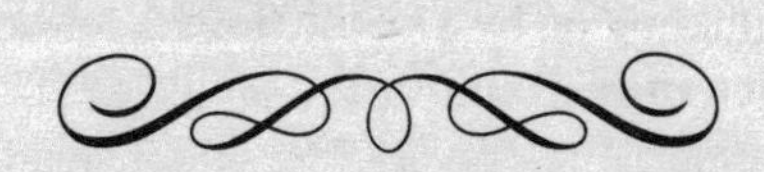

"Mama!" Flynn cried out, reaching his arms over the side of the wagon. "Hold you!"

If Melody had heard her son, Reeve would be surprised. The shock and the grief had to cut to the bone.

The creaking of his saddle leather when he got off his horse and Flynn's distressed cries were the only sounds that filled the anguished silence.

He crossed the yard quickly, then stood behind Melody. He wanted to touch her in comfort but figured it would be best to simply be there.

Despair had to be slicing her off at the knees but she stood tall with her back straight and her features set.

"Why, you wicked girl," Dixie murmured, allowing her gaze to roam over Melody, from head to toe and back again. "Devil give you credit, breaking your daddy's heart, coming home bold as blazes and not just you but a passel of brats." She glanced at Reeve, her gaze roaming subtly where it shouldn't. "And a man."

He'd met this kind of woman before. Unless he missed his guess she was a whore who had become too old to ply her trade and so had latched on to a susceptible widower.

"Marshal Prentis," Melody said in a voice so brittle he wondered that it didn't crack. She didn't look at him. She didn't even appear to be breathing. "Would you kindly take the children to the hotel?"

If it weren't for the fact that her composure was probably holding on by a brittle thread, he would have touched her, offered comfort.

"Of course, Mrs. Travers," he said instead. At least her father would know that Melody had been married. He guessed Dixie had been hinting that she was not.

In time it would come out that Melody had been married to an outlaw, but that time was not now.

"Come with us, Mellie," Libby called gently from where she stood in the wagon bed. "It's not a time to be alone."

"I'll be along."

Reeve noticed the effort it took for her to speak those few words. Her lips trembled ever so slightly.

Another woman might have collapsed where she stood. In spite of her delicate appearance, Melody Dawson was as strong as iron.

While many had gone from girl to woman sheltered and coddled, Melody had grown up among thieves and ruffians. Through it all she had gained a sense of integrity, not lost it.

Joe walked up and touched her elbow. "Come on, Melody."

"I've got to speak with my father alone, but I'll be along."

"Not on your life!" Dixie Dawson claimed her husband by latching on to his coat sleeve and tugging him down the walkway.

"Papa?" Melody hurried after her father.

"You've done enough damage for one lifetime, young woman." It was fair to say that the stepmother actually growled.

"Papa, don't you want to meet your grandsons?"

The man stopped and turned. His eyes brightened for an instant but they still seemed drawn and weary.

"Grandsons?"

"Those brats don't have anything to do with us. They'll only cause trouble."

"I'd like to see—"

"Come along, Porter." Dixie pulled Mr. Dawson down the path. He didn't protest again even when his wife shooed him up the front steps of the house across the road as if he was a chicken being put away for the night.

Melody's shoulders trembled; her hands twisted into white fists.

"I'm home for good, Papa," she called. "I'll be staying at the hotel until I get settled."

"Your mama left you the house," Porter Dawson answered while his wife tried to drag him inside. "The back door is open."

"You old fool," he heard Dixie grumble. Without trying to hide what she did, she yanked her husband's ear. "Keep your mouth shut."

"The sky's clouding up. We'd better get the children out of the weather before it snows," Reeve said, touching Melody's shoulder to urge her toward the wagon.

"I don't know him. He's my father, but he's not the

one I left behind." She looked up at Reeve, her amber eyes wide and hurting. "My daddy was so strong. Whatever happened to him is my fault."

"We can talk about it later. First we need to get the children fed and settled."

He wished that she would lean into him for comfort. It would feel natural to hug her close. The one thing he wanted at this moment was to ease her grief. He knew, of course, that he couldn't. It was impossible.

All one could hope for was to wade through the pain. To come out on the other side stronger, and if not exactly healed, at least able to feel life's joy again.

He knew she had the strength to be all right in the end, but all of a sudden it felt wrong to leave her.

He'd spent his life being a protector, but he'd never felt the need to watch over another person who wasn't kin. Maybe it was because of the children, her own and the ones she had taken on. Or it might be that her inner strength combined with her delicate beauty touched him in a way he hadn't been touched before.

Whatever it was that called him to her, he could not abandon her, just now, to pick up the threads of her life alone.

Reeve sat on his bed and took off his boots. It was late, the fire in the grate had fallen to embers and it was well past time to get some rest.

Unfortunately, restlessness had been his companion much of the evening, keeping him pacing the floor and watching the snow drift beyond the window.

Melody was in a fix, and he wondered what he could do to turn things around. She hadn't returned home to the welcome of her parents as she had expected. Even the parent she had left was in no position to give her support.

It wouldn't be right to ride off, leaving her and the children with their lives in an upheaval.

He wouldn't do it.

Still, ignoring his obligation as a US marshal weighed heavily upon him.

He could take a few more days. After that it was his duty to get back to work, to bring law and order to a wild land. There was still the matter of a couple of Traverses who had escaped justice. He'd need to apprehend them.

A quiet knock sounded at his door. He crossed the room and opened it.

"Miss Libby? What are you doing out in the hall at this hour?" He was surprised to see her at his door, a lamp in hand and her bare toes peeking out from under her sleeping gown. "You ought to be in your room."

"It's Melody, Marshal Prentis. I don't know where she is. She fed the baby an hour ago, then went out. She hasn't come back. She hasn't cried yet like she ought to, either. I'm right worried."

"I'll walk you back to your room." He crossed to the bed, sat down and yanked his boots back on. "I reckon she's gone home. She probably needs some time alone. Would you mind tending the others for a while?"

This late at night, the hotel was quiet. Only a few snores came from behind the closed doors along the hallway.

"I'll let you know when I find her. And, Libby, you did right to come to me."

"I didn't have anyone else to turn to." She opened the door to her room, then stepped inside. Closing the door halfway, she peered around it. "I wish…well, I wish I wasn't too young to marry you, but since I am, there's Melody. Joe and I have been watching, and we think you would suit her just fine."

"I'd be honored if she favored me that way, Libby, but the truth is my profession makes me something of a nomad and Miss Dawson needs to settle. I'm afraid we wouldn't be right for one another."

Even if they were right, even if she was the one person in the world who was perfect for him, he had a penance to pay. He might never be able to make amends for what he had done to his family, but he would spend the rest of his life trying.

Melody's mind recognized the fact that the night was frigid but somehow she didn't feel it. She didn't feel anything at all. Wind shot snow at her face and caked the toes of her boots, but she was already numb, body and soul.

Mama…just the name in Melody's mind cut her heart to shreds. No matter the pain, all she could think of was going home.

She carried a lantern that she had borrowed from the hotel through the darkness. A circle of light surrounded her, making the snowflakes swirling about glitter. There had been a time when the shimmer and sparkle would have delighted her. Now it only made the knot in her chest constrict.

Mama had been partial to snow. She used to catch the flakes on her tongue and spin about with her arms spread wide. Then, pink-cheeked with cold, she would dash into the house to bake something warm and cozy. Cookies most of the time. On days like that, Melody would have the joy of cracking eggs and dumping them into the batter, stirring it all up then licking the bowl clean.

How could a cherished memory become a pain so sharp that it dried up her well of tears? If only she could let them out, the cramp in her chest might ease. Maybe living with the Traverses had so dulled her emotions that she no longer reacted to them.

She entered the house around the back, through the mudroom then into the kitchen. Setting the lantern on the table with a quiet click, she glanced about a room that Mama might have stepped out of only yesterday.

Lit softly by the lantern's glow, her apron hung on its peg. Mama ought to be here, wearing it, taking something out of the oven or sweeping the floor. Melody ought to be hearing her mother's voice, singing while she went about her chores.

With memories crowding in on her from every which way, she picked up the lantern and hurried out of the kitchen, into the parlor.

Mama sat in the rocking chair beside the fire. Melody saw the picture in her mind as clearly as if it were real. She looked away but there was her mother again, standing beside the window, holding her baby girl in her arms and pointing at the snow falling in the yard.

Melody closed her eyes, trying to ground herself in the here and now. She couldn't let grief overcome her. Her babies depended upon her, the other children, too.

She couldn't fall apart. Remaining strong was the only thing that would insure a stable future.

With a steadying breath, she opened her eyes and looked about the parlor in which she had spent so many happy hours. Someone had been keeping the place up. Probably her father. It smelled fresh, not like someplace forgotten and left to gather dust.

She lifted the lantern high. Once again, it seemed that Mama had only stepped out for a moment. Even her knitting lay in the yellow basket beside the chair, waiting for her return.

"Melody…baby?"

The sound of her mother's voice made her spin toward the door. In that instant, she realized that her father had been confused. Mama was alive after all.

"Mama!" she cried and ran several steps toward the empty doorway.

Of course, Mama was dead. The voice had been in her mind, a memory so vivid that she heard it.

Once again, pain cut her heart, as though Papa had just now delivered the news. She bent in half, her knees giving out where she stood. The sob that had been clogging her heart for hours broke free.

She needed something to hold on to, something that was Mama's. She crawled to the knitting basket and plucked out the half-finished project with the needles still crossed midstitch.

Kneeling, she clutched it to her heart, and rocked to and fro.

"Mama," she sobbed, holding back none of the grief now. "What happened to you?"

Her mother was dead and she didn't even know

why…or how. Had she been ill? Had there been an accident?

Lifting the yarn to her face, she let her tears flow into it. The unfinished garment smelled like Mama. She breathed deep and wept, feeling that if she opened her eyes, her mother would be there.

She pulled the wool away from her face to look at it. What project had Mama been pouring her heart into at the last?

Her fingers shook as she rolled open a scarf. A name had been embroidered on the bottom edge. *M...E... L...O...D...* The *Y* had been started but not completed.

She bent her body over the scarf, bowing her head so low that it touched the floor. She began to shake and sob.

Heartache so intense that she thought she would never recover from it crippled her. If she were given a choice of staying here and living with this loneliness or going to live with Mama, she would choose…

"Mama…" Her voice cracked. "Mama."

"Melody." A hand touched her shoulder, and then stroked her hair. "I'm taking you back to the hotel."

She felt strong, warm arms reach beneath her, then lift her from the cold floor. A part of her wanted to resist his touch, but another part wanted to hide in his embrace.

"I want my mama, Reeve." She buried her face into his neck and felt his collar become damp with her tears. "I need to tell her how much I miss her…how sorry I am."

"I know you do." Reeve's breath grazed her hair. "Tell her now."

For all the good that would do. "She can't hear me now. I committed a horrible sin running away with Ram. All the sorry in the world won't make up for that."

"I've been where you are… You aren't alone… I'm here."

And all of a sudden something shifted inside her. She couldn't even say what it was. Pain still sliced her heart, but with Reeve here, so strong and dependable, life didn't seem so hopeless.

As he carried her out of the house and through the snowy night, she let her tears fall.

Reality was no longer tangible. Nothing was as it should be. Vivid memories of Mama collided with the harsh realization of her passing. How could her mother be gone from the earth and yet so present in her heart?

Melody's eyes ached. Her chest felt heavy with misery and disbelief.

A white fog clouded her mind. Fight as she might against the debilitating vapor, nothing seemed secure any longer.

Nothing except Reeve. Reeve was secure. His voice whispering comfort in her ear as he carried her back to the hotel was the slim thread grounding her to the here and now. Just when she thought she might be overwhelmed, his voice whispering across her cheek reminded her that life would go on. It had to.

He carried her through the dark hotel lobby and up the stairs. She thought he would set her down outside the door to her room but he walked past it.

His footsteps padded down the hall with the muffled shuffle of leather on wood. Opening the door to his room, he carried her inside then closed it quietly behind him.

He set her upon the mattress. Propriety, and past experience with a man, demanded that she protest, screech and run back to her own room. Instead, she clung to his neck, holding on to him a moment longer than she ought to.

Gently, he removed her shoes. She sighed and closed her eyes.

What was wrong with her? With Ram, she'd always slept with one eye open, always on guard.

"Rest now, darlin'. I'll keep watch on the children… You get some sleep."

Sleep…she couldn't…wasn't certain she ever would again, but at some point she must have. Her eyes opened slowly, feeling gritty. Her head ached, but she was no longer weeping.

A fire, banked low, glowed in the hearth. Reeve sat in a chair beside it with his arms propped across his chest, his legs stretched out with his boots crossed at the ankle. His chin dipped toward his chest in sleep.

Amber light painted his face, and blue highlights glimmered in his dark hair. The US Marshals badge pinned to his shirt shone softly in the dim light.

There was a blanket pulled over her shoulders that hadn't been there before. It made her feel safe and warm. A week ago she would have never trusted a man, especially a handsome one. Being alone with him in a bedroom would have had her fighting like a cornered cat. But instead of fighting, all she wanted to do was watch the kiss of firelight warming Reeve's face.

She was exhausted to the bone. Tomorrow, she would need to figure out what she would do with her life, but for now she would drift back to sleep knowing that, until then, Reeve would be sitting there.

A tune, hummed low and off-key, woke her before dawn. Truth, cold and hard, crashed upon her as soon as she opened her eyes.

Mama was dead.

If only she could sleep the rest of the day…or the week, or however long it took to deal with the grief, but that could not happen. The children needed her.

Across the hotel room, Reeve stood with his long legs braced wide, swaying before the fireplace with Seth in his arms.

Her infant fussed and flailed. It wouldn't be long before his hungry cries woke the hotel guests.

"I know, little man. I'm not much of a singer… hummer, either, for that matter. My mother never let me do it around my sisters…said it made them fret."

"I know you're making that up." Melody eased to her elbows, then wriggled up against the backboard. She reached out her arms. "I'll take him."

With a half smile, he sat down on the bed near her knees and handed the baby to her. To her very great surprise, she returned his smile.

"I'm sorry things worked out for you like this," Reeve said. "There are times when all a body wants is to go home and be safe."

She unwrapped Seth from his blanket and placed it over her shoulder. Reeve looked away while she freed her clothing so the baby could feed.

"Thanks to you, I am home," she said, pulling the blanket modestly around her.

"Not the way you expected to be." She held very still when he reached over and touched a matted hank of hair that flopped in front of her face. He tucked it behind her ear.

She must look a horrid mess. As of this moment, she was done with looking bedraggled and horrid. Three years of living with the Traverses would not keep her that way and neither would grief.

From now on she was putting all that behind her. Once again she would become the smiling person her parents had named Melody.

"No, it isn't," she admitted. "But it was foolish of me to think I could come home a grown woman and fall into my parents' arms like I was still their little girl."

"I reckon there's times when we want nothing more than to turn the past around."

Of course, he would know that. He'd lived her pain. Shadows haunted the depth of those brilliant green eyes.

"Yes, we can want it, but the fact is—and you know it as well as I do—that it can't be done."

"We move on, though."

"You seem to have, Reeve."

Seth cooed, let his lips fall away from her nipple then rooted for it again. "I hope you've been able to find your peace."

"Most days, I have. Some days…well, they're still hard. Of all the folks you forgive in your life, I reckon it's hardest to forgive yourself. But for the most part you get there."

"There's no choice, is there? Not when others depend upon you."

"You're a strong woman, Melody. You'll have a good life."

All of a sudden she wondered what it would be like if he were to stay in it.

A picture flashed in her mind of the pair of them waking together in the morning, touching each other without restraint and greeting the day with a kiss.

It seemed right…as though it were meant to be.

Watching him ride away from Cottonwood Grove might be harder than she expected.

The urge to lean across the mattress and kiss those weatherworn lips was distressing. It confused her. She didn't want to be touched—and yet she wanted it more than anything.

Besides the fact that she had demons to deal with, his future and hers were on separate paths. Sadly, a kiss would make his leaving that much harder. The last thing she needed right now was another ounce of emotional turmoil.

"According to my father, I have my mother's house. That's something…a place to begin, at least."

"You did say your mother wanted to fill the house with children. You'll do her honor by raising them here. Eventually, you'll feel happy again."

"Do you?"

"Most days… And you have the children. Someday you'll remarry."

"Oh, no!" As grateful as she was for Flynn and Seth, she could not risk allowing another Ram into her life. "I believe I'll be better off on my own."

He gazed at her somberly for a long time while she looked silently back at him.

Seth stirred and broke the moment, but not before she was struck with the confounding thought that she might not be happier on her own, after all.

Chapter Five

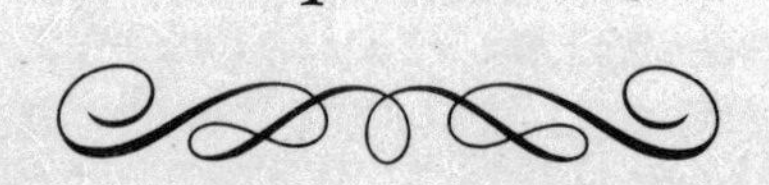

"Is this a castle?" Pansy squeezed Reeve's hand as they walked into the entry of the big white house. "Am I a princess now?"

"You've always been a princess," Joe answered, his eyes as wide with wonder as the little girl's.

It was easy to understand the children's awe of the place. From what Reeve had seen, it was the largest home in Cottonwood Grove. How many bedrooms did Melody say it had? Eight…and all spread out over three stories?

To the children of the Broken Brand, it would seem like a palace. Clearly, Mr. and Mrs. Dawson had intended to raise a large brood here.

"Where's the king and queen?" Pansy let go of his hand and dashed across the large, comfortably furnished room. She hopped onto a red chair beside the fireplace and sat with her legs dangling.

"There's no king. Only a queen," Joe said, pointing to Melody, who had just blown in the door with her boys and a gust of cold wind.

"You is a queen, Meldy?"

"Joe is just teasing you, love." Melody gave Seth to Libby then plucked up Flynn's hand and placed it in Joe's. "See that he doesn't try the stairs, will you?"

"Can I show him how they work? He ought to know."

Melody nodded and smiled. If the shadows of last night lingered, she didn't allow them to show.

She sat on the chair with Pansy and gathered the child onto her lap.

"This isn't a castle. Just a big house. It's where I grew up and so will you."

The big house was plenty cold. It would take a lot of firewood to heat the place. This room alone had two fireplaces, one at each end of the room.

Whoever had been taking care of the house had left nice stacks of wood beside each one. If it had been Mr. Dawson, perhaps he hadn't truly given up hope of his daughter's return.

He knelt down beside the hearth and listened to Melody tell Pansy about the house and the yard.

She took off her bonnet. Blond hair spilled over her shoulders and reflected golden streams of cold morning sunlight coming through the arched window behind her.

The sight took his breath away for a moment. Melody was beautiful. He must have had dust in his eyes that first day, thinking she was haggard and worn.

If he'd ever seen a more radiant woman, he couldn't recall her. Even in her grief, Melody's loving spirit warmed the folks around her.

Children who might have been cast into a bitter world now had a home because of her.

Just in case her smile wasn't sunny enough to warm

the day, her eyes were captivating enough to make him want to stare at her longer than was proper.

While he knelt and stacked kindling and wood together, he watched her from the corner of his eye.

Her skin was fair with a riot of freckles dusting her nose and her cheeks. Thick, golden hair draped over her shoulders. It covered her chest in loopy curls. Even though she was thin, her breasts were full.

An inappropriate vision filled his mind. He ought to snuff it out, but he was a man and couldn't help but savor the image that his brain conjured.

Were those breasts also dusted with pretty freckles or were they pale…smooth as ivory?

"I'll go upstairs and lay the fires in the other hearths," he said because his thoughts were leading him to even more visions that were making things uncomfortable down below. There was a time and place to indulge that type of yearning, but right here with five children getting acquainted with their new home was not it.

"Thank you, Reeve," she said. It was the look in her eyes that thanked him more than the words. They shone up at him with a warm amber glow that shot straight to his heart.

He took to the stairs, grateful for the four cold hearths he found. He needed some time to settle his insides.

Somewhere along the way, Melody Dawson had gone from a victim in need of aid to someone he cared for.

They had become friends. That much was easy to admit, but if he wasn't careful she would steal his heart, bit by bit.

That was something he could not allow. He'd be leaving soon. He wanted to be able to do that free and clear with no lingering attachment holding a portion of his soul in Cottonwood Grove.

A sudden banging of piano keys brought him back to his chore. A composition of Flynn's, no doubt.

He smiled. He tried not to. There was an attachment forming there that would be hard to break, as well. But how was a man to keep a straight face when a peal of baby giggles was the song accompanying the tune?

Melody stared out the parlor window, watching the house across the street. It was late afternoon and still she hadn't had a glimpse of her father.

There was so much she needed to know that only he could tell her. She was doing her best to smile and go about life as her mother would want her to, but there was an ache in her soul that kept her smiles on the surface only…

The Broken Brand had taught her that—to smile for the children's sake even though her heart grieved.

What had happened to Mama? She wouldn't take an easy breath until she knew.

Maybe not even then. Nothing about life was going to be easy anymore. How on earth was she going to support five children? All she owned in the world was this house and the clothes that Reeve had purchased for her.

Children needed to eat. They needed clothing and schoolbooks. They ought to have toys and treats.

This morning, Reeve had brought pastries from

town, putting the children in pure sugar heaven. Once he was gone, how would she get by?

Coming home was not at all how she had imagined it. Mama was going to be the one to feed everyone. Papa was supposed to be the one to protect them all. She was the one who was going to heal in the safety of their care.

All of a sudden, she was Mama and Papa both. What was she going to do?

Turn the house into a hotel? A boardinghouse?

Perhaps she could take in laundry. If she sharpened her rudimentary cooking skills she might turn the downstairs of the house into a restaurant…or maybe she and Libby could learn to sew dresses.

It was all too much. Her mind was a muddle. Even at the ranch, there had been Granny Rose and Great-Aunt Tillie to turn to.

"Mama!" Flynn careened into her legs and hugged them. She patted his head, smiled that practiced smile at him before he rushed off again, laughing and toddling after Pansy.

Just this moment she didn't know how she was going to survive. For now she would begin by discovering what had happened to her mother. Until she knew, she couldn't really settle anything else.

"Libby," she called. "Can you watch the children for a moment?"

"I'll do it," Joe answered, peeking his head around the kitchen doorway.

Joe was a good boy. She only hoped the folks of Cottonwood Grove would see that and not hold his past against him.

Melody went outside and closed the door behind her. The sun was shining. Patches of snow glittered along the brick walk leading to the gate.

The girl she used to be would have stopped and looked, pleased at how snow in sunshine twinkled like a treasure of diamonds.

Just now the only treasure she wanted was her father's arms about her, comforting her and telling her what had happened—to him and to Mama.

She crossed the road and strode up the walk of the house where her father now lived.

She knocked. Nothing stirred inside.

With any luck Papa's wife was not at home. She needed to speak with him alone.

She knocked again, louder this time. A curtain in a front window stirred. Footsteps retreated from the door. She heard voices—perhaps an argument. She couldn't be sure.

"Hello?" she called, then pounded on the door with her fist.

Inside, a door slammed. Seconds later the footsteps returned to the front of the house. Her stepmother was angry—very angry if the shoes slapping the floor were anything to go by.

She raised her hand to knock once more but the door flew open before her knuckles hit wood.

"What do you want?" Dixie Dawson's stare settled on her as hard as a frozen nickel. If those steel-gray eyes had ever crinkled in laughter, it was likely decades ago. The creases on her face seemed set in perpetual anger.

What had happened in her life to make her such a bitter woman? Melody wondered.

Right then and there Melody determined that she would laugh more often and more deeply. Joy would be her new middle name, because quite frankly, she had so much to be joyful over.

Growing up, she had been known for her laughter. Folks used to comment on what a delight she was to be around.

“I’d like to speak with my father, if you please.”

“Well, I don’t please.” Her father’s wife began to close the door, so Melody slipped her foot over the threshold. “Your father is indisposed.”

“I’ll wait.”

“Strumpet! Keep to your own side of the road… Go away and don’t come back.”

“I intend to see my father.”

“And I intend that you will not. In case you believe that your mother’s passing is what broke him, it wasn’t. It was you. You selfish wretch, you won’t get a moment with him.”

Dixie slammed the door on her foot, crushing her boot between the door and the jamb. Pain gave her no choice but to yank her foot free. The door banged closed.

No doubt, it was true that she had devastated her father by what she had done, and her mother’s death had brought him to his knees. But the man she had known all her life had been strong; he would have rallied.

Unless she missed her bet, it was Dixie who had broken him. At a time when he had been vulnerable and in need of comfort, the woman had moved in and made him all but her prisoner.

She pounded on the door with her fist until she heard the bolt on the other side slide into place.

"Blast it!" Ordinarily, Melody did not cuss, but all she had gained for her effort was a hand that hurt worse than her foot.

The miserable woman was not going to keep her from seeing her father! If she had to break a window and climb through, that is what she would do.

Aha! As luck, or more likely, Providence would have it, a copper pail with a long-dead flower wilted over the edge was set inches to the right of the door.

Dixie Dawson was about to discover that Melody was not as withered as the posy.

It was a shame to break the window that her elderly neighbor used to sit beside while she watched life parade by in front of her house, but some things couldn't be helped.

Melody lifted the bucket and swung her arm back, preparing her pitch. Mrs. Cherry would understand.

"I hope you aren't planning on breaking the law," came a deep voice from close behind her.

Reeve caught her hand and uncurled her fingers from the copper handle.

"I reckon I was—and still will if that horrid woman doesn't let me see my father."

"There are ways to get what you want without breaking into someone's home."

"Will you arrest me? She's the kidnapper."

"This is his home. She's his wife."

Reeve didn't look angry. She studied his face for

a moment. Amused is more what he appeared. That didn't mean he wouldn't do his duty and throw her in the hoosegow.

"Would you have arrested me?"

"I'd rather have dinner with you."

"You didn't answer—" Just then she smelled the delicious aroma of roasted vegetables and pumpkin pie coming from a pair of covered trays sitting on the porch near Reeve's boots. He must have brought dinner from the hotel.

All things considered, she would rather eat dinner than go to jail, as no doubt Dixie would press charges.

"All right for now," she said, frustrated at the angry tears welling in her eyes. "Let's get the children fed. But, Reeve, I won't let her get in the way of being with my father."

"And you shouldn't." He picked up the trays and handed one to her. "Just do it within the confines of the law."

Confines? Stuff! She would be with her father no matter what law she had to break.

It was still an hour before supper. Reeve made good use of the time by holding Pansy on his lap and listening while she told him a story—a very long, detailed story about a dog…or maybe a cat.

He listened and nodded, pretending that everything the child had to say made perfect sense, but he was distracted.

From where he sat at the dining table, he could see Melody's reflection in the kitchen window. She opened a cupboard then closed it. She picked up a teacup and pressed it to her heart, squeezing her eyes shut. After a moment she shook her head then opened her eyes. After giving the cup a quick kiss, she set it on the counter.

Maybe he shouldn't be watching her without her knowing it, but he couldn't look away. Especially when she clutched her skirt, lifted the fabric and stared at it, stroked it.

Unless he missed his bet, she was struggling to put away the ugly part of her past and embrace the present.

He knew something about that kind of struggle. He dealt with it daily. It was why he spurned a comfortable life in favor of chasing criminals. Every time he turned the key on a jail cell, he felt his father's approval.

"Pansy, that's a fine story. I'm sure Libby would like to hear it."

"I tell Libby!" She wrapped her small arms about his neck, squeezed and then dashed up the stairs in search of her sister.

Reeve coughed outside of the kitchen door to alert Melody that he was coming in. He didn't want to startle her.

Seconds later, he walked into the kitchen to find her smiling and putting on an apron.

"Dinner won't be long," she said, tugging the apron strings into a bow behind her back.

"Do you have a moment?"

"Of course." She smoothed her palms over the apron, looking at him with the hint of a frown. "But I've got to say, breaking someone's window, especially if they deserve it, wouldn't be the worst crime ever committed."

"I'll admit that some crimes are worse than others, but a crime is still a crime. It's something else I wanted to talk about, even though it's not my business and you can say so."

"Speak your mind. You have my consent."

This was not going to be easy.

"It's my feeling that you need to talk about what happened to you at the ranch." She looked away from him, out the window. In the reflection he saw her eyes close, as though she wanted to shut away the memory of that time but, of course, could not.

"I can't."

"I know what it's like, having the past eat at the joy of the present. I've been where you are… It will go easier if you talk to a friend. You can talk to me."

"There are some things that are better left alone."

"So they can fester? Melody, don't let Ramsey Travers keep you at that ranch."

She looked at him, her lovely brown eyes simmering with shame. He knew that feeling all too well.

"The things that happened were not your fault."

"I could have stood up to Ram when he became violent… I never did. I ducked my head, took the blows, waiting for his anger to pass and praying that I wouldn't be hurt too badly. I'm ashamed of that, Reeve. I was a coward."

"How many times did he beat your son?"

Her cheeks flared, red and splotchy.

"He never touched him."

"Why not?"

She shrugged one shoulder. "It was an easy thing to direct his anger away from Flynn."

"And toward you. You are a brave woman, Melody Dawson. I admire you greatly."

"How can you? I'm damaged inside." She crossed her arms across her middle. "Do you know that as much as I like you, I'm also frightened of you? Even here, safe at home, I'm a coward. Would you like to know why? I'd like for you to touch me but I'm frightened of it."

"You touched my hand the other night at the hotel."

She shrugged her shoulder again.

"I knew that wasn't easy for you. You were brave to offer me that comfort."

"It seemed right, then."

"Let me touch you, Melody."

She backed away from him. "It's nearly time for supper."

"It's time to free yourself from Travers's ghost." He reached out his hand, palm up. "Give me your fingertips. I won't hold on. You can take them away whenever you want."

She gazed up at him for a long time. He thought she wouldn't, but then she surprised him. Slowly, lightly, she pressed her fingertips to his palm.

After a full minute she still hadn't withdrawn her hand; she simply stared at her fingers on his skin.

"May I close my hand over yours?"

She gave him a hesitant smile and nodded.

He curled his fingers over hers, returning her smile. "You have lovely hands, Melody. Soft and competent."

"Work-worn, you mean."

He shook his head, stroked his thumb over the calluses on her palms. "I mean that they are the lovely hands of a woman who gives herself to others."

He lifted one of her hands to his mouth then kissed her open palm.

Her eyes widened, then her expression softened.

She touched his cheek shyly, ran her fingers over the line of his jaw.

Slowly, carefully, he touched her shoulders and drew her to him. He held her loosely, giving her the freedom to pull away if she wanted to.

A tremble ran through her shoulders, then she relaxed and laid her cheek against his chest.

After a moment, she stepped away from him. She was smiling.

"I do admire you, Melody. You have more courage than you know."

"It's the most curious thing. Just now, I believe I saw the back door hit Ram in the behind as he was leaving."

He grazed her cheek with his knuckles. To his relief she didn't flinch.

"You are a good friend," she said and he felt as if he had swallowed a grapefruit.

"A man can't have too many of those," he answered, instead of pulling her into his arms and kissing her.

If only he hadn't made that mistake that had ruined his family, he might... He might nothing.

He had made the mistake and it had ruined his family. He would spend the rest of his life trying to make it right in the only way he knew how.

He wished he had Melody's courage. If he had, he might consider another way of life, one that included a home and a family.

* * *

Melody studied him from across the dinner table. He couldn't quite judge her expression. The moments they had shared in the kitchen had been intimate, but he wondered if, in the end, he had frightened her. It hadn't seemed so at the time, but perhaps in retrospect, she regretted letting him touch her.

She smiled at him, but it was short of being genuine.

The night that she had stepped out of the hot spring he'd seen her true smile. It had shone through the darkness and warmed him.

He would have a hard time leaving Cottonwood Grove without seeing it one more time.

"When the children are asleep, will you walk with me?" he asked. "I could use the night air and the company."

She tilted her head to the side, apparently considering the offer.

"I'd enjoy that." If he saw right, her smile was a flicker away from being true.

Two and a half hours later she stood beside him on the front porch, clutching the hood of her coat close to her face. She looked as pretty as a portrait in a frame.

Judging by the scent in the air, snow wasn't far off.

"It's mild for this time of year," she said, then shot him a wink and a shiver.

"When those snowflakes begin to fall they'll be warm instead of cold." He played along.

She surprised him by slipping her arm through his as they walked down the front steps. There had only been a whisper of hesitation when her fingers curled over his arm.

"Little bits of sunshine falling from the night sky," she continued. Suddenly she smiled up at him, bright and true.

"Something's different about you all of a sudden." Very different. It could not have all come from what happened before dinner.

Here was the woman coming out of the hot spring—but then again, not quite. This Melody was playful, flirting. He hoped she was flirting.

"Do I have the pleasure of meeting the girl you were before Ramsey?"

"Please no!" She laughed out loud. The sound tinkled through the dark. It tiptoed through his heart and stayed there. "She was vain and so selfish. You wouldn't have liked her."

"Something's happened. You look—"

"My baby smiled at me for the first time," she said in a rush.

She hugged his arm as they walked past the last house on the road. The curve of her breast molded his arm.

By dickens! She was flirting.

Dainty, glove-covered fingers pressed his sleeve. He covered them with his hand and squeezed. He was definitely flirting back.

Pretty lips nipped pink with chill smiled up at him. All of a sudden the night didn't seem so cold. Maybe snowflakes really would fall warm instead of icy.

"Seth was feeding, making those contented little

sighs they do, and all of a sudden he turned from my breast, looked me in the eye and smiled."

"I've heard my nieces make that sound. It is touching."

"Yes, but it's more than that." She let go of his arm and looked up at him. "Seth was born under the worst of conditions, but when he gave me that smile…well, it was like he said none of it mattered. In spite of the decisions I have made, who I was forced to become, all he needs is me. I can raise these children and I will. I'll do a good job of it, too."

"You'll need an income." A courageous spirit was well and good, but there were practical matters to be considered. "The government has a program—for women in your situation—"

She arched her brows at him.

"Reeve, the government has done more than enough. It's time for me to stand on my own. Otherwise I'll be no better than I was before I ran away. I'll forever be a taker when the children need a giver—when I need to be a giver."

"What will you do?" A lamp in front of the hotel reflected golden light on her face. The nippy air blushed her cheeks and reddened the tip of her nose.

He wanted to kiss her—and badly.

Couldn't, though. It wouldn't be wise. He was leaving tomorrow—outlaws to catch, his own family to provide for.

"I'm going to open my home. I'll run a boardinghouse. It makes sense with the house being so large. I have room for at least four boarders."

"Make me one of them."

"But you're leaving tomorrow."

He shook his head. "The day after." Assuming he worked up the gumption to get on his horse. "Cottonwood Grove is central to where I travel. I want a place where I can come and roost now and again. I get good and tired of hotels."

"I don't know." A frown set her mouth in a provocative pout.

Surely she had no idea how much he wanted to kiss her. A snowflake drifted from the clouds. It settled on her bottom lip then melted. He wondered how she would react if he did.

"It seems a lot of money to spend when you'll only be passing through now and again."

What would she do if he licked that drop of moisture away? He slid his arm around her back and drew her in close. Three more snowflakes dusted the halo of hair that slid out from under the brim of her hood.

She didn't look frightened.

"It might be more than now and again." He dipped his face toward hers, slow and cautious, hoping that she wouldn't push him away. She fit under his hands as if she was meant to be there. "All of a sudden, I don't want to leave."

She sighed and closed her eyes. Her breasts grazed his chest. It was easy to feel how full and firm they were even under heavy coats.

He touched her lips with one finger, then he leaned in for a taste of bliss.

"But you will leave." Her eyes opened, warm amber

glistening in the dim light of the lantern hanging beside the hotel door. "You have to."

He nodded, then took a long, hard step away from her.

"I've got to… If I had a choice—"

What would he do if he had a choice? He'd kiss her for certain. Those moist lips, glistening in the lamplight, would get thoroughly compromised. He'd tip back her hood and bare her hair. Then he'd remove the pins one by one and run his fingers over the tresses, then bring her long hair to his lips.

What devil had gotten into him, showing him in vivid detail things that could never be his?

He would not kiss her. Not now, not ever. But he'd dream of it, probably every cold, lonely night on the trail. While he stared across the campfire at some criminal, he'd be seeing Melody.

"Life is complicated enough right now without adding heartache to the mix," she pointed out, with a shake of her head and her eyes downcast.

"You'll keep me a room, though? I'll pay up front for a year." Even if he couldn't be with her in the way he wanted to, he would know she had at least that bit of income.

"Why would you do that, Reeve? You shouldn't. What if you don't get back this way?" In spite of her protest, he saw relief wash through her.

"I'll be back. Besides, a government program pays for it."

"The government is unusually generous these days," she said with a frown. The gesture made her face even prettier than usual. As much as he tried to remember how bedraggled she had looked leaving the Broken Brand, all he saw now was luminous beauty.

Just went to show, things were not always what they first appeared. Years ago, it looked as if the only way to support his family and atone for his sin was to work as a US marshal. The job suited him fine. Life on the move hadn't been horrible.

If he were honest, and honesty was something he stood for, he would have to admit that renting the room for a full year had not only been to give Melody and the children an income. He wanted to see them again.

What was there to say he couldn't make a living some way that didn't involve tramping about the country? But even as he thought it, he knew it was only wishful thinking.

In order to feel his father's approval, and see it in his mother's eyes, he had to arrest bad people. He was a lawman to the bone.

"I'd better get you home," he said. "The snow's coming down faster."

"I can find my way back. No point in you walking away from your front door."

He glanced through a parlor window. A fire roared merrily in the hearth. It would be warm and welcoming inside. It was tempting to get out of the cold, sit in a chair and put up his feet to warm.

But he had a duty to see Melody home, just as he had a duty to put criminals away.

Duty ruled his life. That didn't mean it wasn't as tempting as hell to think about settling down, courting Miss Dawson, living a full and easy life.

He'd do well to remember that he had sacrificed easy when he'd betrayed his parents.

Melody slipped her arm into the crook of his elbow for the walk home, but this time there was no squeezing. No flirting.

Just snow coming down harder and colder.

Chapter Six

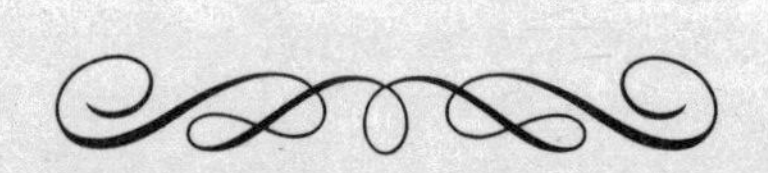

It had been harder than Melody expected, leaving Joe and Libby at the schoolhouse. She had half hoped that the snow would continue through the day so that they could remain home just a little longer.

But the day had dawned bright and sunny so the morning saw them all headed toward the bright red schoolhouse three blocks away. With their backs straight, elbows locked and fists clenched, Joe and Libby looked like walking logs. A body would think they were facing a prison sentence rather than higher education.

Their apprehension was understandable. They had never been to school, had never even seen a classroom.

She felt like an executioner, marching them up the stairs and through the front door at a time when all the other students were already seated.

The teacher welcomed them with kindness.

A girl near the back yanked on her neighbor's braid then whispered in her ear. The gossip receiver giggled.

A boy at a desk near the stove pounded a fist in his hand, sizing Joe up.

Oh, dear. What would happen when it came out, and it would, that Libby and Joe were the children of outlaws?

"Lord, give them courage," she whispered as she walked home holding Seth and pulling a wagon with Flynn and Pansy bundled in blankets.

As outsiders, they would need it. Cottonwood Grove had been a wonderful place for Melody to grow up, but her parents had been loved and respected in the community. It wouldn't be the same for Joe and Libby. All they knew of society was what they had learned from social outcasts.

There was no help for it, though. This was Cottonwood Grove not the Broken Brand. Here, children went to school.

In an attempt not to dwell on worrisome things, Melody let her mind drift back to last night. To her almost kiss with Reeve.

The kiss that never happened had been more intense and more sensuous than any she had ever shared with Ram, even before she knew who he really was.

Pushing Reeve away last night had been no easy decision. A bit of her heart had broken when she did. Falling into his arms, letting him soothe and protect her, would have been so easy.

She shook her head. Indulging in what was easy would not make her the person that her family needed her to be.

Coming to her front door, she helped the babies out

of the wagon then followed close behind while they scrambled up the slippery steps.

Maybe someday, if Reeve really did come back around—

"Papa!" she gasped.

Her father sat in a chair beside the fireplace, rubbing his hands in front of the flames.

"Melody…baby." His eyes misted, and he clapped his chest with one open hand. "Is that my grandson?"

"This one, and that one trying to roll himself up in the rug, too." She could barely catch her breath. How had he escaped his wife? "You might just as well get used to calling little Pansy, here, yours, too."

A clinking of mugs came from the kitchen. A moment later Reeve strode out carrying a cup of coffee in each big fist.

"Look who's come to visit," he said and handed her father one of the mugs. He offered her the other but she shook her head.

"How did you manage it, Reeve?"

"I didn't bash in a window." His handsome grin made her regret that she hadn't kissed him. "Better get your visiting done quick. Your stepmother went out, but there's no telling for how long."

Her father stretched out his arms for the baby. She laid Seth in them, then sat down on the raised hearth, facing him.

"Come out from under the carpet, Flynn. Come meet your grandfather." The hump that was her little wild man moved this way and that but didn't emerge.

"I tried to see you yesterday, Papa. Your wife wouldn't allow me in."

"I know, Mellie. We fought over it. I'm grateful that your man was watching for Dixie to go to the…well, wherever it is she goes this time of day. He walked right in and brought me over."

"There's so much I need to know, Papa, about you and Mama."

"It appears that there's a bit I need to know about you, as well."

"I'll care for the young'uns while you two get caught up." Reeve picked up Seth then bribed Flynn out from under the carpet with the promise of a treat. Melody was only half paying attention to them and barely noted that Pansy skipped along, clapping and laughing.

"I wish I could take back the hurt I caused." Her apology was too small considering her crime. "I don't deserve your forgiveness…but, Papa, I'm so sorry."

"Oh, stuff. You're my baby. There's no blame or forgiveness between us." He leaned forward and cupped her cheeks in his palms. Hands that used to be firm and strong were now frail, the skin paper-thin. "I'm grateful that you didn't come to any harm… You didn't, did you?"

She ducked her head and her father's hands fell away.

"I ran away and got married. I left a note but… well, Ramsey took it. He was an outlaw, Papa. I tried to come home, but—"

Sorrow contorted her father's face. He shouldn't have to bear the burden of her sin. He didn't need to know it all.

"I couldn't. The ranch where we lived was remote. The worst of it was that I missed you and Mama dreadfully. Anyway, I'm a widow now. I've gained a pair of sons and three others to go with them."

"I suppose it's all come out right in the end, then."

Not quite. Mama was not here and Dixie was.

"What happened to Mama?" It was hard to ask. She was afraid to know. Words choked under the lump swelling her throat. "When did she die? How?"

"It must be a year…no, more than that. It's all fuzzy in my mind now. But it was the fever that took her. It swept through town and killed a few others, too. Mrs. Cherry across the road was one. Your mama went to nurse her then came down with the same thing."

"I'm so sorry I wasn't here. I ought to have been."

"It's good you weren't, Mellie. You might have caught the fever, too. I'd have lost you forever, then. Your boys would have never been born." He tipped her chin up. She had been staring at the floor, trying to hide her grief. "It all worked out the way it was supposed to."

Melody dashed her sleeve across her damp cheek.

All of a sudden the front door flew open with enough force to hit the coatrack and tip it over.

"Mr. Dawson!" Dixie Dawson crossed the room with her fisted hands riding her hips. "I expressly forbade you to come here."

Reeve stepped out of the kitchen holding Pansy. He must have stashed Seth in the cradle beside the stove.

Flynn charged out of the kitchen with his mouth smeared in strawberry jam. It appeared that he had waggled his hands in the jar up to his wrists. Bright red jam dripped off his fingers, thick and gooey.

"Mess," he babbled and smacked his lips. "Mess, yucky."

Unfortunately for Dixie, she ignored Flynn while she focused her ire on her husband's disobedience.

With a lunge, Flynn wrapped himself in Dixie's ivory-colored satin-and-lace skirt. He twisted his face into the folds and smeared his hands over a flounce of trim.

Melody figured she ought to put on some show of apology, but really, anyone who burst into a home where toddlers lived did so at their own risk.

As far as Flynn was concerned, any piece of cloth would suit his needs.

"Why you nasty little heathen!" Dixie cried. She lifted her hand, palm open, clearly intending to strike.

Melody lunged up from where she sat. Outlaws and outcasts at the Broken Brand had never managed to lay a hand on her child. Blamed if she would allow his wicked step-grandmother to do it.

She rushed forward, fist balled and ready, but Reeve was quicker than she was. He caught Dixie's arm on the downward swing then forced it back.

"The boy didn't mean you any harm, ma'am."

"For all the difference it makes. This gown is ruined!"

"You've a wardrobe full of frippery. You won't even miss this one," her father muttered.

"What did you say? I'll not hear another word out of you, Mr. Dawson." Dixie scowled at her husband. "You'll be buying me two to replace this one, mark my words… Let go of my arm, Marshal."

"I reckon you owe this little boy an apology for frightening him."

Melody knew that Flynn's tears were not likely due to fright, but the fact that Mrs. Dawson stood on the rug that he wanted to crawl beneath.

"Apologize to a child? Are you mad?"

Reeve let loose of her arm in order to comfort a sniffling Pansy.

"If he were mine he'd be facing a few moments with a switch."

"Let's be very clear on one thing." Melody scooped up Flynn. Strawberry-flavored fingers poked into her mouth, which made the threat she was delivering garbled. "He is not yours. If you even think about laying a hand on him, I'll shoot you where you stand."

If the hitch in Dixie's breath was anything to go by, that last bit came out clear enough.

"Or…she'll send for the law." Reeve shot Melody a frown.

"When did you learn to shoot a gun?" Her father stared at her in openmouthed shock.

As well he would be shocked. The little girl he remembered would never have known how to shoot, but a Travers bride…well, it was required.

"You heard the threat, Marshal. See that this woman stays away from me and mine. I'm a respectable lady." She cast an arrogant glance over Melody, judging her, tidy bun to polished boot. "Not a wanton like some. Come along, Mr. Dawson."

When her father hesitated, Dixie snagged him by the sleeve and tugged.

"Papa, you don't have to go… I have room. Stay with me and the children."

"Over my dead body!"

If only murder were not a crime and a sin! She could nearly consider it.

"She can't force you if you don't want to go. Isn't that right, Reeve?"

"Since when does a lawman side with a slattern?"

"I'll have a word, Mrs. Dawson," Reeve said, setting Pansy on the floor then escorting her father and Mrs. Dawson to the front door.

Reeve spoke quietly, but Melody was determined to hear every word they said.

"In my line of work I meet all kinds of women. Many of them are respectable in every way…like your daughter, Mr. Dawson. I'll tell you, she's faced a lot these last couple of years. You can be proud of how she's handled her life."

"I know a fallen woman when I see one," Dixie announced with a scowl at Melody.

"You felled down, Meldy?" Pansy asked. "Get ouchy?"

"No, darling, I didn't fall. Go and play with Flynn under the rug."

She scrambled underneath. Two humps rolled about, giggling.

"I've also met the other kind," Reeve continued. "Those who sell their bodies until business dries up and then they latch on to lonely widowers. I've seen your kind before, Dixie. If I hear that you are taking advantage of this man you will answer for it."

"I'm his wife, legally wed. You have no power over our personal business, Marshal."

"Mr. Dawson." Reeve turned his back on Dixie, blocking the nasty glare she was stabbing Melody's father with. "You ought to move home with your daughter. You'll be happier here."

"I made my choice and married Dixie. It's best for everyone if I go home and keep the peace."

"It's not best for you, Papa," Melody answered, because even though she was not supposed to hear the conversation, she did. "This is home."

"*Was* home," Dixie snapped. "Come, Mr. Dawson, we belong across the road."

She shoved her father out the door and pressed him forward with a hand to the small of his back.

"Don't you ever let me catch you over here again."

While Melody watched from the front porch, her stepmother herded her father into the house. Even from across the road, she heard the bolt slam into place.

"I'm so worried, Reeve. She's turned him into someone I don't know. My father used to be a rock."

"I've seen it happen—a lonely man and a greedy woman."

"He won't be lonely long. No matter what, I'll have my father back under my roof."

"Can't say I'm comfortable with the sound of 'no matter what.'"

As friendly as she felt toward Reeve, she was not about to reveal to a US marshal the unlawful acts that had just popped into her mind.

Silence stretched long and accusing. She might as well have confessed that in her imagination not a single pane of glass in the house across the street remained intact. And that Mrs. Dawson's eye was blackened and her closet raided by babies.

Reeve placed his rough, muscular hand on her shoulder. She wished she could burrow into the security of his touch.

"Promise me, Melody, that if you need help you'll call on the law. I'll let the town marshal know what's going on before I leave."

She nodded because it wasn't quite as strong a commitment as agreeing verbally.

How could she say how she would react in situations that had yet to arise?

"How did the children settle into school?"

Trouble was brewing there. Since she didn't want to burden him with things he could do nothing about, she kept that worry to herself.

Late in the afternoon, Reeve walked beside the streambed. Too bad it was too cold for fishing. He'd enjoy nothing more than easing his mind by settling back against a mossy log with a pole in his hand, letting troubling ideas wash away with the current.

But since there was no grassy knoll or pole, and for that matter no fish, he was stuck with contemplation. There was a fallen log near the water so he sat down on the cold surface and shivered in his coat.

From here he could see Melody's house, all three stories reflecting the afternoon sunshine. Someone peered out of an upper-story window. From here he couldn't tell who it was. He turned his attention to the water flowing icily by.

Until recently, the course he had set for his future had been uncomplicated. It was comfortable, predictable. He had been satisfied with the roaming life that allowed him to make up for the sins of his past.

Then along came a certain little lady with honey-colored hair and a smattering of freckles across her nose. She had blown him off course.

Now all he did was doubt the ideas that had kept him true to his cause.

The best lawman was a single lawman. A family kept a man's heart at home when he needed to be single-minded in the pursuit of law and order. A wife and children made a man cautious when he needed to take risks.

Lately, he'd been wondering whether or not he could do both, or if there might be another way of honoring his parents.

"You are looking mighty dour on this beautiful afternoon, Marshal Prentis," called a feminine voice from behind him.

He pivoted to see Melody coming toward him with a cup of steaming comfort gripped in each of her hands.

Ah, coffee. Life just went better with the dark, rich brew.

She wore a coat with fur trim decorating the hood. Her nose was pink with cold. She sat down beside him and handed him the mug.

"There's nothing that a cup of this won't help." He raised his mug in a toast.

"To our futures, then!" she said with a smile warmer than the mug he tipped against hers. "Mine making a home for the children, and yours making the world a safer place for them to live in."

"To our futures," he agreed, but hell if he didn't see the image of a different future flash through his mind. A future they shared.

"Which one of our futures are you frowning at, Reeve?"

He hadn't realized that he had been.

"It's the past more than the future." He took a long draw on the coffee. It was easy talking to Melody. "It's a hard time of year, just before Christmas. Always reminds me of the day my father was killed."

"That would be spring for me, when I broke my parents' hearts. I wonder why it's harder then than at other times. What happened, happened. The time of year doesn't make it any more or less real."

"Maybe it's the smells and sounds that bring us back in time, closer to the loss."

"Or just the idea of an anniversary. There's something about the 'this time last year' idea that makes it seem like you ought to remember and relive things."

"I reckon that's it as much as anything," he said, but there was more to his heavy heart than that. Melody was stirring up a desire that he didn't want to have. A desire for a home and a family of his own.

When days turn blustery, when holiday cheer warms the house, a man should be home with his own kin, not wandering the countryside in search of people to arrest.

"I believe that your father sees you, Reeve. I know that from wherever he is, he is so very proud of the man you've become."

He believed that, too. It's why the thought of giving up marshaling was so troubling.

"You came all the way out here in the cold just to cheer me up?"

She blushed.

"That and to give you something."

He raised his mug of coffee again.

"Not that."

She looked nervous, tangling her fingers together in her lap but holding his gaze.

"Thank you for everything you've done for me, Reeve."

"Just doing my job. Watching out for women and children is part of what I do."

"And you do it well, but what I mean is…"

She leaned forward and quickly kissed his cheek.

"Thank you for helping me to stop being frightened to do that."

She stood up quickly and took his empty mug.

"Won't you come for supper?"

"I'd like that, Melody. Thank you."

"See you at six, then." She gave him a bright smile then walked back toward the house.

He watched her go. She hadn't bound her hair and it swayed across her back with her quick gait. It caught the golden rays of the afternoon sunshine.

He was going to miss her.

Reeve folded the telegram he had received regarding a train robber in Iowa into four neat creases and placed it in his saddlebag. From his hotel window, he paused in his packing to watch the full moon come up huge and round through a haze of clouds.

He glanced around the room with a frown. This was

his life: a bed not his own, an empty dresser and only as many belongings as could fit into his saddle packs.

For the first time, he wasn't anxious to be on the move, eager to bring the next criminal to justice.

That, he reckoned, had everything to do with Melody Dawson.

When he rode out tomorrow before dawn, memories of her would fill him up, make it hard to get his life's vision back.

He was a US marshal, first and foremost. That came before anything—or anyone.

Melody had invited him to dinner and to see his room. She must have spent all day making it up for him. No doubt she wanted his approval.

He'd admire it, say how he looked forward to coming back, but he didn't believe that he ever would. If leaving gnawed at his insides every time as much as it did now, he'd be better off staying away.

He shouldn't be calling on her tonight, but here he was, closing his hotel door and quick-footing it toward an easiness he'd only ever known in Melody's presence.

If, later on, he suffered for indulging in it, so be it.

From three houses down he spotted her trim yet curvy silhouette in the window. She lifted her baby toward the ceiling, wriggled him then lowered him and kissed his cheek. She did it over and over because, he guessed, the baby was smiling.

He went up the steps then knocked on the front door. While he waited, he glanced at the house across the street. The windows were dark. The place looked cold and dreary.

Melody opened the door, no longer holding her infant.

She clasped both of his chilly hands in her warm ones.

"Welcome home, Reeve." She shut the door behind him while he took off his coat and hung it on the coat-rack. "Since you are a paying boarder now, there's no need to knock, just come on in."

"Smells like heaven."

Or like home. He filled his lungs with the delicious scent wafting out of the kitchen.

"I hope it's half-edible." She wrung her hands in front of her, looking nervous but smiling. "Fancy cooking was not something I ever learned, but an old friend stopped by this afternoon and showed me a few tricks."

"I'm pleased to hear that old acquaintances are calling."

"Jillie and I were close once. I hope we can be again. It seems like coming home was the right thing to do. Thank you, Reeve. Without you I don't know what we would have done."

He knew he should remind her that he had just been doing his job. That would have been the truth in the beginning. But if it were the truth now, he wouldn't be standing here stuffing his heart back in his chest because she was smiling at him.

"My pleasure," he replied.

She tilted her head to the side. Her happy expression reminded him of a twinkling star.

She tapped her bottom lip with one finger. He wished it was an invitation to give her a kiss, but he knew better. More than likely, she was just mulling something over in her mind.

"Just as it's my pleasure to rent you a room," she said, and none too soon. Another second and he might have pounced upon her mouth, mindless of good sense and the children in the house.

With some effort, he turned his attention toward the dining table, where Joe and Libby sat with a small chalkboard between them. Joe squeezed a worn-down piece of chalk while Libby clutched an eraser.

The pair of them looked as perplexed as chicks in a rabbit's nest.

"What's the trouble?" he asked, taking the chair beside Joe.

"Sums," Joe grumbled, one hand tangled in his hair. "Back at the ranch, Aunt Tillie only made us read and write."

"Come on, Joe," Libby said. "I'm not going back to school until we've learned at least a little."

"I reckon I don't want to go back to school at all."

Melody, who had gone into the kitchen, peeked her head around the corner.

"Nonetheless, you are," she declared. "Write down the numbers four and nine, then tell me what they total."

Melody returned to her task in the kitchen, but called out, "I'm listening."

"I don't need to know. I've got by fine without sums so far."

"And who's going to hire you for any job when you grow up?" Libby asked.

"I'll find work that doesn't have a hill of beans to do with sums."

"What kind of work did you have in mind, Joe?" Reeve asked. There were a few jobs that didn't require math, but none that would make a bright boy like him happy.

"I'll be a US marshal, just like you, Reeve. I'll throw bad folks in jail. Don't need sums to do that."

While Reeve considered how to respond, Flynn clutched his pant leg and scrambled onto his lap. The boy grabbed a spare hunk of chalk then pounded it on the writing tablet.

"Look, even Flynn wants to learn sums," Libby said.

"More like he wants to grind chalk to powder," Joe mumbled.

The last thing Reeve would advise Joe to do was to become a US marshal.

That would not have been his advice last month, before ousting the criminals from the Broken Brand. Now, somehow, encouraging the boy to spend his days and nights on the trail with no one for company but outlaws and mad coyotes seemed wrong.

"You'll need quite a bit of education if that's what you have in mind."

Joe looked him hard in the eye for a long moment.

"I really do want to put outlaws away…so I reckon nine plus four is—" he plucked the chalk from Flynn then wrote on the board "—thirteen. Can I do something else now, Melody?"

Melody reemerged from the kitchen with a dab of flour on the tip of her nose.

"You can subtract four from nine."

"You sure a marshal needs to know this stuff?"

"This and plenty more. Even if you don't use the

skills on a daily basis, you'll need it for your own self-respect."

Joe wrote nine, the minus sign and four on the chalkboard. Before he could write the equal sign, Flynn slammed his hand on the board and smeared the equation.

"Five," Joe said. "Just about the age you'll be when they make you start cramming your brain full of numbers."

"You're smarter than you know, Joe," Libby said. "I wish I was catching on to sums as quickly as you are. What's seven plus three? That one's got me stumped."

She was right. The boy was smart, but so was Libby. Without Joe even realizing it, she was encouraging him to a higher standard.

Flynn wriggled down to the floor, then toddled to the divan where Pansy played with a curly-haired doll. It looked old. Reeve figured it must have belonged to Melody.

Pansy screeched when Flynn grabbed the doll's dress. She stood up on the cushion and held it high over her head.

"Meldy!" she cried. "Help!"

"Reeve..." Melody peeked out from the kitchen again. This time there was a dot of flour on her cheek. "There's a rag doll under the rug. Will you fish it out and give it to Flynn?"

And so the evening went with the occasional spat but more laughter than tears. A delicious meal, then everyone gathered nice and snug by the fireside while the wind huffed against the solid house.

The only occasions he had ever felt this content

were the moments he spent with his sisters and Sarah's children. He suspected that he was born to be a family man. It wasn't easy, knowing that he had killed that kind of a future by making a mistake so many years ago. Just one wrong thing spoken to the wrong people had changed the course of his life.

When he left tomorrow, he would picture Melody and the children just this way—and the sorrow of leaving them would cut his heart to the quick.

With the children bedded down for the night, Melody turned her attention to washing the dishes.

Well, maybe not all of her attention, a goodly portion of it was focused on Reeve's smile, the pull and stretch of his muscular back under his shirt and the deep sound of his voice. The low tones rippled through her, making her belly feel as if…as if she ought to focus more effort on washing dishes.

The spot on the pot she scrubbed had vanished, but she kept at it for another minute while she gathered the gumption to take Reeve upstairs and show him his bedroom. Oddly, it seemed an intimate thing to do.

Silly goose, the agreement between them was simply business. There was no need to read any more into it than that. He paid her rent money and she gave him a room.

All over the country, women earned incomes providing rooms for boarders. They did not lose their hearts in the bargain.

From the parlor, she heard her mother's music box begin to play. She squeezed her eyes shut and remembered Mama and Papa spinning about the parlor to the lively tune. Her heart swelled, not in sorrow, though.

Had Papa ever sneaked over and opened the box? Did his toe ever tap to the memory of Mama and the music?

Hers did. The melody wrapped her up, and she began to sway, still scrubbing the pot.

A big, warm hand curled about her cool, sudsy one. Reeve's strong fingers wrapped firmly around her hand. What a wonderful thing it was that she didn't mind his touch—rather, she welcomed it.

The pot fell with a splash into the soapy water.

Slowly, Reeve turned her about and placed his other hand at her waist.

"May I have the pleasure of a turn about the parlor, Miss Dawson?"

"Why, yes, sir. The pleasure would be all mine."

It had been ages since she danced. The grin she flashed him came from a source of joy that had been dormant in her life for far too long.

He spun her out of the kitchen, past the dining table and into the parlor. She laughed and he laughed in answer. His eyes shone down at her, brilliant green and suffused in high spirits.

These were among the best moments she had ever spent in this room. It was glorious to realize that good times had not died with Mama. Life and joy could go on.

"You have a way with the polka, Reeve."

"I have my sisters to blame for that."

If, on this very rug, she hadn't spent so many years dancing with imaginary swains, perfecting the steps to all the stylish dances, she might have stomped on Reeve's toes. His grin down at her was that distracting.

He dipped her backward, sideways, and quick-stepped her about to the tinkling tune. At times, his broad hand slid up her back. Once and again, he drew her forward so that her apron's bodice grazed his plaid shirt.

Still, the most intimate step of the promenade was when he held her at arm's length and simply gazed into her eyes.

A meeting of bodies was tantalizing, but a meeting of souls…well, that was spellbinding.

Was she a fool to be drawn in when there was no future for them? Would it be such a horrible thing to let her heart have its way again?

Yes, very foolish. She had known Reeve for such a short time. But there was nothing to say that she could not enjoy this moment, feel the joy and keep the memory to cherish later on.

The moment that she decided that she hadn't a solid bone or firm muscle left in her body, that she was composed of wax, he waltzed her up the stairs, down the hall and into his bedroom.

Chapter Seven

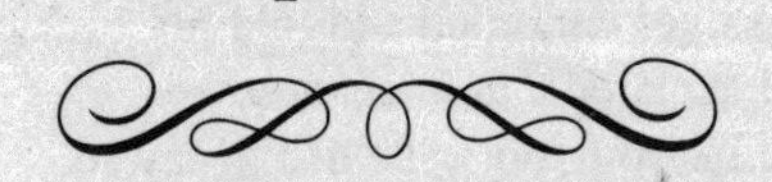

As soon as the music faded, his hands fell away from her waist. Breathless, Melody stood beside the bed and gazed across the mattress at Reeve.

With the children asleep and the music box wound down, the house was quiet. Only the wind blustering under the eaves softened the utter stillness.

Absently, she fluffed a pillow.

She had spent the afternoon scrubbing the third-floor room. The linens smelled like lilac and the floor shone with its recent polish.

"I haven't had so much fun since…since forever," she admitted.

"I care for you, Melody."

Blazes! In a special way?

She had to look away. Her gaze flitted to the dormer window, then the fireplace and the rug woven in a blue flowered pattern lying on the floor in front of the hearth.

"I hope you like your room," she answered because there was nothing else that felt right to say.

Staring out the window at the fat full moon she tried to find her breath, calm her pulse.

She cared for him, too, but a woman shouldn't set her heart on a man who would flash in and out of her life.

Reeve's gaze remained fixed on her. She felt the heat of it warming her face. Unable to resist, she glanced at him again.

Oh, she shouldn't have. His mouth lifted in a half smile. His eyes darkened and told her everything his voice had declared a moment ago.

"I care for you, too." She had to say so.

All of a sudden the confessions seemed to leave them both speechless. No doubt he regretted what he had said. How could he not, when their futures lay in different directions?

"This used to be my bedroom," she declared in order to ease the uncomfortable silence.

She didn't regret saying that she cared for Reeve, exactly. It was the truth, after all. The time she had spent with him had been healing.

In every way he'd proven to be a decent man. One who wore honor along with his badge. Not like her late husband, who, she was certain, dragged about a spaded tail in the great below.

"I thank you for your trouble." He reached across and covered her fingers where she had, without knowing it, continued to stroke the pillowcase.

"I wish I could be that pillow, Melody. You know I do."

She nodded. "If things were different... But you have outlaws to catch and a family to provide for."

He let go of her fingers but raised his hand to touch her cheek.

"It's just a fact," she murmured while he reached across to twirl a strand of hair that had slipped from the coil at her neck, "that you need to be on the move and I need to stay put."

"I wish that weren't the case." He let go of her hair and took a step back from the bed.

Admitting that they felt something for each other had probably not been wise. Parting would be easier if they had been levelheaded enough to leave things unsaid.

Staying silent would have been more reasonable, but in the end, there was something about Melody and Reeve that fit, that just felt right. It seemed as if she had known him for years rather than weeks. If only it really had been years, she might be more at ease with her feelings.

This attachment, for all that it had developed in such a short time, went soul deep. Parting might be the right thing, the logical thing, to do, but it was going to hurt like the devil.

After the moment they had shared over the bed, they had come downstairs, and like proper friends, sat at the dining table laughing and talking over spice cake and coffee.

She supposed allowing him to stay so late was acceptable, given that he was a legitimate boarder.

Hours flew by. During that time she didn't bring up the conversation from upstairs, and neither did he. That didn't mean that the words didn't hang between them.

They were there in a shared joke or a story from

each other's past. Getting to know one another more deeply, time fell away.

When the grandfather clock in the dining room struck five o'clock, she glanced at it in surprise.

With a look of regret, he stood to take his leave.

Stuff! Why did life beyond this room have to come knocking with the dawn?

Reeve stood, walked to the coatrack and shrugged on his duster.

Bidding him farewell was a misery. Standing beside him at the front door, Melody felt that her heart was bleeding.

"When do you expect to be back this way?"

Soon, please say soon.

"It's hard to know." He glanced at his boots, and she had the impression that he didn't want to tell her that he wasn't coming back at all.

"Well, when you do, your room will be waiting."

I'll be waiting.

"Melody…I—"

"What part of the country are you riding off to this time?" she asked, wanting to prevent the truth from being said out loud. Knowing was hard enough; she didn't need to hear the words. "What desperado are you hunting down?"

"There's a bank robber in Iowa—and don't forget a couple of Traverses still on the loose."

"The sooner you capture them, the more secure Joe will feel. He's still apprehensive."

"Tell him not to worry. I'll send word when they're behind bars."

Send word? This really was goodbye. She was not

going to cry, absolutely was not going to shed a tear. This man had returned her life to her. The least she could do was send him off with a smile and a kind wish.

Saying goodbye was the sensible thing to do. All of a sudden, she hated being sensible. It felt like a bony fist squeezing her heart.

She plastered a warm smile on her face, but it ached.

"I wish you a safe trip." She hugged him quick around the ribs, then stepped back and opened the door to the wee hours of a cold, windy morning.

The fat full moon sat on the horizon directly behind him. With his face in shadow it was hard to read his expression.

Just as well. If he showed a kernel of the regret that she felt at his leaving, she might fling herself into his arms and never let go.

That wasn't what either of them needed.

"Be safe, Reeve. Take care," she murmured, unable to resist pressing her hand over his heart for an instant before she closed the door.

She also could not resist running to the window to watch him walk away, to memorize the way of him.

His strides were long, his pace quick. Wind blew the opening of his coat so that it flapped like wings. He had to slam his big, rough hand on top of his head to hold his Stetson in place.

She pressed her fingers to her throat to hold back the sob that constricted it.

Reeve clutched his hat to his head with one hand and his coat lapels together with the other. He strode against the biting wind toward the gate glowing white in the light of the setting moon.

It seemed that even the elements wanted to hold him here.

He reckoned there was a chance that he was the biggest fool to wear a badge. The fulfillment of every forbidden dream he'd ever had waited on the far side of that closed door.

He flipped up the gate latch and shut the gate behind him.

There were US marshals who were married, plenty of them. Over the years he had convinced himself that they were selfish, irresponsible even, for leaving their families behind to chase low-life criminals across the country.

How many times had he vowed to himself and his family that he'd never marry? His sisters had laughed themselves silly at this assertion. Someday the right woman would change his mind, and they would not be pleased to miss out on a sister-in-law because he was pigheaded.

Until the right woman stepped out of a hot spring, a bedraggled goddess in the moonlight, he had believed that his siblings were the misguided ones.

He paced four hard strides down the fence line.

Pigheaded was not a quality he admired.

He stopped, then pivoted toward the house. Melody stood at the window, outlined softly by lamplight, her hand touching her throat.

Curse it!

He bounded over the picket fence and raced across the yard.

Before he reached the door, it flew open and Melody rushed out.

She opened her arms. He drew her in, backed her against the wall and felt her heart beating against his shirt. Her hips grazed his belly. He shifted his weight to ease the swelling her nearness caused.

"I don't know how to make this work between us." He cupped her face in his hands. It looked small and delicate between his palms. "But I'll damned sure find a way if you'll have me."

Good sense told him he'd lost his mind, but better his mind than his soul.

Her lips parted, in surprise, he reckoned, but there they were, glistening and only inches away. And by hell, he was going to have a taste of them.

Let her reject him if she was bound to, but not before he showed her how it could be between them. How much she had come to mean to him.

Slow and easy was how he ought to go in, but there was nothing slow, or even tender, about his feelings just now. He was hungry in a way he had never been. And she, gazing up at him, her eyes open wide in question, was his feast.

He lifted her from the porch with one arm around her back and claimed her mouth, deep and hard. Spice on her lips and spice in her soul captured him. He would never be the same.

After a long moment, he released her mouth, but when she took a breath and appeared about to say something he kissed her again. If she was going to turn him down he didn't want to hear it. That possibility didn't bear considering.

Wind, cold and penetrating, pelted his back. He drew Melody closer, kissed her more ardently.

Since he couldn't kiss her into silence forever, he let her go, sliding her slowly down the front of him until her toes touched the porch. She could not have failed to notice the way he had hardened because of her.

"You know I want you, Reeve." She looked up at him, her eyes shimmering amber in the lamplight that spilled out of the open door. "But I won't hold you. You have your calling—and your family."

"I won't say there aren't some things I need to sort out, but I love you, Melody."

She blinked wide and clutched the lace collar of her dress. She shook her head.

"I need time and so do you."

Wind howled across the porch; it slammed the front door against the coatrack inside. When it toppled, the clatter might have been his heart shattering.

The woman he could not do without, the one he would turn his life inside out for, was refusing him.

He took a step backward, gathering himself. He nodded, drawing on professional discipline to turn and walk away without making an emotional outburst that would only make this more difficult on her.

She'd been through too much. She *did* need time. He ought to have recognized that.

If it broke him, he'd give her time—and distance.

Turn and walk away, he told himself. *Wish her well as you go.*

He got his feet to shuffle backward, but his heart was a mite slower getting over the rejection.

"Reeve, wait!" She caught his sleeve. "You misunderstand me. I just need some time. Everything has happened so quickly between us, but that doesn't mean that I don't want you. Go… Take care of what you need to, and I'll do the same. Then, if we still feel the same, if you still want me, I'll be waiting."

"I'll always want you."

She wrapped her arms around his chest, clinging tight and nuzzling her head over his heart.

"Off with you now." She pushed away from him, dashing a smear of moisture from her eye. "Let's see how we feel after some time."

Leaving was misery. Would he be able to do it time and again as his profession required? Some sort of a choice had to be made. Just now he couldn't think of what it might be, but Melody was right about needing time. Not to know how he felt about her or what he wanted, but what he was going to do about it.

He opened his arms then drew her under the folds of his coat. She trembled against him so he soothed her slender back with his open hands. He felt the bump of her ribs under his palms. All he wanted in the world was to protect her, to give her and the children a secure, happy life.

"Don't change your mind about me while I'm gone," he whispered, dipping his head and nuzzling her neck. He breathed in her scent, letting it fill him and storing the memory of it for the lonely times to come.

"Don't you, either."

"I'll be back before you notice I'm gone."

Since stalling wouldn't get him back here any sooner, he turned, hunched his shoulders into the wind and walked away.

Going through the gate, he heard her voice call out.

"I love you, too, Reeve!"

Once more he leaped over the fence and dashed up the porch.

After half a dozen kisses, and a caress as searing as a blazing match head, he managed to walk away once again.

He turned at the gate, hating like the devil to go beyond it.

"You wait for me, Melody. I'm coming back to make you my wife."

Just then dawn pinked the horizon, calling him to be off. He should have been on the trail a couple of hours ago.

He hurried along. When he glanced back, she was no longer on the porch. She had returned to her position behind the window.

She kissed her fingertips then pressed them to the glass.

"Wait for me," he called, but doubted that she heard him over the howl of the wind.

Chapter Eight

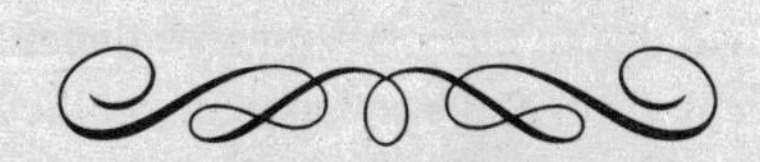

Winter whirled about the house and swirled against the windows for three days after Reeve left. On the morning of the fourth day, Melody opened the front door to a layer of hard frost on the ground.

It was time to venture to town, to do more than walk the three blocks to see the children off to school.

Today she would gather her courage, hold her head high and visit the butcher, the banker and the dress shop, and, thanks to her absent boarder, buy Christmas presents.

It was intimidating, going out alone. Coming home had not been what she expected. She could not just pick up where she had left off.

The pace of things would take some getting used to. It had been a long time since she had been around people running here and there, horses and wagons creaking down the street and strangers' voices coming from every which way.

In the end, there was nothing to be gained by isolating herself. It would only make her neighbors curious.

At some point her past would become known, but the longer it took for that to happen, the better.

After asking Libby to watch the children, she put on her coat, her hat and her gloves.

She stepped onto the porch, fighting the urge to go back inside, lock the door, draw the curtains over the windows and stay where it was familiar.

People were going to stare at her, wonder what had kept her away from home so long. Surely they were already speculating on why she had returned to Cottonwood Grove with five children and no husband.

She wondered how they would react when they discovered she was an outlaw's widow. Not well, she suspected.

She hurried down the front steps. Staying inside, safe and comfortable, would only make her weak.

Turning onto the main street of town, she felt eyes upon her. Somehow, she hadn't noticed the staring when Reeve had been with her. His big, bold presence and his badge had drawn all the attention.

"Walk with me, Reeve," she murmured, pretending he was still beside her and not goodness only knew where.

If she closed her eyes, she could imagine his long strides speaking his authority, daring anyone to think badly of her.

Pretending that he was with her was a silly game, she knew, but when she went into the dress shop, she imagined him looking at this ready-made dress and that one.

Silly, yes, but when Mrs. Gilmore, the dressmaker,

HARLEQUIN™ READER SERVICE—Here's How It Works:

Accepting your 2 free Harlequin® Historical books and 2 free gifts (gifts valued at approximately $10.00) places you u
no obligation to buy anything. You may keep the books and gifts and return the shipping statement marked "cancel". I
do not cancel, about a month later we'll send you 6 additional books and bill you just $5.44 each in the U.S. or $5.74
in Canada. That is a savings of at least 16% off the cover price. It's quite a bargain! Shipping and handling is just 50
book in the U.S. and 75¢ per book in Canada.* You may cancel at any time, but if you choose to continue, every month
send you 6 more books, which you may either purchase at the discount price or return to us and cancel your subscrip
*Terms and prices subject to change without notice. Prices do not include applicable taxes. Sales tax applicable ir
Canadian residents will be charged applicable taxes. Offer not valid in Quebec. Books received may not be as show
orders subject to credit approval. Credit or debit balances in a customer's account(s) may be offset by any other outstar
balance owed by or to the customer. Please allow 4 to 6 weeks for delivery. Offer available while quantities last.

If offer card is missing write to: Harlequin Reader Service, P.O. Box 1867, Buffalo NY 14240-1867 or visit: www.ReaderService.com

NO POSTAGE
NECESSARY
IF MAILED
IN THE
UNITED STATES

BUSINESS REPLY MAIL
FIRST-CLASS MAIL PERMIT NO. 717 BUFFALO, NY
POSTAGE WILL BE PAID BY ADDRESSEE

HARLEQUIN READER SERVICE
PO BOX 1867
BUFFALO NY 14240-9952

looked her over, Reeve's imagined presence told her she was brave and lovely and that she deserved a new dress.

"Good day, Miss Dawson—but it's Mrs. now, is it not?"

"I'm still just Melody, Mrs. Gilmore. Same as before."

How blatantly did that lie show on her face? she wondered.

"Is there something I can help you with?"

"Which dress do you like?" she mentally asked of her invisible marshal.

"The red one." She nearly felt his breath blow her hair.

Very bright and bold, she thought. She remembered the night in the kitchen when he had taught her not to fear his touch. He had told her that she was brave and that he admired her. She remembered it so well that she really could hear his voice.

"Buy the red one," her imaginary companion urged, again.

It was interesting how heated the memory of his voice made her feel, even with miles of the unknown between them.

"I'll try on the red one."

"What a lovely choice."

The seamstress handed her the dress. The expression in her eyes was searching. She wanted to know how it came about that Melody was suddenly home, with children and no husband—and escorted by a US marshal.

Eventually, her sorry past would become known, but

she was not ready for that yet. Only once the Broken Brand became a distant memory would she be ready.

She stepped behind a privacy screen, holding the dress. The garment was pretty—the prettiest thing she had seen in a long time. She put it on, feeling the slide of the linen over her arms and chest.

The sensation made her imagine big male hands gently stroking her skin.

It was a sad and sorry fact that although she had been a married woman, she had never really been made love to. She'd had sex, but that was not the same thing at all.

If the day came for her to be with Reeve, she knew she would not shy from his touch. She would welcome it with a joyful heart, and a willing body.

"Buy it," her imaginary Reeve urged.

"I'll wear it when you come home," she promised him, but not out loud.

She purchased the gown, then stepped out of the shop into the icy afternoon. A man rushed by and tipped his hat.

She nodded back. Common, everyday social activity was coming back more easily than she had expected it to.

Next, an old man sauntered past. She was the first to offer a greeting.

Things seemed to be looking brighter. In her mind, she saw Reeve's approving grin.

Her next stop would be the First Bank of Cottonwood Grove. She needed to open an account. She would have to give her real name.

It was time to leave Reeve behind. Thinking of him

had given her the courage she needed to begin her journey to town, but now it was time to do it on her own.

She was a bit nervous. Appearing confident while she walked into the bank would not be easy. But what had been easy since she ran away with Ram?

Even loving Reeve was complicated.

As intimidating as it was, she was going to open a bank account, and she was going to give her married name.

She was going to become a woman whom her parents would be proud of.

A woman who would be a good match for Reeve.

Walking to town had become easier, but no matter how many times Melody did it, there were things that she would never take for granted.

Before the Broken Brand, she had never appreciated the fact that she could have a yearning for a can of peaches, go into the general store and then ten minutes later be licking peach juice from her lips.

Walking down the boardwalk this morning, pulling Flynn and Pansy in the wagon, she felt as content as a bee in a spring flower bed. Never mind that this was the first day of winter.

The day was full of things she had never truly appreciated before.

Just seeing Dr. Melton's front door gave her deep-down comfort. For as long as she lived she would never take for granted the fact that if one of her children needed medical help, the doctor was only a few moments away.

And now there was Reeve. The memory of him telling her he loved her, the scent of his skin when he held her close and the heat of his lips claiming hers made her feel warm all over.

Fate, she reckoned, had a sense of humor, giving her an outlaw and then a lawman.

"Cookie, please, Meldy!" Pansy called when they rolled past the bakery. "Cookie! Cookie! Cookie!"

"Cuk!" Flynn mimicked then launched his quick little self over the wagon side.

He ran to the bakery door then reached for the door-knob. "Cuk, Mama!"

Another wonderful thing about town was that when one's child asked for a common treat, a mother could provide it.

Melody recentered Seth in the sling hung over her shoulder and opened the bakery door.

Pansy and Flynn stormed inside, dashed across the cozy dining room then pressed their noses to the glass on the large pastry cabinet.

"Is there something I might help you with, Miss Dawson?" the young counter girl asked. Her stature was so small that her blue eyes barely peered over the top of the display case.

"That's Mrs.—" Melody caught herself. While she wanted to make it clear that she was a widow, she did not want it known whose widow she was. "Well, I'm a widow now."

The door opened and the bell hanging over it jingled.

"Mellie!" Jillie, coming in with her cheeks blushed by the nip of the outdoors, rushed forward to embrace her. "What timing. I had a spare half hour to idle away, and now I won't have to do it alone. Let's sit and have a chat."

Nothing sounded more wonderful than spending an idle moment with a friend. And she would, just as soon as she separated Flynn and Pansy from the glass.

"If you have a rag, miss," she said to the counter girl. "I'll wipe away the smears."

The girl scowled at the previously sparkling glass. "No need, ma'am. What can I get for you?"

"Tea, but not too hot." She would be lifting the cup over Seth, asleep in his sling, as she drank. "Three—no, make that four white cookies and one piece of chocolate."

"I'll have my usual, Mary." Jillie pointed to a table next to the window that had four chairs placed about it. "This will be just like the old days."

Melody settled Flynn on a chair but he scrambled off—three times. Well, not quite like old times.

"Let's try this." Jillie removed the scarf draped around her neck and tied it to the chair and around Flynn's squirming belly.

Mary brought the tea and cookies, set them on the table then disappeared into the back room.

Pastries ought to keep her little wild man still for a few moments, and Pansy tended to be a nibbler. The cookies would probably keep her busy for a while.

"I can't tell you how I've missed doing this with you, Mellie," Jillie mumbled over a mouthful of cookie crumbs. "The years you were gone weren't nearly as lively."

"I've missed you, too, Jillie."

She picked up the cookie that Flynn tossed on the floor. She considered dusting it off and handing it back to him. It was probably cleaner than anything he had eaten at the Broken Brand, after all. But this was a new time, a new life with new rules. She set the cookie on the table out of reach.

"Tell me all about what went on while I was away."

Jillie related this story and that, but it was hard to fully appreciate town drama because Flynn's attention had been drawn to the door behind the display case, and how it slid open and closed. He was, in fact, fascinated by it.

"And then Mrs. Hilton—you recall her, the dreadful flirt—well, she set her cap for..."

Jillie's voice went on and the tale was a good one, but across the street she spotted her stepmother speaking with Mrs. Olsen, the wife of the general store's owner and Cottonwood Grove's most prolific gossip.

"Oh." Jillie glanced out the window, following Melody's gaze. "If there's a bigger busybody than Mrs. Olsen, it's your stepmother. If one of them has discovered a secret, it will be known all over town by this evening."

More than likely, the fact that she had been married to an outlaw was by now no longer private business.

"Jillie, the truth is, I have a secret." She glanced sideways at Flynn. He was working at his binding but not making much progress with it. "I'm afraid that what Dixie has to say will be hot gossip. I'd like you to hear it first."

"Well, no need to look so green over it. You're home, safe and hale and in time to celebrate Christmas with me. I can't imagine that anything that old harpy has to say will matter much. Nothing you can tell me will make a difference."

From across the road, Melody watched Mrs. Olsen drop the fir garland she had been attaching to the window, cover her mouth with one hand then give a slow, sorrowful shake of her head.

Mrs. Olsen was clearly and thoroughly scandalized.

"All right, then… You recall that I ran away with Ramsey Travers?"

Jillie nodded. "He was a handsome one. As much as folks had to say about it, we girls were all jealous that you were the one who snatched him up. I'm sorry for your loss, Mellie."

"Don't be. The fact is, Ram was an outlaw—he and his whole family." She took a breath, needing to tell her friend the story even though Jillie's face had gone from pink to milk white. "I lived on an outlaw ranch, with criminals as kin."

"Meldy!" Pansy said, yanking on Melody's sleeve. "Look!"

"Not right now, sweets, I'm speaking with my friend."

"But—"

Whatever Pansy wanted would have to wait. Jillie was withdrawing from her. Her eyes were no longer warm with the joy of having tea with a friend. No doubt she was considering the social implications of associating with the wife of a criminal.

It was understandable. Poor Jillie would be looked down upon for being seen with her.

"It's okay, Jillie. I suppose it will be for the best if we don't socialize."

"Bad Flynn," Pansy muttered under her breath.

"I don't judge you. Honestly, I don't. But I've got a beau… He's courting me. I can't think he will want me to—" Jillie stood up, wringing her hands in front of her. "I'm truly sorry, Mellie."

"Chocolate mouth," Pansy muttered.

Had she left the chocolate bar within reach? If it kept the child happy for a moment longer, let her eat it.

The bell on the door jangled with Jillie's hasty exit.

Melody buried her face in her hands, but she would not weep. All along, she knew that the secret of her marriage would surface. It would be unreasonable to expect her friend to risk her reputation and her young man.

"Pansy have chocolate, too."

"You and Flynn share, baby," she mumbled absently.

Fabric shuffled and small shoes pattered across the floor.

It would be nice to hide behind her fingers from the world, but life was out there waiting to be lived. She would not cower, lily-livered, in fear of what others had to say.

She would laugh through the scandal. It couldn't last forever, after all. When Reeve came back, she would be the strong woman he deserved. If she was not, she did not deserve him.

The front door burst open; the bell rang madly.

"I'm a horrible friend! Can you forgive me, Mellie? No matter what— Oh, dear!" All of a sudden Jillie started to giggle, wagging her finger at the pastry case.

Oh, dear…what? Melody shot her glance to Flynn's chair and found it empty, the scarf lying in a heap on the floor.

Oh, please don't let him have— Slowly she shifted her gaze.

"Flynn!" she gasped. "Pansy!"

A pair of chocolate-covered mouths grinned at her from inside the pastry cabinet. Both children sat happily among the treats, their legs tucked under them. The pair of them were gobbling down goodies in their chocolate-smeared fists as fast as they could manage.

What could she do but laugh along with Jillie, even though she would, no doubt, be banned from the bakery.

Mary hustled out from the back room. She screeched, apparently not appreciating the humor of the situation.

And maybe it wasn't funny. After this, in the eyes of the town, Melody would not only be a heathen, but she would be raising them, as well.

She laughed harder, blessing Jillie for laughing along with her.

Whatever came from now on, she was well and done with crying.

Melody stood on her front porch, arching her back and working out the aches from a long morning of hard, wonderful work. Very soon the house would be ready for paying borders—well, ones that would actually live here.

Sunshine touched her face, but she only felt the warmth in her imagination.

A drip of ice-cold water from a melting icicle hit

her scalp. She shivered, then stepped off the porch and walked to the small plot of earth on the south side of the house that would become the garden, come spring.

Right now, the ground was still too hard to do anything but dream of carrots and sweet potatoes.

And dream she would. She would dream of green trees, bountiful crops and lush summer warmth. Mentally, she saw the children, carefree and running barefoot in tall grass.

Later on, once the children, free from every care, had tumbled into bed for the night, she would dream again of tall grass, of being hidden in it with Reeve and nothing between her skin and the cool night breeze but his warm hands.

Dreams were a poor substitute for a flesh-and-blood man.

She sighed, glanced down at a dirt clod and tried to crush it under her boot, but it was still frozen.

Reeve had only been gone for a few weeks, but it seemed much longer. Christmas had been a joy, spent with the children and Jillie, but she felt his absence keenly.

How long, she wondered, would it take for him to return? Would he write? It wouldn't surprise her if he could not. Running after her former relatives would take him to some of the most isolated areas in the country.

She knew the places they would hide—dirty, barren stink-holes where dangerous things happened.

If Reeve meant what he had said about marrying her, worry was something she would have to get used to.

"Ouchhhh!" She heard the complaint from three houses down the street.

Without a doubt, the distressed voice belonged to Joe. The bitter cold day and reality crashed about her head.

"He didn't steal anything, Miss Jeffers! I know he didn't." This time it was Libby who screeched.

"'Cause you was in on it with him," scolded a voice cracking in adolescent indignation.

"That's enough from the lot of you," Melody heard the schoolteacher, Miss Jeffers, say.

She marched into view, dragging Libby by her left ear and Joe by his right. Twelve students followed, looking like a pack of overwrought bees.

Melody wanted nothing more than to smack the smirk from the face of the boy in front. He seemed to delight in riling everyone up. Too bad that bit of indulgence would only illustrate that she was, in the end, an outlaw's bride.

Gossip that she had hoped would soon die down would instead blossom with new life.

Both Joe and Libby raised a fuss under the teacher's pinching fingers, but they did not break free as she knew they could have. They had been through much worse in their young lives.

"Mrs. Travers," Miss Jeffers declared, "we have a situation."

Melody heard a door open. From the corner of her eye she saw Dixie step onto her front porch, arms folded across her chest and an eyebrow raised. Her lips pressed together in an expression that fairly shouted, "I knew they were no good."

A curtain beside the front door drew aside revealing her father's face, wrinkled in concern.

Miss Jeffers released Joe and Libby. They scrambled to Melody's side, standing stiff and bristling with indignation.

"What's happened?" she asked, certain as could be that Joe and Libby were innocent of whatever had occurred. They had been eager over the past few weeks to put the sins of their parents behind them.

"Outlaw Joe stole my marble!" Randolf Sweeny, the nasty boy out front, stood a head taller than Joe. The slant of his eyes and the narrow twist of his mouth bespoke mischief.

"Ain't no—" Joe growled, then collected himself. "I'm not an outlaw. And I did not steal a marble."

"You can trust Joe, Miss Jeffers," Melody said. "In spite of where he couldn't help coming from, he is a good boy."

"That may be so, but Joe refused to empty his pockets."

"He shouldn't have to!" Libby stomped her foot, her cheeks pulsing red with anger. No doubt, this behavior was what earned her the pinched ear. "He didn't do anything wrong."

"We have a witness," Miss Jeffers stated with a glance over her shoulder. "Butler Buchanan, step forward and tell Mrs. Travers what you saw."

Hearing her married name made her feel as if she had a burr in her corset, but apparently, she was not going to be so easily rid of it.

"Outlaw Joe—"

"That will be enough of name-calling, young man,

unless you want your ears boxed, as well." Miss Jeffers stared the culprit down. "Now, relate—truthfully—what you witnessed."

"Saw him take the marble from Randolf's desk when he wasn't looking. He put it in his pocket. Now he won't empty his clothes 'cause he's a Travers and guilty as sin," Butler declared, scooting beyond his teacher's reach.

Miss Jeffers sighed and looked at Melody. "If you will convince the boy to turn out his pockets we can all get back to the classroom."

The last thing she was going to do was single out Joe for this humiliation. Still, the truth had to come out, and she figured the guilty party was not Joe.

"I'm sure Joe will have no problem emptying his pockets—when everyone else does the same. Isn't that right, Joe?"

"Yes, ma'am." Joe swallowed hard. "That's right."

"I'd like a description of this marble, Randolf," Melody said. "Just to make sure we find the one that's gone missing."

"It's blue with two red dots, top and bottom."

Joe emptied his pockets. A rock and a twig fell out.

"Students?" Miss Jeffers turned to her class.

Pockets fell open to the afternoon light.

No marbles tumbled to the ground, but—

"Butler, what is that you are hiding in your fist?" Melody pointed to the hand that he quickly hid behind his back.

"Step forward, young man," Miss Jeffers demanded. "This minute. Don't make me come for you."

The boy shuffled forward, walking the walk of the condemned. He uncurled his fist to reveal the missing marble.

"I didn't steal it!" Sweat beaded his forehead despite the chilly afternoon. "Randolf made me take it!"

"Please, do tell us why he would want his own marble stolen," the teacher said, her patience clearly nearing an end.

Randolf scuffed his shoe in the dirt. "'Cause we wanted to catch him before he really took something."

"The pair of you will apologize to Joe—and to Libby. You will serve an hour of detention for the rest of the week, as well."

"My mama said not to talk to—" Randolf could not finish because Miss Jeffers snatched his ear.

"Please accept the apologies of the whole class." The teacher turned her gaze on Joe, then Libby. "If you don't wish to return to class today, that will be acceptable."

Miss Jeffers pointed her finger in the direction of the schoolhouse. "March!"

"I have to go back," Joe told Melody. "That's what Reeve would do. Face up to his troubles."

Joe straightened his slender shoulders, took a deep breath and followed Miss Jeffers.

"I'll go back, too. Just to watch out and be sure he's safe." Libby took several steps, then stopped and turned. "Because that's what you would do."

All of a sudden Melody couldn't find her breath. She watched Joe and Libby walk away, posture straight and heads not bowed in shame.

Every moment of every day she wished that Reeve

was here, but never more than right now. She was more proud of the children than she could say. She wanted nothing more than to share this with him.

Chapter Nine

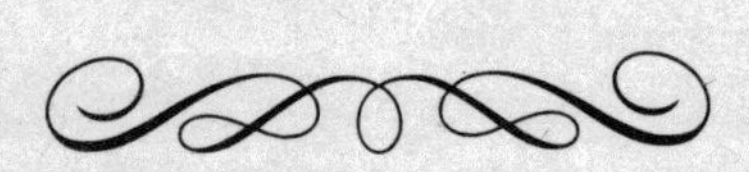

On occasion, life took the course of a tumbleweed in a windstorm.

Until a few days ago, events had been moving along as Reeve had intended them to. The last of the Travers gang were, he figured, no more than two days ahead of him.

Just as soon as they were in custody, it had been his intention to go home. Home to Melody.

He reckoned it shouldn't have, but it came as a surprise to him that life on the trail was not what it used to be. In the past he'd never been lonely in his own company. He'd never felt anything but satisfaction in his line of work.

Separation from Melody had made one thing clear: wherever she was, was where he was meant to be.

What he couldn't quite figure was how he was going to be where he was meant to be, when where he was required to be pulled him in the opposite direction.

If all had gone according to plan, he would have been in Cottonwood Grove this very minute, courting Melody, convincing her that she was his woman.

No period of waiting would change a thing, as far as he was concerned.

Then Tuesday came and with it frustration. He'd stopped at one of the four post offices where his family sent him mail. There was a letter from Mildred.

Even knowing that his youngest sister tended to be dramatic, the hair on his neck stood on end when he read what she had to say.

According to his sister, Mother was gravely ill, the landlord was evicting them in order to move his own parents into the house and Sarah was expecting again—sick all day, and her husband had gone for a drink at the Muddy Sipper and never returned home.

Today, a week after reading the letter, he slipped off his horse, nearly as lathered as the beast was. He pounded up the stairs to his mother's house, opened the door with a crash then strode inside.

"Mildred!" he shouted.

Surely half of the things she reported were an exaggeration. It wouldn't be the first time she had invented some drama only because she missed him and wanted him to come home. His youngest sibling was a delight and a terror all at once.

"Marshal Prentis!" Mrs. Cooper, the housekeeper, bustled into the parlor, wringing her hands in her apron. Normally, her complexion was as cheerful as peaches, but today she looked pale, worn. "Praise the Good Lord you've come in time."

His heart crashed.

"Mother?"

"The fever broke last night, but the poor dear is

weak. Certainly in no condition to be put out on the street, I can tell you that."

"She won't be, Mrs. Cooper." He took off his coat and placed it on a wall hook, then did the same with his hat and gun belt. "What about Sarah's husband? Did he come home?"

"No, but it's a blessing if you ask me."

The house was unusually quiet. Normally the place was alive with women's voices speaking all at once.

"Where are Mildred and Delilah?"

"This morning, as soon as we knew your mother was going to make it, Delilah went to look for a place for us all to live. I can tell you, it's slim pickings and high rent. Hopefully Mildred has had better luck with her errand."

Something cold shifted in his belly, making him feel slightly nauseous.

"And what, exactly, is Mildred's errand?"

Mrs. Cooper's gaze dropped suddenly to the floor, as though she had spotted an errant crumb that had escaped her attention.

"Mrs. Cooper?"

"She's gone to try and change Mr. Sweeny's mind."

"And how does she intend to do that?"

"I shouldn't like to make a judgment, but she was wearing her most fetching dress."

The clock downstairs chimed midnight, and so far, the family had not been tossed out into the dark.

Sweeny, his heart as hard as a silver dollar, had given them two more days. He claimed it was because Mrs. Prentis was ailing, but Reeve couldn't help but shiver at what sort of feminine wiles Mildred had called into play.

Reeve and his sisters gathered in chairs about their mother's bed, listening to the rhythm of her even breathing while she slept.

"She sounds worlds better than last night, Reeve." Mildred gazed across the bed at him.

"The wheezing is gone," added Delilah.

"There were times when..." Sarah crossed both arms over her middle. "I won't even say the words. Let's just be grateful that she is getting well and Reeve is here to set everything in order."

That comment brought him up short and quick. What if he hadn't been here? Anything could have happened to him alone in the wilderness. Then what would have become of his mother, sisters and small nieces?

He wanted to marry Melody—and soon. But did he even have the right to ask? How was a man to protect his family while his job kept him away from home for long periods of time? If the criminals he hunted had their way, he'd never make it home at all. He might end up in a cold, shallow grave without his wife even knowing.

"There's something different about you, big brother." Mildred peered at him across their mother's slumbering form. She stood, then she rounded the bed and bent over to peer closely at his face. "Don't you all see it? His expression softened just now."

"As though he were remembering something," Delilah observed, "or *someone* special?"

"You'd best watch your heart, if that's the case." Sarah frowned hard at him. "One day you think life is the buttons, then the next it's all come unraveled."

"Don't worry, sis, I'll find out what's become of Edward."

"I've got my guess, and if it's true he can just stay where he is." Sarah's voice was full of indignation but her eyes welled with tears. "I reckon I don't want him back."

Still, the man had to be found and held accountable, at least for the financial support of his family.

Mildred stood behind his chair with her hands on his shoulders. She bent her head close to his ear to speak. "Don't think you'll get away without telling us about your new lady."

Sometimes he believed that his sisters were emotional bloodhounds.

This was not the time to discuss Melody, as much as he wanted to. The problems he had come home to were enough of a trial for one night.

"What went on with you and Sweeny?" he murmured.

She smacked his cheek, but tenderly, then went back to her chair.

"Only a bit of friendly persuasion. Nothing that you need to be concerned about… And in the end, here we are, at least for a couple of days. I'm sure you'll have everything sorted out by then, Reeve."

It was going to take more than a few days to see his family resettled.

Getting back to Melody was not going to be as quick as he had hoped. First thing in the morning, he would write to her, let her know that she was ever in his heart and he would return as soon as things were settled here.

Possibly, while he was here, he'd come up with some sort of resolution to his career issue.

"Son." His mother's voice, muffled from the blanket tucked around her, was a welcome sound. From what he'd been told, she hadn't spoken in a week. "Don't keep us in suspense about your lady."

Late in the afternoon, rain dripped off the eaves of the front porch, slow and steady.

Melody breathed in a lungful of damp earth. She raised her shawl over her head, braced her hands on the porch rail and peered around the side of the house at her garden.

After the hardest winter that anyone could recall, the ground had finally thawed enough to allow the first green shoots of spring to poke up from the earth.

At long last, the bare branches of the cottonwoods had begun to flush green, and much to the delight of the children, the creek that ran along the edge of her property had become swollen by spring rains. Summer and warmer water for swimming could not come soon enough for them.

From where she stood, she could see Joe sitting on the grassy bank, hunkered under an oilcloth and gripping a fishing pole. It seemed that every day brought some new wonder to Joe and Libby. Joe's new passion was fishing.

The boy did catch a few fish, but mostly, she reckoned, he enjoyed seeing the water rush by. Water had been as scarce as laughter at the Broken Brand.

"He's a good boy when you get right down to the heart of the matter," said a voice from behind her.

Melody ducked her head back under the porch roof to smile at her boarder, who sat in a rocker with his hands folded over the head of the walking cane that she suspected he didn't really need.

Hyrum Stewart was a retired US marshal who had blown in one night in January, along with a bitter snowstorm. When the marshal had wanted a quiet place to enjoy his later years, Reeve sent him her way.

The only correspondence she had received from Reeve was a telegram to let her know that Hyrum was on his way.

That had been three months ago.

Sometimes, an ugly voice in her head tried to persuade her that she had not heard from him for one of two reasons. The first: time and distance had changed his mind. The second: something horrid had happened to him.

If something had happened to him… That was too painful to dwell on, so she closed her mind to it and wondered about the other option.

She had certainly not forgotten him. She dreamed of Reeve day and night.

The man she remembered would not have forgotten her, surely not.

She would not let herself believe that she had misjudged a man again. Reeve was a man of his word. He'd said that he would come back, and he would.

A miserable winter might have delayed him. And she knew firsthand how hard the land could be. Still, it was hard to banish terrifying thoughts, especially when they crept in during the worry hours just before dawn.

Melody shook her head. When he returned, and he

would, she might become the wife of a US marshal. She would need to learn to live with the constant dread.

She shook herself. It was spring. New life was emerging, green and sparkling in the rain. Reeve would be here soon.

"He *is* a good boy," she said to Hyrum. "I only wish the other boys his age could see it." Melody sat down in the chair across from him, sighing and listening to the gentle drum of raindrops.

"I wouldn't worry. Those boys will come around." Hyrum's blue eyes crinkled at the corners when he smiled. "He's still a stranger, and to tell you the truth, Miss Mellie, they're jealous of the life he's lived."

"How could they possibly be?" That was absurd.

"They're young and ignorant. Don't know a real outlaw from a dime-novel character."

"Let's hope they never do."

"Cottonwood Grove is as peaceful a place as I've seen. Miss Dixie, across the way, is the closest they'll likely come to anyone truly corrupt."

"If only she'd broken some law." Melody drummed her fingertips on her knees. "Just anything I could use to bring my father home."

"You still speaking with him through his bedroom window at night?"

She shook her head. She had managed a few short conversations sneaking over after dark and tapping on the glass.

"Dixie must have found us out. Last night the window was nailed closed."

"I wouldn't fret over it, Mellie." Hyrum reached across the way to still the nervous tap of her fingers.

"A woman like that is bound to go back to her old ways sooner or later and forget all about her husband."

She prayed that it would be sooner. How long would it be before Dixie sapped every last bit of joy from her father's life?

"I wouldn't worry about Reeve, either." Hyrum sat back in his chair with a grin. "He'll be along soon as he can to make you his, right and proper."

"Were you married while you wore the badge, Hyrum?"

Hyrum slapped his knee and laughed out loud.

"Yes, indeed! To a woman who was rougher and tougher than I was, I'll swear. And she was a beauty to go with it."

"How did she manage the anxiety? She must have hated it, not knowing if you had come to harm while you were away."

"She never let on if she did. More's the time she pushed me out the door to be on my way, said it was worrisome always having me underfoot." Hyrum paused for a moment while he seemed to look back at his memories. "It does take a special kind of woman to be married to one of us. There's some that can't handle it."

She sighed deep and hard. She loved Reeve so desperately. She simply had to be one of the special ones. If she wasn't, she would just have to make herself that way.

"Put away your frown, Mellie. You'll do just fine if the need comes." Hyrum had a smile that made a body feel peaceful. It seemed to say that he had been through life and things *did* work out in the end. "Who's that out in the rain?"

He leaned forward, and she turned in her chair to look up the street.

"It's your sweet little friend Jillie, unless I miss my mark." He waved and Jillie waved back. "Say, I hope you girls aren't planning some grief for your stepmother. Nothing illegal, at any rate."

Well, wasn't he just like Reeve? She stood up, bent at the waist and kissed the top of his bald head.

Age hadn't dulled his perceptions, apparently.

Jillie had, in fact, come out in the rain to help her devise a scheme to bring her father back home.

"You girls can't up and haul a man over here against his will." Hyrum, propping his elbows on the dining table, bent forward and gave Melody a stern stare. He swung his head to look at Jillie, who sat beside him. He gave her the blue-eyed what-for, as well. "Kidnapping will land you both in jail. Then what will become of your papa?"

Melody listened for any sign that Libby or Joe might still be awake. She didn't want to set a bad example as a schemer.

All was well. With Joe snoring as loud as he was, even if Libby were awake, she wouldn't hear a thing.

"It wouldn't be against his will." She didn't think so, at any rate.

"It'll have to come from his own mouth. Otherwise that harridan will say you kidnapped him." Hyrum rapped his knuckles on the table. "I'll do what I can to help, just as long as we don't break any laws."

"You sound like Reeve," Melody said, repressing a longing sigh. "You lawmen must be cut from the same cloth."

"It's a brotherhood, is what it is."

"I might like to meet one of those brothers," Jillie said with a playful grin at Hyrum.

"Don't you have a young man already?"

"I have one, but I wonder how much of a man he is." Jillie frowned and folded her fingers before her on the table. "He nearly broke it off with me when I chose to keep my friendship with Mellie. I lost some esteem for him."

"He's decent to the core," Melody said. "And he did come around in the end."

"He's not as big and bold as your Reeve."

"There's all sorts of ways to be bold, young lady." Hyrum lowered his bushy brows at her. "Standing up for you at the risk of his reputation is something."

"I suppose. And I was fond of him, before all this."

"You'll find that again, Jillie. He'll be a good, safe husband."

She would always know where he was—behind his desk at the bank or warming her bed at home. Jillie would never have to wonder or worry.

"He's very handy with a bat and ball," Melody added in the face of her friend's less than enamored expression. "All the girls sigh over him. It's impressive being the star player on the town's baseball team."

"Getting down to business, ladies," Hyrum said. "How do we get your father from over there to over here without any misconduct?"

"I could ask Dixie to tea," Jillie suggested. "You

bring your papa back here and explain on the way that he has to say the words that he left of his own free will."

"Dixie hasn't got much use for other women," Melody observed. "I doubt she would accept. Besides, she'd smell a rat, for sure, knowing we're friends."

"I'll invite her to lunch," Hyrum volunteered. "Even though I'm an old fart, it would appeal to her vanity. I could let on that I've got some money in the bank. That might get her out of the house."

Jillie leaned sideways and hugged Hyrum around the neck. "Maybe I should be courting you instead of James."

"Could be that's so," Hyrum said with a grin and a wink. "I'll play my part in this as long as you girls stick to this side of the law."

"There's still the problem of getting inside the house," Melody pointed out. "My stepmother keeps it locked tight as a bank vault."

"I suppose I'll head on to bed." Hyrum stood up. "I might not want to know what the pair of you come up with."

She'd do her best to remain above legal reproach—for Hyrum's sake and because that's what Reeve would expect of her.

Still, the plain fact remained: one way or another, her father was coming home.

It was late when his damned wife finally walked into her bedroom. She'd forced him to stand behind the window curtain for an hour with the window open.

Guess she didn't care that the rain blew inside and got him wetter than a cat dumped down a well.

She'd care soon enough. He'd make sure she paid for this and a whole list of other things. No wife of Ramsey Travers was going to run out and not pay the price.

While he watched as cunningly as a phantom from behind the curtain, she lit a bedside lamp, then turned it down low. She eased off her dress, slowly and wearily. With her back to him, she draped the pricey-looking garment on a wall hook.

She had filled out some, as if she'd had plenty to eat while he had survived on rattlesnakes and whatever other vermin he could scrounge while lying low from the law.

Hattie turned toward him, although she didn't know it. Her shift didn't quite hide the body that she no doubt, by now, considered her own.

Her breasts were full, her waist slender and her hips round. She reminded him of the girl he'd kidnapped to be his bride. It was hard to see the resemblance to the broken-in woman he'd left waiting for him at the ranch.

Lamplight shone on her face. It revealed one bare pink shoulder when she sat down on the bed. It wasn't right for a man's wife to have a healthy glow when he looked like a tumbleweed that had rolled across hill and dale.

It rankled to see the difference between them. There had been a time when he was the good-looking one. Women used to remark on his handsome looks. All it took was a wink to get them tumbling into his bed.

Lightning glared bright white through the bedroom window. If Hattie had looked up, she would have seen him standing there with his fists clenched. But she gazed down with her hands folded in her lap, as if maybe she was saying her prayers.

Probably thinking of that marshal he'd heard tell of. The one she was sweet on, and him in a lather over her.

The very same marshal who had taken away the two things that belonged to him—his woman and his ranch.

He'd get even with him for that, and enjoy every second of it.

His wife slid into bed still wearing her shift. She pulled the quilt up to her chin and closed her eyes. It only took a moment for her to fall into a deep, hard sleep.

Even so, he approached the bed with caution. If she discovered him now it would ruin his plans.

By rights, he ought to be able to pounce upon her in the plush clean bed, startle her and watch her mud-brown eyes grow wide with fright.

He ground his teeth and felt the tic pulsing in his jaw. Thanks to Marshal Prentis, his would be a bed on the cold, hard ground with his snoring cousins for company.

Patience was a virtue, he'd been told. For a man who set no store in virtue, patience was a damned nuisance.

For the sake of settling the score, though, he'd try it out.

Jack and Dwayne, his only free kin, had pointed out that the person he ought to get even with was Colt Wesson, since it was him who burned the ranch down.

Any fool knew you didn't go up against Colt and his big knife. It would be hard to enjoy one's proper retribution with a blade in the gut.

Better to deal with Prentis first, and then take his

time breaking Hattie again, good and proper this time so she'd never wrong him again.

He leaned over the bed, close enough to feel the heat of her skin. His nose grazed her neck. He nearly cracked his teeth, he ground them together so hard. Beneath the rose water she had on, he could almost smell the tang of her blood, almost feel the warm smear of it on his knuckles.

He straightened quickly, retreating across the room. If he acted too soon he'd only get a portion of what was coming to him.

Lightning blanched the room as soon as he hooked his knee over the window frame. Thunder shook the house. Hattie turned in her sleep. Her shift sagged, revealing one plump, vulnerable breast.

He eased backward out of the window, hating the act of patience that was required in order for him to get his full due.

"Look out, Hattie. I'm coming for you," he said in a singsong voice, walking backward across the yard and getting dumped on by buckets of rain.

Chapter Ten

"I don't see any help for it but to break the glass," Melody said, standing before her father's bedroom window.

"We've pried and budged it every which way," Jillie said, nodding her head in agreement. "That nail isn't coming loose."

Her father peered at them from behind the glass, his expression puzzled. It had been days since she had spoken to him through the crack in the window frame, and she feared that he was slipping into some sort of mental decline.

She only hoped that she would be able to explain to him that he must say that he was coming home of his own free will.

"Hyrum won't like it." Melody tapped the glass. US marshals were such sticklers for every letter of the law.

Her father tapped his thumb on the other side of the pane then crossed the meagerly furnished bedroom to sit on a cot that served as his bed.

Jillie hustled to the corner of the yard, kicked at this

and that, and then hurried back with a satisfied smile on her face.

"Won't you look at this pretty rock I found?" Jillie turned the dirt-encrusted stone in her hand. "It will be just the piece for my collection."

"I didn't know you had a rock coll—"

Jillie hurled the rock. The window shattered.

"Oh, dear!" Jillie dusted her hands on her skirt. "I don't know my own clumsiness."

"Accidents happen." Melody shrugged, then climbed carefully through the window. "I'll meet you out front."

She watched until the blue plaid flare of Jillie's skirt rounded the corner of the house.

Melody spun about and approached her father.

Standing before him, she cupped his hands in hers.

"Are you ready to come home now, Papa?"

Her father glanced about the dull, dirty bedroom.

"It'll cause trouble, Mellie. I ought to stay here."

"I have a room ready for you. It's clean, and there's a real feather bed." She glanced at the worn rag that served as his blanket. The current Mrs. Dawson would answer for this.

"I don't dare."

It nearly broke her heart to see the apprehension in his eyes. How had Dixie turned this once-strong person into a man who didn't dare?

"Please, Daddy, come home. I need you."

She drew her father up. To her relief, he didn't resist.

"As long as you tell people you have moved out of your own free will, she can't hurt you."

"It's not me I care about, Mellie. I made a choice, a

wrong one, and now it's mine to live with. But Dixie is a greedy woman. She has her heart set on your house. When you came home, her lawyer was only a month away from taking it from you. It's you and the children I worry about."

"Papa, the children and I have lived with far worse people than your wife." She drew him a step closer to the door. "Trust me, I can handle her. All you need to do is say you have come home of your own free will."

"All right, Mellie." He let her lead him into the hallway.

Glancing about while she led her father through the dining room and then the parlor toward the front door, Melody became angry. Heat suffused her in a red-hot wave.

While her father had been confined to the poverty of his room, Dixie had surrounded herself with every sort of decadent luxury imaginable.

It looked absurd, but a crystal chandelier hung in the modestly sized dining room. Lace and purple velvet covered everything but two walls.

And the smell! It was difficult to take a breath with a cloying mist of perfume weighting the air.

Melody hurried to the front door and turned the doorknob. It didn't open.

This really was a prison.

"This lock only opens on the outside."

"There must be a key."

"Dixie always keeps it in her pocket."

"Papa! What if there was a fire? How would you get out?"

His answer was a blink, then a frown of confusion.

The shifty way to do things would be to take her father out the broken window in his bedroom. But by Heaven, there was only one way he was leaving this house, and it was through that front door, tall and proud.

She tapped on the front window. "Jillie!"

Jillie's face appeared on the other side of the lace curtain.

"I need you inside."

A moment later Jillie stood beside her.

"Let's sneak out of here quick," Jillie exclaimed with a yank on her arm. "I hear your stepmother's voice from a block over, and she's spittin' mad over something."

"There's only one way my papa is leaving here, and that's through the front door, which is locked. The key is in Dixie's pocket."

"Oh, my word."

"I'll understand if you want to go out the back window before things get… Jillie, I'm pretty sure I'm going to do something that Hyrum won't approve of."

"Do what you have to. I'll be here to lead your daddy out as soon as you open the door."

Melody rushed back through the house then slipped out the broken window. With both hands, she yanked her skirt free of the shard of glass that snared it.

She reached the front porch in the same instant that Dixie rounded the corner with Hyrum at her heels. He appeared to be doing his best to coax her into behaving in a reasonable manner.

Well, let her come, then. Let her steam down the street in all her wicked anger. Melody had a good deal of anger to meet her with. And hers was righteous anger!

This house was no better than the Broken Brand. Her father was going to walk out the front door, even if she went to jail over it.

Melody stepped off the porch and met Dixie on the path still littered with last season's dried flowers.

"Get off my property," Dixie hissed.

"Gladly, as soon as you give me the key to your front door. My father is coming home. We'll leave you to your—" she slashed her hand toward the house behind her "—selfish overindulgence."

"Try and get it from me." Dixie's lip curled in a rouged sneer. Her fingers fisted and then flexed.

It seemed safe to assume that her stepmother had been involved in a ruckus before.

There was no going back now. She wouldn't, even if she knew a way.

Dixie lunged. Melody sidestepped her but grabbed her about the waist in an attempt to shove her hand into the pocket of Dixie's green satin gown.

Together, they went down. The breath rushed out of Melody's lungs when Dixie landed on top of her. Pebbles and stones ground into her backside. She arched her back, then she yanked on Dixie's bodice, which sent the woman toppling.

Melody pounced across Dixie's hips, holding her in place while rifling in the deep pocket for the key. It wasn't easy with her larger opponent bucking and punching.

It had to be in here! All of a sudden a crimson petticoat covered her head. She came close to suffocating in its perfumed frilliness. With Dixie's cusswords ringing in her ears, she searched harder for the key.

For a middle-aged woman, her stepmother was strong. She bucked, twisted and pulled Melody's hair until she thought it would give at the roots.

Just when she feared that her father had been mistaken about the key, her fingers closed about a three-inch piece of metal.

She yanked the key free and held it high in the air.

"Take that, you old besom!" she shouted, working her head free of the clinging petticoat.

Victory, she had to admit, was sweet.

A big, solid hand clasped hers. It swallowed up her fingers and the key.

She glanced up and behind her.

"Reeve!"

"You came back?" was the only pitiful thing she could think of to say.

With gentle pressure, he squeezed her hand and lifted her up. She held tight to her prize, the key. Dixie's malodorous petticoat fell away from her shoulders.

"You waited?" he answered. His Stetson looked dusty, evidence that he had ridden long and hard to get here.

She nodded because her throat had closed up too tight to speak.

With a leap, she launched herself at him. He caught her up in his arms and lifted her. His hat fell off when he buried his face into the crook of her neck. The hard circle of his badge pressed into her breast.

Reeve's arms about her felt like a dream, but not of

a vaporous sort. If Dixie had walloped her in the head and she was hallucinating, it was as solid as reality.

"I was worried." His mouth moved against her hair. "I was afraid you'd given up."

Pulling away, she peered deep into his eyes, hardly believing that the green sparkle was real and not in her imagination.

"I was afraid you'd been killed by outlaws."

"It seems to me that a US marshal should pay more mind to protecting the innocent than cavorting with assailants," Dixie grumbled.

"It wasn't you I was cavorting with, Mrs. Dawson." Reeve shot Dixie a frown. "As I saw it, you attacked Melody.

"Later on," he whispered into Melody's ear before he set her back on her feet, "I guarantee some cavorting. Mellie, I missed you."

"Nothing illegal about defending oneself," Hyrum declared, reaching down a hand to Dixie, who, flailing about in the dirt, resembled an angry red ant.

She slapped his hand aside, shoved her skirt down over her knees then scrambled up.

"And who would believe the pair of you? She has you both under some sort of spell, the wicked creature."

A fist banged on the far side of the front door.

In her joy over seeing Reeve she had nearly forgotten that her father was waiting behind the locked door.

She dashed past Dixie. The woman had to be addled because, even with Reeve and Hyrum standing by, she lunged for the key.

Over Dixie's screeching objection, she unlocked the door.

Her father emerged, arm in arm with Jillie. He blinked, not having seen the sunshine in a long while.

"I'm going to believe her, Dixie," her father said. "I saw you attack my baby girl. I have something to say, and I want these lawmen to witness it. I'm leaving you. I'm going home with my daughter, and I'm not coming back."

"You old fool! I don't know why I married you in the first place."

"Your reason, I'm ashamed to admit, has become perfectly clear." Her father let go of Jillie. He approached his wife, his posture no longer stooped. Melody wanted to leap and cheer. Here was the man she remembered. "It took me a while to accept it, but the truth is, you saw a lonely old man and wanted what was his. I could have been any widower with means."

"I took care of you, and for what?" Dixie spun about. "I'm done listening to your blithering."

"I'd listen to this if I were you." He walked toward Melody, plucked the key from her fingers then tossed it to Dixie. "Keep this house—it's yours with my blessings. But don't even glance at my daughter's house again. It will never be yours."

Dixie huffed and pointed her narrow nose up a notch. She marched up her front stairs, then paused before she went inside.

"You stupid old man, we could have had everything." She slammed the door.

No doubt, what the harpy means is that she could have had everything, thought Melody.

If Papa was distressed over the parting with his wife he didn't let on.

All of a sudden her father seemed taller and stronger, as if some hard years had rolled off him.

"How'd you get inside the house?" Hyrum asked, his frown indicating that he suspected something illegal.

"It was the funniest thing," Jillie said, her wide eyes reflecting innocence. "I found the prettiest rock for my collection. I was showing it to Mellie and, well, all of a sudden it slipped from my hand and broke the bedroom window."

"It's the truth. I saw it happen. So Papa invited us in, and there you have it." Melody shrugged. There was not a chance in Heaven that the pair of US marshals would believe the story, but she smiled charmingly at them both in hopes that it might sway them.

"I don't see any witnesses to say it didn't happen that way," Reeve said with a glance around. "Do you have a large rock collection, Jillie?"

"That rock was to be my first. I guess that's why I was so excited and let it fly out of my grasp."

"What a shame that the gem is probably trapped in Mr. Dawson's old room," observed Hyrum.

"Maybe I'll collect buttons instead." Jillie shrugged one shoulder.

"For safety's sake, at least." A tall, pretty young woman, whom Melody had failed to notice in the ruckus, slipped off the back of a sweet-faced mare.

The girl rushed forward, her red hair flying loose behind her. She stopped in front of Melody. Green eyes that were an exact match to Reeve's narrowed on her.

The girl nodded her head, clearly weighing Melody in the balance. All at once she grinned. Her arms shot about her, hugging Melody tight and rocking back and forth.

When Melody thought she'd faint from lack of breath, the girl pulled back. She kept a good tight grip on her hands, though.

"I'm Mildred Prentis, the youngest sister." The girl turned to glance back at Reeve. "I adore her! On behalf of all your siblings, I give our consent."

Melody set the ingredients for her mother's Special Day Cake on the kitchen counter. She knew that Mama was smiling down, seeing her house full of people, just as she had always dreamed it would be.

It had taken some time, but at last, she was able to think of Mama with joy and not sorrow. Lately, she felt Mama's cheerful presence in every corner of the house.

Closing her eyes for a moment, she listened to the sounds of life going on in the parlor and imagined her mother's spirit happily visiting among those gathered.

Papa's laughter rang out over something that Reeve's lively sister had said. She couldn't tell what it was, but her heart swelled. She hadn't heard her father laugh in a very long time.

Flynn banged out a tune on the piano. Someone must be holding Seth and tickling him, for she heard his giggle.

Life was nearly perfect. If only she could hold on to it just this way, she would not be unhappy.

"Can I give you a hand?"

She turned to smile at Reeve, suddenly feeling shy. How odd that she should feel this restraint for a man she well and truly loved. She'd been dreaming of this day for months, imagining the scent of him, longing for the deep timbre of his voice.

Maybe if he'd written, if they had stayed in touch… But just now, it seemed as though they were starting all over again.

Her initial reaction to him earlier today had been pure emotion. She'd attacked him in an embrace because, illogically, she feared that the moment might be just another dream.

Now, with time for emotions to even out, how did she even know he still wanted her in the same way?

"Can you cut the fat into the flour?"

"You'll have to teach me."

She handed him the pastry cutter. Flour from her fingers dusted his knuckles. He wrapped his hand around her wrist for a moment. He stared down at her, his amazing green eyes searching hers.

Silence stretched. Not the comfortable silence between close friends, but the awkward kind. He let go of her wrist.

"I hope you don't mind that my sister will be staying here," he said, breaking the strained moment.

"I love a pleasant surprise. It's wonderful having her here." And it was. Mildred was a bright spirit spreading goodwill with her easy laugh and warm smile. "I'm amazed that she wanted to leave your mother and sisters."

If Melody had been blessed with siblings she would never have left home.

"There wasn't much of a choice, after the episode with Mr. Sweeny—and Edward."

He gave her a puzzled look, arching a brow as

though she ought to know who Mr. Sweeny and Edward were.

"A surprise…? I don't understand. I wrote to you about bringing her here."

"You wrote?" He had written?

"Of course." He frowned.

"I didn't get your letters, only that one telegram about Hyrum."

"I guess I don't want to know what you must think of me." He dropped the pastry cutter into the bowl. "You must have figured that I—"

"I always believed you'd come back… I never doubted you." Not enough to tell him about, at any rate.

With big, flour-dusted hands, he drew her in. She leaned her head against his chest, listening to the steady thump of his heart. She felt the rise and fall of his lungs and breathed in the familiar scent of him. This was what she had waited for.

"I'll admit I was scared that something had happened to you," she confessed. "That I would never even know what happened."

"I'm sorry for that. It's a burden you shouldn't have to carry. I've a couple of ideas for making a living some other way."

"I'll never ask that of you, Reeve. Your job is part of who you are."

"Might not be… Mellie, I—"

"What have we here? Is a chaperone in order?" Her father strode into the kitchen, his voice sounding playful.

"Indeed it is, sir." Reeve stepped away from her. "I wonder if I might have a word with you in private?"

The men walked out of the kitchen, Reeve's head tipped down toward her father and her father's ear turned up toward Reeve.

Feeling replete, having indulged in a fine meal topped off with Special Day Cake, Reeve stood at the front window of Melody's parlor gazing out at the clear, warm night.

The stars blazed like diamonds in the dark sky, making him think of the dainty ring with the shiny stone tucked into his shirt pocket.

From upstairs he heard the sounds of the house settling in for the night.

Hyrum and Porter spoke quietly in the upstairs hallway. A brief silence was followed by the clicks of their closing doors. Melody's voice, softly muted, drifted down from the third floor. He heard her laughing with Mildred, who had been given his room.

It was well past the time he ought to have been on his way to the hotel, but the adults had lingered beside the fire until after midnight.

Mildred had wanted to get to know everyone, and they, in turn, had wanted to make her captivating acquaintance.

What Reeve had been waiting for, what he would have, by the saints, was an hour alone with Melody. There was so much that needed to be settled, to be rekindled.

It was no wonder that Melody seemed reticent where he was concerned. The wonder was that she hadn't tossed him out on his ear, given that for all she knew, he had taken his kiss, and a bit more on that last night, then gone upon his merry way.

He'd meant to have private time with her long before now, but it wasn't easy, not with this growing family needing to get to know one another and taking their time doing it.

He was still set on marrying Melody, but it grated on him that he hadn't asked her in the proper way. Last winter he had blurted his intentions, then hightailed off. He'd only meant to be away a month, but life had not gone according to his plan.

From behind him, he heard the rustle of skirts and petticoats descending the stairs.

Love me, Mellie. Feel the way you did before.

He turned and saw a vision in red coming toward him. He reached his hand out to her. She took it, but shyly.

And why not? They hadn't known each other long before obligations had separated them. Since he'd asked her to wait for him, they had spent a much longer time apart than they had together.

Still, right there, beneath her hesitant, blushing smile, was the woman he had fallen in love with.

"Do you still want me?" he had to ask, for the question was burning a hole in his soul. "I didn't mean to be gone so long. I missed you every single day."

"I missed you, too."

He let go of her hand to stroke a strand of blond hair that slid across her temple. With the backs of his fingers he traced the curve of her cheek. It felt firm and smooth under his knuckles.

She had filled out some. She looked so pretty that

he couldn't breathe. When she smiled at him it was with a healthy sparkle.

If only he could breach the constraints that time and distance had caused.

Here and now was the time to lay his soul on the line, to be rejected or loved.

"I never properly asked for your hand." He cleared his throat. "I spoke with your father. He gave his consent."

Again, with the back of his hand, he traced her smooth cheek, trailed his fingers across her shoulder and then down her arm to clasp her fingers in his.

He went down on one knee, then fished in his pocket for the ring.

"Melody Irene Dawson, will you do me the honor of becoming my wife?"

She covered her face with work-worn fingers that looked delicate, nonetheless. She nodded. When she peeked out at him, her cheeks were dotted with tears.

"I will." She extended her hand, and he slipped the engagement ring onto her finger.

She looked at it, wonder evident in her smile.

"I've never had an engagement ring before, or a wedding ring, either."

"Can't say I'm sorry about that, but your husband never gave you a ring?"

"Ram gave me one, but it was one that he had stolen so I refused to wear it." Her eyes took on a faraway expression, as though she were visiting some dark memory. "I paid an ugly price for that decision, but it was worth it."

He stood up, taking her face in his hands. He looked hard into her eyes.

"Melody. My Mellie." There was something he needed to make her understand. "I will never treat you harshly. As long as I live and breathe no one will."

A shudder went through her. He'd bet his badge that it was from relief.

"Clearly, you found the self-reliance you were after, and I respect you for it. I admire all you've done on your own. But I need you to know that I protect what is mine, and you are mine. You don't have to do it all on your own anymore."

But what if she did? How could he promise her that he would always be there? His was a dangerous occupation. Men died in the line of duty all the time.

"I am yours, Reeve." She pressed the ring to her heart. "Because I'm giving myself to you of my own free will."

In that instant, from one heartbeat to the next, the last thread of hesitation in her demeanor vanished. Her eyes softened, her lips trembled and he knew that she had handed him her future—and her trust.

He drew her into his arms and kissed her, deep and hard. It stirred up his body good and tight. It touched him, soul deep.

"You promised some cavorting," she whispered, apparently reading his mind—or the change in his anatomy.

Her anatomy must be warming up, as well. He heard the shortness of her breath, felt it heating his lips.

"Yes, ma'am, I did."

He led her by the hand to the big chair in front of the

fireplace, turning down the lamps in the room as he went. A big log cast a dim glow over the chair.

He sat down, then drew her onto his lap.

Outside, the wind began to blow, gentle at first but quickly becoming wild and erratic. Something, a tree branch perhaps, banged against the front door.

A storm might be on the way, but here in front of the crackling logs, life was sweet.

Melody's gentle fingers sifted through his hair. Lips, full and lush, kissed him. He kissed them back and felt a bit intoxicated, as though her mouth had been drenched in smooth, warm whiskey.

It was as if the time and distance that had separated them had never happened.

A delicate dusting of freckles on her cheeks caught his eye when she smiled at him. What else could he do but kiss a few of them?

"Before the year is out, I'm going to kiss each and every one of your freckles," he promised.

"That's lovely, Reeve." She tapped her mouth with one finger. "But only after you've worn out my lips."

He gave it a good effort, but it didn't appear that wearing out would ever happen. Even after a half an hour of tasting, nipping and probing, each kiss was more exciting than the first.

Again, what was a man to do? Even though he couldn't have all of her just now, he needed more than wild, hot kisses.

He pressed her back, into the crook of his arm. He caressed the curve of her waist, stroked the swell of her hip.

Then, because she was his, with his ring twinkling

on her finger, he claimed her by pressing his hand to the plush swell of her left breast. Through the layers of clothing, he felt her nipple rise against his palm. He gave it a gentle twist then slid his hand to the right breast.

She sighed, her pleasure at his touch evident.

With a wink, she flipped open the top three buttons of her crimson dress, inviting him beneath her chemise with a smile.

Tenderly, as though he were opening the gift of a lifetime, he freed the buttons to her waist. He drew the fabric aside to reveal a lace corset and beribboned dainties.

Melody tugged the ribbon. He spread the fine, sheer cotton, exposing her breasts. Could it really be possible that this exquisitely formed woman was his to love? That he would be allowed to cherish this lovely body for the rest of his life?

"You take my breath away, Mellie."

She really did; it was not just an expression.

A tiny drop of moisture pearled at the tip of one pale round breast. When he suckled, swirling his tongue around the sweetness, he was damned sure his heart had quit as well as his breath.

"I reckon we've cavorted all we can with a house full of relatives and boarders upstairs," he forced himself to admit.

She sighed and nodded.

"It'll be misery going back to the hotel, but I'd best be on my way."

"I just got you back, Reeve. I can't let you go just yet." She closed the fabric of her dress but didn't fasten anything back together. "Stay with me for a while. Tell me everything you wrote in those letters."

"It'll take till dawn."

"Good." She tucked her head beneath his chin and snuggled in. "I want to hear every single detail."

He gathered her closer, cherishing her warmth and the weight of her cuddled against him.

"I'd been gone from you a month, within days of arresting the last two Traverses, when I got a letter from Mildred. You might have noticed that she has a flair for the dramatic."

"I have. It's charming."

"I reckon it can be, but at the same time, it's hard to gauge what is fact or fancy. Unfortunately, every last bit of her letter turned out to be hard, sorry fact. The problems at home took months to sort out. I hated being away from you, Mellie. It's not something I ever want to do again."

"You might not be able to help it."

Because of his career, was what she clearly meant.

"Well, I raced home to find Mother near death with a fever, the landlord ready to evict, my sister Sarah pregnant and her husband missing."

"I'm so sorry, Reeve. Please tell me that everything is all right now?"

"More or less. Mother is healthy, praise the Good Lord."

"Where are they living?"

"Until the baby comes, Mother, Sarah and her brood, and Delilah will be living together in a house that I leased. I'm hoping to move them to Cottonwood Grove once the baby comes, if that's all right with you."

"I can't think of anything I'd love more." She wriggled against him, then squeezed her arms around his ribs. "But what happened to Sarah's husband?"

"Mildred happened." Melody arched a slender brow at him. "I had forbidden her to leave the house…but she's Mildred, and so she did. Here the rest of us were, packing to move to the new house, when she burst into the parlor on Edward and jammed her little ivory-handled Deringer into his back. She forced him to admit that he had lost his soul to drink, cavorted with a strumpet from the Muddy Sipper and outright sold his soul to the devil.

"Mildred would not let him up off his knees until he groveled for Sarah's forgiveness."

"It sounds to me like your baby sister broke a few laws. What did you do?"

"I took off my badge for as long as it took the fool to believe that Mildred would pull the trigger. After he'd taken a good long look through the gates of Hades, I put the badge back on and let him walk away under the condition that he never return and that he never press charges against Mildred."

"I'm sure Mildred only meant well."

"No doubt, but what my sister intends and how things work out…well, you haven't heard the story of the landlord, Mr. Sweeny, yet."

"I'm sure I'll be on Mildred's side."

He laughed, couldn't help it. "Wait until you hear the story."

Melody's dress gaped open, since she hadn't buttoned it up. He slipped his hand inside and curved his fingers over her breast, just for the comfort of it.

"The first day that I got home, tuckered as a worn-out pup, Mildred was not at home. The housekeeper told me that she had gone to convince—hell, charm is what it was—Sweeny into letting them stay. Well, what to my sister was simple flirtation, to the landlord was an invitation to behave inappropriately. She made it home untouched, but a few nights later, I caught Sweeny climbing through Mildred's bedroom window."

"Please tell me she wasn't hurt!"

"I didn't take off my badge that time. Sweeny went to jail nursing a lump on the head that Mildred gave him and charged with every crime I thought would stick."

"I love you, Reeve." He felt her heart beating against his palm. "I'm so happy that your family will be coming to live here."

"You hold my heart, Mellie. You and no one else." He kissed her temple and felt the fine strands of her hair on his lips. "I love you and everyone who comes along with you."

"You mean the world to them, too, especially Joe."

"He seems to be thriving. The town accepts his and Libby's past?"

She shrugged. "There have been some problems. I'm just glad you're home, Reeve. Things ought to smooth out now that you are."

And so they sat, talking quietly of this and that, until an hour before sunrise.

If this was how the rest of his life would be, he thanked the Good Lord for it.

Chapter Eleven

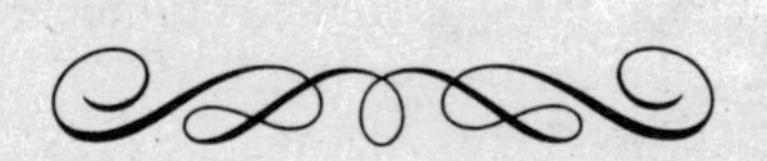

Ramsey Travers jerked his shoulder, dislodging his cousin Dwayne's pointed chin. He peered harder through Hattie's parlor window with Dwayne's breath huffing hot on his ear.

The lace window curtain barely blurred what went on inside his wife's, and therefore his, house.

"I believe you're going to need a new wife, cousin," Dwayne whispered.

Jack Travers yanked Dwayne out of the way and took his place peering over Ramsey's shoulder.

The humiliation that Hattie was putting him through made him see red. He'd heard about that "seeing red" business before, but had never experienced it until this moment. Hell, he was damn near seeing purple.

"The way I see it," Jack declared, as if he had the right to, "is that Ram needs to set this wife straight. Ain't the Travers way to let a wife get away with kissing another man."

"Well, she don't rightly know that Ramsey's alive. Don't you recall that we told her he was dead?"

"Doesn't much look like a devoted way to grieve."

What he wouldn't give to punch his worthless kin in their yapping mouths... His fists nearly ached with the need. But that would cause a ruckus since the pair of them would fight back. The wind would cover some of the noise, but the marshal, involved as he was in cuckoldry, would still hear the blows and grunts.

To rouse the marshal now wouldn't be wise. If he didn't want to end up in jail with the rest of his family, Ram would have to be canny.

"Well, my, my, what do we have here?" A sultry feminine voice came from out of the dark.

Startled, Jack fell against the wall.

Ram wanted nothing more than to shoot his imbecile cousins. He regretted the happenstance that made them kin, which meant that he could not.

"Mind your own business, lady," he said to the woman, who he suspected was not a lady at all. The rouge on her cheeks, fancy dress cut too low—dead giveaway. He couldn't figure what a whore was doing in this dull town.

"This un's kind of pretty if you don't mind that she's old," Dwayne said, looking the woman over and nodding. "Maybe you could cart her off and marry her instead. I'll say the words all legal-like."

"I have a wife, you moron."

"Don't look to me like she knows it," Jack said with a glance back through the window.

"Why don't you gentlemen come quietly off the porch so we can discuss the problem without being overheard."

"My problem is not your concern." Ram shot the

whore a withering stare, but she was right about getting his stupid cousins off the porch.

"Oh, indeed it is, much more than you might guess." The woman sighed and gave a lewd yank down on her bodice to reveal more of her shriveling charms. "That woman—your wife—is my stepdaughter."

"That makes you and her related, Ram," Dwayne declared. "Reckon you can't cart her off. You want a bride, Jack?"

"Not that one." Jack appeared to shiver. "I'm looking for a young and juicy one—no offense intended, ma'am."

She didn't look offended. Could be she didn't even notice what his fool cousins were talking about. Could be that her attention was so focused on him that she wasn't aware of anything else.

"Why would you help me get even with Hattie? You'd turn on family?"

"She's not my family. Why don't you boys come in out of the wind. We can discuss things at my place."

"You got a brothel, right here in this pure little town?" Jack looked as though he didn't believe it.

"I'm not that kind of..." The denial died on her lips because she was just that kind of woman and they all knew it. "Well, boys, come inside and let's see what can be done about your situation."

"I been denied a woman's charms for a long time. Thank you, ma'am. I reckon old Ram might need some comfort, too, seeing that his wife has taken up with a US marshal."

"Dwayne, if you aren't the stupidest—"

"Let him be, Mr. Travers. Come inside my very humble home and we'll put our heads together and see what can be done about your wife."

He already knew what needed to be done about his wife. Blood on his fists and another brat in her belly, nothing less would do.

If this woman knew a way to go about that, he'd listen to what she had to say. It wasn't as if he could just walk up to Hattie and deal with her as he wished, not with the high-and-mighty Marshal Prentis wrapped tight around her.

It wasn't easy, but he'd bide his time, plan his moment, then give Hattie her due and the marshal his.

"You are a handsome devil, Ramsey Travers." The woman, whose name he didn't even know, slipped her arm through his, as though she were a lady and he a gentleman. The image tarnished when she pressed the curve of her breast against his arm and her voice became a practiced coo. "I can't imagine how your wife could even glance at another man."

For all that the woman was an old whore, maybe, if he played her right, poured on the Ramsey Travers charm, he and his cousins could quit their secret camp beside the river. It wouldn't be a harsh price, warming the painted woman's bed, in order to sleep in a soft place.

It rankled that Hattie, Mrs. Unfaithful, had forced him and the boys to sleep on the hard ground while she got a big old house to live in.

Things were far from even between them, but soon they would be.

* * *

Melody sat on a log beside the stream, watching a horde of gnats hovering over the water.

Reeve had been home a week. The wedding was the day after tomorrow. There was nothing she wanted more than to walk down the aisle and vow her future to him.

She swatted at a dragonfly buzzing about her head and sighed. If only she could go into her marriage without conflicting emotions shadowing her joy.

There was no question about the quality of the man she was going to marry. No indeed, she could not have dreamed a man better than Reeve.

It was the children she was concerned about. Reeve was everything to them, the same as he was to her. Could she allow him to be a major part of their lives when he might be taken from them at the whim of an outlaw's bullet? Or a lightning strike? Or a snakebite? Or a mad coyote?

She shook her head, trying to see through the confusion. On the other hand, would it be selfish of her to deny them the best thing that had ever happened to them in order to avoid pain that might never come?

Maybe she was weak. It would be hard when he went away, doing everything by herself and dealing with the constant worry, too. Was that really something she could handle?

Yes, certainly. She had been managing before. All the time Reeve had been gone she had been the one to hold things together, to give the children, and now her father, a home to thrive in.

A shadow fell across her back, spreading across the water, long in the afternoon sunshine.

"Dreaming of our wedding night?" Reeve touched her shoulders, his big long fingers stroking, easing her tension.

He sat down behind her on the log, splaying his muscular thighs on either side of her.

"That is never far from my mind."

"We'll have a good life, Mellie."

Yes, better than good.

Perhaps her misgivings were simply due to things moving along so fast. This time last year she had belonged, quite literally, to an outlaw. Very soon, she would give herself to a lawman.

She had barely gained her independence, and now she was about to give it away again… But that was not true, as she thought about it. Reeve wanted to give of himself, not take away who she was.

Perhaps the wise thing for her future would be to wait, but wait for what?

Until the shadow of Ram's abuse no longer haunted her? Until she was able to ignore the fact that Reeve might be taken from her? That, one day, not only her life, but the children's, as well, might be shattered across her husband's grave?

If that happened, would she have the strength to put it back together again?

No one could guarantee what would happen in the future. It was just as likely to be blessed as not. Her dreams of a wonderful husband and more babies to love were coming true.

Dwelling on the positive was a far better way to live.

"All I know is that I love you, Reeve."

"I reckon that's all that needs knowing."

"I can't imagine life without you."

"I'm yours, Mellie. Never doubt it."

That was all anyone could say. The day after tomorrow, she would give herself to a lawman and let life happen as it would.

"I can't believe that everything is coming together so quickly," Melody said, standing beside the bedroom window of the room where she and Reeve would sleep. She gazed down at the wedding gown draped across her bed, looking like a ruffled cloud.

A spring breeze, warm for this early in the day, blew through the open window and stirred the lace.

"This is the most breathtaking thing I have ever seen!" Libby stroked the air over the dress but didn't touch it.

"Mama said to give it to you." Mildred petted the satin bow over the bustle. "But she only wanted you to wear it if it made you happy."

It made her beyond happy. The gown was Reeve's mother's way of giving her blessing, just as Papa had given his.

"I wish she could be here for the wedding."

"Nothing but doctor's orders and an abandoned pregnant daughter to fuss over would keep her from coming," Mildred said.

"I'm so honored to wear your mother's dress. I can't say how much it means to me. When I walk down the aisle wearing her gown and my mama's veil, it will be like they're both with us."

"Once Pansy sees this gown, you'll never convince her that you aren't a queen," Libby declared with a laugh.

"And why would you want to?" Mildred added, laughing, too.

What a joy it was, hearing Libby's laugh in return. The infectious sound was becoming more common as time passed.

With Reeve home, standing as Libby's protector and acting as her father, the attitudes of the townspeople had begun to change.

There was a great deal of difference between being an outlaw's girl and being the daughter of a respected US marshal. Day by day, Libby was healing from her past, as they all were.

"Mama!" Small footsteps galloped down the hallway toward Melody's bedroom. "Mama, where are you?"

"In here, baby," she called back, unable to keep the smile from her voice.

Because of Reeve, this little boy would have a happy, secure life. He and Seth would never have to grow up the way Joe and Libby had. They would never hear a mean-spirited word or feel an angry father's fist.

Maybe she ought to feel some sorrow that Ram was dead, but all she could manage was relief.

Flynn rushed into the bedroom with Pansy at his heels. He skidded to a stop and grinned when he saw Mildred.

Everyone adored Reeve's sister. Her lively spirit had captivated them all, from Hyrum to Seth.

"Mild!" Flynn cried and made a dash toward her.

All at once his attention shifted.

"Cloud… Fun!" he declared and made a leap for the bed.

Mildred scooped him up, twirling about while tickling his belly.

Childish laughter filled the room.

"Is that your queen's dress, Meldy?" Pansy approached the bed cautiously and, like her sister, let her hand hover over a bit of lace.

"That's my wedding gown. You can touch it, love. Gently, like this." She guided Pansy's fingers over the row of softly shimmering pearl buttons.

"Touch! Touch! Touch!" Flynn wriggled to be set down.

"Oh, no, you don't!" Mildred said. "You'll only put those pretty pearls in your mouth."

"Pearls in mouth!" he agreed with glee.

"Let's learn a happy day dance instead." Mildred set Flynn down but kept a grip on his hand. "What do you say, Pansy? Want to learn the Dancing Tree?"

"What's that?"

"Well, it's like this. Let Libby hold you up to the window so you can see the trees by the riverbank. See how their branches wave back and forth in the breeze?"

Pansy nodded.

"That's what we are going to do. All of us, we can practice and perform the dance at the wedding reception tomorrow."

Mildred raised her hands over her head. She swayed back and forth, waving her arms.

Fascinated, Flynn copied her. Melody, Libby and Pansy did, too.

It felt wonderful, really, to wave one's arms about in carefree abandon. Her only concern was that she was going to break into tears while reciting her vows tomorrow.

"Throw your arms this way and that. Pretend that the wind is tossing them, and then all of a sudden waggle your arms up and down… And don't forget to close your eyes and wag your head," Mildred instructed. "It's the best step in the dance."

Libby started to laugh. She doubled over.

In a moment everyone was laughing in the way that, when you tried to stop, it made you laugh even harder.

"Now that we all know the Dancing Tree," Libby declared between giggles, "we can teach it at the wedding reception."

"Na-nak!" Flynn exclaimed, suddenly dashing back into the hall.

"Snack for me, too!" Pansy rushed after him.

"Come on, Libby." Mildred looped her arm through Libby's. Together, they trailed the little ones. "I don't know about you, but I feel I've earned a bite to eat."

The girls, one tall and one petite, continued giggling all the way down the hallway.

Melody walked to her wardrobe. Carefully, she took out her mother's veil. She paused for a moment to gaze at Reeve's clothes hanging beside hers. Tonight would be his last night at the hotel. The only thing of his that remained there was his wedding suit.

She touched the sleeve of one of his shirts, brought it to her nose and breathed deeply. If she closed her eyes, it was as though her groom stood beside her.

With a sigh, she closed the door. She crossed to the bed and set the veil beside the gown.

"I believe you two were made for each other." She kissed her fingertips then touched them to the veil. She did the same to the dress. "Thank you, mothers."

Male voices drifted up from below.

"A fishing trip is what a man needs the day before his wedding," she heard Reeve declare.

She crossed to the window and leaned against the frame, watching the scene below.

Three men and three boys walked slowly toward the river with fishing poles slung over their shoulders.

Hyrum and her father walked together, nodding their heads.

"Wish I'd thought of fishing on the day before my wedding," Hyrum said.

"It's a soothing thing to do to calm the jitters."

"Why were you jittery, sir?" Butler Buchanan asked.

Melody covered her mouth to stifle her laugh. She wanted to hear the rest of this conversation. Her heart warmed seeing Joe going fishing with friends. Especially since the friends were the two boys who used to badger him.

With Reeve's return and their engagement announced, both Butler and Randolf had come by to make amends and bury the hatchet.

"That's a question for another day, young man," her father said.

"Why not now? I'd like to know," Randolf insisted, arching a brow.

Joe kept quiet. Even from the upstairs window she saw his ears flaming. As young as he was, Joe knew things that most youngsters might only wonder about. Like everything else at the Broken Brand, privacy had been sadly lacking.

With her thoughts now turned to her wedding night, Melody watched her betrothed.

The man was everything that the Creator had intended a male to be. He sauntered with a smooth, easy gait. She couldn't help but smile, watching his narrow hips, the strength of his broad shoulders. She felt half-giddy.

What miracle had made this man hers? Her heart swelled as she watched his winning way with the old men and the boys. Truly, she felt it expand in love.

To be honest, her heart was not the only organ feeling the draw. No indeed. Yearning for him shot straight to her feminine parts, coiling and impatient.

Watching him, wanting him—her wedding night seemed a year away.

Reeve leaned against the doorjamb of the house that already felt like home. Tomorrow he would move into the top-floor bedroom that he and Melody had prepared for themselves. He watched the sun go down behind the trees that lined the riverbank.

It was a beautiful sight, with the evening breeze rustling the cottonwood leaves and making them shimmer, sending puffs of white fluff floating over the land.

This was a place he was happy to call home.

He didn't know what to do yet about his calling. He'd taken some time off to see his family settled. When that time ran out, he wondered if he had it in him to resign.

Cottonwood Grove, the people living in this house—his family—would be hard to leave behind.

He knew men who did it. Some of them didn't mind. Hyrum was one of them. He'd been a happily married marshal for many years.

"Papa." There was a yank on his pant leg near his knee. "Catch Pansy a fairy?"

The little girl, his soon-to-be daughter, hopped up and down, pointing her finger at a cottonwood puff floating over the porch. He reached out and snatched it in his hand.

"Here you go, princess."

She giggled, spun about then dashed off into the parlor to show off her prize. He heard Mildred fussing over it, admiring it. After a moment, his sister launched into a story about fairy kings and queens.

There had been no question about bringing his sister to live here. Even if she had protested, he would have insisted. It was a relief to know that when he had to be away, Melody would be watching out for her.

It was his hope that sleepy Cottonwood Grove would tame Mildred a bit, but not too much.

"Look, Reeve." His bride-to-be walked up to him from behind. Standing close, she nuzzled her blond locks against his shoulder. She cupped a small box in her palms. It was wrapped with a neatly tied red ribbon. "It's a wedding gift from Jillie."

He looked up and spotted Jillie standing in a corner with James beside her. The pair of them smiled and waved.

Poor James was smitten with Jillie. Devotion was etched in every line on his face.

The object of his affection, while clearly fond of him, did not appear to feel the same ardor. She had hinted that she had her heart set on a bolder sort of man. Jillie didn't know how lucky she was to have a man with a safe career.

What, Reeve wondered, would it be like to spend one's days in a slat-backed chair? He had to give James credit for it. Just the thought made Reeve's back ache and his nerves twitch.

All around, the room buzzed with conversation. Excitement over the wedding infected everyone, except for Seth, who slept upstairs in his trundle.

The house was brimming with gifts from folks all over town. It seemed that Cottonwood Grove was overcoming its fear of the former outlaw family.

"It doesn't weigh much." Melody gazed up at him and his heart tripped. He doubted that James was the only one with devotion stamped all over his face.

At three o'clock tomorrow this exquisite woman would be his wife. What stroke of good fortune had made him that lucky?

"Open it up. Let's have a look," he said.

Slowly, Melody pulled the ribbon. As always, her fingers moved with feminine grace. The fabric wrapping fell away revealing a small brass bell.

He felt her sudden intake of breath. "It's so lovely! Aren't those cottonwood flowers engraved around the edge? And look here, it's our names, Reeve and Melody Prentis."

She hugged him tight about the middle, then dashed off to give her friend a tearful hug. Reeve followed to give Jillie thanks of his own. He left the door open to let in the fresh evening breeze.

After he thanked Jillie for the gift, he sat down on the couch between Hyrum and his soon-to-be father-in-law.

Their advice about the wedding night lasted about three minutes before Pansy screamed high bloody murder and Flynn copied her.

"Witch!" Pansy screeched, running to Reeve. She buried her face in his pant leg, sobbing.

"Witch!" Flynn repeated, but toddled toward the woman standing in the doorway.

Beside him, he felt Porter stiffen.

"What are you doing here, Dixie?" Porter demanded.

"Witch," Pansy hiccuped and dared a glance toward the door.

Reeve stroked the child's small, trembling back. "It's not a witch. Look again, princess—it's the neighbor from across the road."

It was fair to say, though, that Dixie did look like a witch. Wearing black from scalp to boot, with her hair parted severely down the middle and tied up in a bun at the back of her neck, she played the part. All she needed was a wart on the tip of her nose.

"I've come to offer my apologies to your daughter, Porter." She held out a jar of something, apples, or maybe peaches, with a bow tied about it. "I've brought a gift."

Melody scooped up Flynn and carried him with her to the front door. She did not invite the witch inside.

"Why are you wearing black? What happened to all the fancy clothes I bought you?" Porter asked.

"I'm in mourning over my lost marriage, naturally." She wiped her eye, even though there had been no tear to smear away.

She turned her attention from Porter to Melody.

"I beg your pardon for the way I treated you," she said stiffly. "I do hope you will forgive me."

Odd, that her words were full of apology, but not her eyes. They looked as cold as ever.

"What do you suppose she's up to, Porter?" Hyrum whispered, leaning across Reeve.

"Can't rightly say." Porter frowned and squinted his eyes. "Not what it seems, I can tell you that much."

Dixie extended the jar to Melody, who stared at it but made no move to take it.

"Peach! Peach!" Flynn squirmed, reaching for the jar and whining.

"For pity's sake, I didn't make it myself. Look, it's from the mercantile, sealed good and tight."

Melody stood silent, still as a rock.

"Can't say I blame you." Dixie tried to sound contrite, but there was that bitterness to her voice that was probably habit. "I've been hostile to you in the past. I freely admit that I was jealous."

Dixie stooped to set the jar on the porch. "Keep it with my good wishes."

"I don't reckon you have any good wishes." Porter stood and walked toward the door to stand beside his daughter.

"You have every right to be angry. I've been difficult since your daughter came to town. As I said, I was jealous."

"Witch!" Flynn declared and clapped his hands.

Dixie laughed.

In Flynn's defense, the woman did cackle. Everyone in the room suddenly grew quiet.

"And to think that if I hadn't been so…so selfish, this sweet little boy might have been my own dear grandson."

"She doesn't mean that," Hyrum murmured.

"Witches tell lies," Pansy whispered back.

"I want to believe you, Dixie," Melody said. "You'll understand if I need some time."

"Of course, dear. I understand." She gave a smile, of sorts, parting lips that resembled a pair of thin red lines. "I don't deserve to be invited to the wedding, but if you'd let me come by tomorrow, when you are preparing, well I'd like to be there, standing in for your mother if that's possible."

"That is not possible."

"Naturally not. But if you need a motherly touch to your hair or want some advice about…well…" She arched a brow and nodded toward Reeve. "I'm only across the way if you change your mind."

With that odd speech, Dixie turned and walked back to her house in the dusk, batting cottonwood fluffs away from her face.

Chapter Twelve

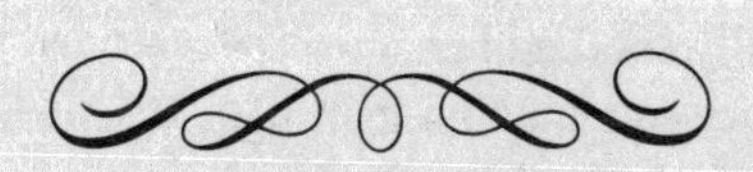

Attempting to sleep was useless. Melody sat suddenly upright in bed and flung off the covers. She stood up, put on her robe and cinched it tight at the waist. She walked out of her bedroom.

Prewedding jitters and Dixie's curious change of heart made her nervous. Her only relief was to pace.

After five minutes, she decided that she would wear out the hallway rug before she managed to relax. She paused beside the upstairs window to gaze across the street at Dixie's house.

The lamps were out, as would be expected after midnight. Nothing appeared out of the ordinary, but something felt off. She couldn't figure out why, but looking at the house made her feel a bit queer.

It concerned her that Dixie's sudden change of heart was an attempt to lure Papa back into the black widow's web.

A curtain at the parlor window drew aside. In the moonlight she saw a dimly shadowed face peer out for an instant before the curtain fell back into place.

It was too dark to read what Dixie's expression might have been, or if it had even been Dixie. She might be entertaining a male caller, which ought to have eased Melody's mind about the woman trying to lure her father.

Still, the unease persisted. She might need a breath of night air. Watching the blink and glimmer of fireflies usually soothed her.

The door squealed on its hinges when she opened it and stepped into the soft warm night.

A movement beside the porch rail drew her eye. A man's figure moved toward her in the dark. She gasped, her heart slamming against her ribs.

It was only Reeve. She laughed in relief.

She needed to forget how Ram used to come upon her in the dark, an evil shadow seeking his twisted entertainment.

"Can't sleep, either?" Reeve asked, drawing her in for a hug. He rested his chin on top of her head and suddenly all the tension inside her drained away. "This time tomorrow night, we'll wish we had."

"What are you still doing here? I thought you'd be at the hotel."

"If I was going to be restless, I figured I might as well be restless at home."

"Shall we walk by the river? See if it makes us drowsy?"

He held her hand. It felt like forever and always wrapped in a bow.

The river was not far from the house, but far enough that it seemed a world away in its peacefulness.

A firefly landed on Reeve's shoulder, blinking for a moment before it flew off.

"That's a sign of good luck," Melody observed, breathing in the moist, fresh scent of the water as they drew closer.

"Luck's been on our side all along." He tugged her closer, whispering in her ear. "Thank you for waiting for me, for not moving on."

"How could I, Reeve?" She snuggled in closer. "You took my heart with you when you left."

"I'm just grateful. You never got any of my letters. Most women would have given up."

She shook her head. "Not on a man like you."

He was quiet. Sounds of the night filled the silence, frogs and crickets singing along with the rippling water.

Sometimes, she noticed, feelings were better expressed without words because when he caressed her shoulder with his long, strong fingers, then kissed the top of her head, she knew just what he was feeling.

The sense of belonging together, that feeling that they were meant to be, was tangible. If she reached out, it would feel as solid as the tall grass brushing her hand.

As soon as they approached the riverbank the frogs fell silent, but after a moment, they began to croak again. A fallen log with moss growing on its north side lay near the shore. Reeve sat on it and drew her down beside him. Hip to hip, they gazed at the clear water rushing past, watching the reflection of moonlight glimmering on the surface.

She thought back to the night that moonlight had

shone on the hot spring, how she had risen from it a new woman. Maybe she had fallen in love with Reeve that very night.

Something rustled in the high grass growing near the log. A raccoon emerged followed by her litter of six. They scurried away into the shadows.

"It's peaceful here, with just the two of us." Reeve touched her chin, then turned her face up and kissed her. "Maybe we ought to stay here until morning."

"Or forever. Reeve, what do you make of Dixie coming by tonight? It seemed so odd."

"I can't say I trust her. But hell if I can figure out what she's up to, or why." He squeezed her hand. "Don't worry about her, Mellie. There is nothing she can do to harm us, or anyone who is ours."

"Let's not think of her anymore."

"I know what I'm thinking of." His grin was suddenly as hot and sultry as the night.

"What?"

"I'm wondering what my bride sleeps in at night. Looks to me like that robe is the only thing you've got on."

It was true. Sleeping garments were too constrictive. It was her belief that slumbering in the altogether was by far more restorative than fighting all night with a tangled gown.

"Well, now." She stood up and walked a few feet toward the water into a stab of moonlight that filtered through the trees. She untied the belt but held the robe closed at her throat. "I suppose you have a right to know my sleeping habits before you speak the vows tomorrow. You ought to know what you'll be sleeping next to before you make that commitment."

"Just so you know, I'm committed, no matter what you put against my skin."

Committed. He might have read poetry to her for hours on end and it wouldn't have meant as much to her as that one word.

He had pledged his love. She had vowed hers. Deep, committed love would solve any troubles that came after, so she peeled the robe away from her body slowly, letting it slip while she watched Reeve's gaze intent upon her.

With the cotton robe a puddle at her feet, she stood before him, naked in the moonlight.

She heard his gasp and her heart tripped over. Her desire for him to touch her became overwhelming. She wanted it more intensely than she'd ever wanted anything. Waiting for tomorrow would serve no good purpose that she could think of.

There were moments in life when a man wanted to spring into action. And there were other moments when he wanted to lasso time, savoring each heartbeat and breath. Reeve couldn't recall an instance when the urge to do both slammed into him all at the same time.

Breathe. That was something he could do, even if it came out as a gasp.

Melody was... Well, pretty words could not describe her.

He sat on the log with his mouth hanging open. She might think he was drooling, and he was, but more than that, he was memorizing her, dumbfounded that this goddess was his to make love to for the rest of his life.

Moonshine glimmered in her hair where it fell in blond whorls over her chest and down her back. It illuminated the outer curve of one breast where it grazed her arm.

If the heat in her gaze was anything to go by, hunger gnawed at her insides, same as it did his.

She twined her fingers in her hair and twirled a lock around one finger, exposing one pert, pink nipple. A moonbeam streaming through the treetops appeared to suckle it.

It was her smile, though, that made him grip the log to keep from falling off. The provocative tilt of her lips plowed through his heart.

She tossed the hank of hair over her shoulder.

With one hand resting on the curve of her waist, she arched a brow. Her figure was firm and trim. Delicate lines, silver in the moonlight, etched her belly. The fine tracings were a testament of her motherhood and, as he saw it, a badge of honor and courage. In a moment, after he'd finished indulging in the sight of her naked body, he intended to kiss each pretty thread.

"I want to see you, too, Reeve. Take off your clothes."

Now would be the time to spring. He shed his trimmings faster than he knew he could.

He scooped her up, feeling the slide of her smooth bottom against the hair of his forearms. He glanced about, searching for a private spot. He was happy to note that this far from the house and this late at night, they could lie open in the moonlight and it would be private.

He carried her to the tall grass because it resembled feathers bending in the breeze. He'd never lain naked in tall grass before. The thought of it made his shaft beat in time with his heart.

"I love you, Melody Irene," he whispered. He shifted her so that her legs straddled his middle. "I always will."

"I love you, too, Reeve." She wrapped both arms about his neck and squeezed tight. He felt her lips smile against his neck. Against his belly, her core felt as hot as a live coal. "I want you to make love to me tonight, but…I'm not sure.

"I reckon, given where you are sitting, not wearing a stitch, that you're pretty sure."

"It's just that you're a US marshal, appointed by the president himself." There was no mistaking the tease in her voice. "Making love without the blessing of the vows, well, it might compromise you."

Once again, he felt the twitch of her lips against his neck.

"I reckon that's true." He cupped her bottom cheeks in his hands, squeezed and stroked them. He discovered a pair of dimples and circled them with his thumbs. He lowered Melody and himself down to the moist earth. The long grass tickled his shoulders as he knelt down. "But there's all kinds of laws, darlin'. There's the ones that men make, to keep things orderly and within bounds."

He drew his hands over the curve of her bottom until his fingers found her feminine crease. He fondled the warmth, exploring her moist, satin-like flesh.

"Then," he said, his breath coming short and hard,

"there's the laws of nature that compel us to do things that are wild and out-of-bounds. Which laws do you reckon we ought to observe?"

Even the frog, whose eyes blinked at her from between blades of grass, would know that there was no decision to be made, not when Reeve touched her that way.

How, she couldn't help but wonder, could a man with such big, powerful hands touch her skin so gently?

She wanted to weep with the beauty and tenderness of it. Reeve would have no way of knowing that she had never been touched tenderly in that spot. That she had been afraid each and every time that Ram was in the mood to have her.

Well, his ghost had no place in this moment. She pushed his memory aside, relieved that it was easier to do than she would have guessed.

"I want to be out-of-bounds with you, Reeve. Right here in the grass. You already have my heart. I want you to take my body and make me your wife."

His thighs, firm and dusted with coarse hair, shifted beneath her. His arms crept up her back. One large, capable hand cradled her head when he lowered her onto the bed of grass.

Looking up, she watched the tall, green blades bend in the breeze, reaching up as though they were trying to touch the moon. Down here, the ground smelled damp and felt cool against her back.

Reeve loomed over her, his knees between her thighs, his hands bracing the earth on either side of her head. His shadow, blocking the moonlight, covered her. His dim image aroused her.

Very slowly he bent his elbows, levering down on his arms. He dipped his head and covered her nipple with his mouth, suckling it until she moaned. She cupped his head in her hands, twined her fingers into his hair. She arched her back, wanting more of his mouth and his tongue.

He nudged her thighs apart and she lifted her hips. Rough fingertips slid over her most sensitive flesh. Circling and caressing, he dipped two fingers inside her.

If he didn't take her in the next second, she might… She didn't know exactly what; it was hard to settle on a coherent thought except that she wanted him, inside her, filling her and claiming her.

He withdrew his fingers. That firm yet velvet part of him nudged her. In a single thrust, he was inside her.

The world came down to this one truth: the joining of bodies also bound souls. The sounds of frogs and crickets dimmed, the smell of the river faded and all she knew was the scent of Reeve, the rasp of his breath and the fullness of him moving within her.

She wriggled against him because she was helpless not to. He answered with a growl and a thrust. They arched together; one thrust, one pulse, one new life.

No spoken vows could be more binding.

Moments later, with her head cradled against his chest, with the sounds of the world settling back into place, she listened to the even pace of his breathing and felt his heartbeat under her fingertips.

"Reeve," she whispered, "there is one very big rule we did break."

"I don't care, but what is it?"

"You aren't supposed to see your bride on the day of the wedding."

He lifted up on his elbow, keeping her head cradled in the crook of his arm.

He looked her over, his fingers trailing the path of his gaze.

"I reckon the sentence for that infraction is life. I'm ready to pay for my crime."

He grinned at her, then made love to her all over again.

If Melody stood quietly before her bedroom mirror, letting her breathing and her heartbeat ebb, if she allowed everyone and everything to fade, she could feel her mother standing beside her.

By looking with the eyes of her spirit, Melody could see her mother smiling over her shoulder, touching her hair then her veil. Mama seemed as real as Libby or Mildred.

"I've never seen anyone so lovely as you," Libby said with a hug.

Her mother's image vanished, but the echo of her love lingered. "This time last year, who would have dreamed we'd be here now?"

Certainly not Melody. A year ago she believed her life would sputter out in a puff of Badlands dust.

"I wish that Cousin Colt could be here. Granny Rose and Great-Aunt Tillie, too. You'd love them, Mildred—" Libby adjusted the old lace veil over Melody's shoulders "—even though they used to be outlaws."

"Probably because they used to be outlaws." Mildred stooped to arrange the hem of the bridal gown. "The stories they must have to tell! I hope to meet them someday."

A hot breeze stirred the curtain, bringing with it the chime of church bells and a peal of distant thunder. It was all she could do to not pick up her skirts and run the three blocks to her wedding.

"It's time to go." Mildred stood up and gave her a hug.

"I only hope Joe doesn't expire before he does his part. He's that nervous about escorting you down the aisle," Libby said.

Melody laughed. Poor Joe had skipped breakfast and been fidgety all morning. An hour ago, dressed up in his new suit, the green tinge about his lips had been evident.

Downstairs, a light knock rapped on the front door.

"I'll see to it," Mildred volunteered, then dashed out of the bedroom. Her footsteps tripped lightly down the stairs.

"I'm sure that Melody has not got the time or the inclination to see you at the present." Mildred's muffled voice drifted up from below.

"I imagine that's so, and I did tell her young man that I was the last person who should deliver his message."

It was the truth. Melody had no desire to speak with Dixie on this of all days, but what message could Reeve have possibly given her? What could be so important that he would send that woman?

Dixie was not on the guest list, possibly the only person in town who had been left off, so why would she have been anywhere close enough for Reeve to give her a message?

"It's all right," Melody called, coming down the stairs and trying to ignore Libby's urgent warning about cats and curiosity.

"Reeve gave you a message?" The notion that this was highly unlikely must have been evident in her tone because behind her smile, Dixie clearly bristled.

"Who was left to do it? Everyone else in Cottonwood Grove is already seated in the pews, watching for your arrival." Dixie reached a hand toward her, palm up. "I understand, truly I do. I respect the circumstances that keep me from the happy event. But in the spirit of peace and the joy of this day, I did agree to carry your groom's message."

The feline inside her was fairly caterwauling, her curiosity was that great.

"Is something wrong?"

"And what could be, on this of all days? It's just that he's planning something special. A surprise. Without the girls, Mr. Prentis won't be able to pull it off."

"This is the first we have heard of it." Mildred glanced at Libby, who nodded her agreement.

"I suppose he must have been worried that in your excitement, you might let on to something." Dixie, her hand still outstretched, caught Melody's. Her touch was cool but not threatening. "You girls run along and the marshal will tell you all the details. I'll walk our little bride to church. We'll be right behind you."

"I don't like it, Mellie," Libby whispered, taking a step closer to her.

"No need to worry, child." Dixie flashed a practiced

smile, the one that had probably earned her living. "I have some things to say to Melody, most of them apologizing, and I'd appreciate a few private moments."

"It's all right," Melody said to the girls, freeing her hand from Dixie's. "I'll see you in a few moments."

It was a damned humiliation, hunkering down in a bush beside the parlor window and peeking through the leaves while his wife prepared to marry another man. He deserved better than this.

She'd put on airs since the Broken Brand. What gave her call to pose this way and that in her fancy gown, as if she was some sort of queen?

He'd married her wearing what she had on when he'd taken her from her home. Even with a few rips and stains, it had been plenty good enough for the occasion. All she'd ever needed was him. He looked finer than she did decked out in her geegaws, anyway.

He brushed a wave of pomade-slicked hair from his temple with the palm of his hand. He smelled good. He wore a suit that had belonged to a former client of the whore's.

Hattie needed to take a good long look at the fine figure of a man she was within moments of betraying. Just because the marshal wore a badge did not make him better than anyone else. Ram had lost count of the number of women he'd bedded. He reckoned that the marshal could count his conquests on a thumb and a finger.

The front door closed. He heard the girls who had been inside hurry down the street.

The devil give her credit, Dixie had played her part

well. That didn't mean he'd give her his wife's house as he'd promised, though.

The more he looked at the place, the more he liked it. He might not be able to live here, given his criminal roots, but it would fetch a goodly price. Maybe enough to buy him another spread like the Broken Brand, where he and his cousins could live in the way they were accustomed to. Raise his boys to rob a train or pick a pocket. Teach them the Travers way of things.

"Let's be on our way." Hattie's voice drifted out of the open window. He watched from his hidey-hole while Hattie touched the whore's elbow. "Dixie, if it is truly peace that you want between us, I'm willing to try. I'd like it if you stayed for the wedding."

Dixie laughed, low and sultry in her throat. Peace, he knew, was the very last thing the harpy wanted.

What she wanted was the house. With all her experience with men she ought to have recognized that he and his cousins were liars. She must figure that since she had, on various nights, shared a bed with each of them, she had cast her snare.

He looked forward to seeing the expression on her face when she discovered that she had been duped. She was, after all, just another fool to be deceived.

Dixie snagged Hattie's arm. Judging by the veins he saw popping out on her hand, she was holding on with force.

Hattie looked surprised. But just wait, the real surprise was about to spring upon her. It was a well-laid trap, if he did take pride in saying so.

"What I want, Mrs. Travers, is your house."

He scrambled from the bush then dashed toward the

porch, grinning with glee. All hell was about to crash down upon his unfaithful wife.

Her comeuppance would be sweet vindication. No doubt she would shed a lot of tears. He hoped so, because it was his right to put them there, just as it was his right to remove them from her face.

Chapter Thirteen

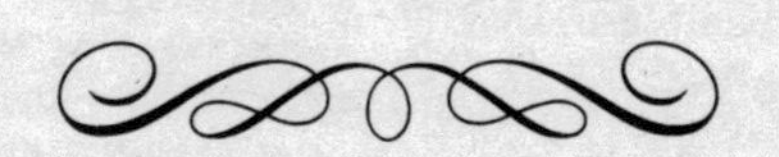

"Dixie!" Melody tried to yank herself free, but the woman's grip latched on to her arm like a pair of bony talons. "This isn't the time for—"

"Oh, this is exactly the time."

Dixie spun her about to face the front door with such force that she nearly lost her balance.

Lightning flashed. It had to have hit nearby because the thunderclap shook the house with an immediate crash.

Dixie let go of her arm to cower and cover her ears. All at once, rain poured down and a shadow filled the doorway.

"Miss me, Hattie? From the looks of you, I'd say you didn't."

The world tilted. Her stomach cramped and lights flashed at the corners of her vision.

"Ram?" To her reeling brain, her voice sounded as if it belonged to someone else.

She reached for the arm of the couch but didn't feel it under her fingertips, didn't feel the wood floor under her feet.

This was nothing more than one of her dreams—a horrid nightmare. As soon as she woke up things would be right again. She would dash through the rain to the church. Reeve would gather her up in his arms and marry her.

The ghost of Ram gripped her chin in a bruising grip. He had never managed to cause her physical pain in previous dreams.

"Reeve!" she gasped, her heart shattering.

"If you want to keep your teeth, you'll never mention that name again."

Black fog swirled in her vision, dulling the dream. She gave herself over to it and drifted down.

Dark oblivion cradled her. Time and trouble failed to exist until Dixie's voice intruded, drawing her back toward the light.

"Well, there she is, all yours." Her stepmother's voice sounded hollow, as if it came from inside a bucket. "Now get her up and out of my house."

"In due time." Ramsey's voice was far too real to be a dream. The floorboards under her cheek felt hard. The scent of rain-dampened earth filling the room dragged her fully back to reality. "But the sorry fact for you is that I've gone and changed my mind about the house. It belongs to my wife and therefore to me. You don't get it, after all."

"We had an agreement!" Dixie screeched, high and shrill. "I made sure she was alone. I get the house!"

Melody lay still, afraid to breathe. Could she pretend to be unconscious, or dead, until someone came looking for her?

"Your fault for working with a Travers." He snickered, making the breath rumble in his throat. Melody had only just been able to forget how that sound chilled her. "We aren't known for keeping our word."

"You won't get away with this."

With her eyes closed, Melody couldn't see what was happening, but she believed that only the three of them were in the parlor.

"What are you going to do about it? Call the marshal?"

"I'd do it if I weren't afraid of sharing a cell with you. This is my house now. If you want me to leave, you'll have to throw me out."

She almost felt sorry for her stepmother. Dixie had no way of knowing that Ram would take great pleasure in doing just that. He'd say she asked for it.

"Don't say you didn't ask me to." A second later Melody heard the sound of a slap against skin, a cheek, she thought. From the sound of the impact, it was Dixie doing the hitting. Next came a muffled blow, like a bunched-up fist plowing into a soft belly.

Not enough time had passed that she didn't know exactly what that last sound meant.

Dixie would flee, doubled over with just enough strength to hobble across the street and lock her door behind her. Perhaps she should have pushed up off the floor and warned Dixie, but experience had taught her that it would have made matters worse for both of them.

For a while, the only sound was rain pelting the earth outside. After a moment, Ram's boots stomped across the floor. He nudged her ribs, but not painfully.

"Playing possum, are you?"

She felt it when he sat down on the couch. Judging by the rustle of the cushions, he was close by. To her horror, the scent of damp boot leather was inches away from her nose.

Paper rustled.

"You've been unfaithful, Hattie."

She wanted to shout that she never had been; that she had believed she was a widow. Instead she lay still, afraid to breathe.

Something crinkled, like the paper being unfolded. He struck her head with it gripped in his fist.

"I have proof. Got some letters here that you never received. Dixie got them from the postmistress. Promised she'd deliver them, but here I've got them and you don't."

The boot shifted closer to her nose.

"I read them over and over while I stayed right across the street. Didn't know that, did you? Me, Jack and Dwayne been holed up over there for the better part of a week."

Her heart nearly stopped. He'd been that close to the boys and she hadn't known?

Rage flared inside her, so hot and strong that she felt the burn of it in her throat. She trembled with it. No doubt he thought she was afraid. He wouldn't guess that he'd stirred up a protective instinct so primal it made her shiver.

He dropped the letter on her head. It slid onto the floor and then lay there, fluttering with her breathing.

"I noticed we have a new boy. I reckon you planned on telling him that the marshal is his pappy?" The couch creaked. He bent down so that she felt his breath, stirring the hair near her ear.

"He's mine, Hattie. A Travers born and bred. He'll be raised to be a proper hellion."

No! No, he would not! If she had to kill Ram to keep that from happening, she would do it.

His straight and perfect nose, the one he was so vain over, was close. One sudden upward jerk of her skull and she might break it.

Ram wasn't used to defiance from her. He would not expect her to attack. An hour ago she wouldn't have expected it, either, but he was not going to corrupt her innocent boys. Not while she was alive.

A warning voice reminded her that she might not be alive for long unless she played the whipped dog.

She swung her head up, fast and hard. She heard a crunch. She rolled. She scrambled to her knees.

Blood gushed from Ram's nose. His cheek was cut where the pin holding her mother's veil in place had jabbed it.

For a second, he stared at her, stunned. In the past, she had never done anything but cower before his brutality.

With her beautiful wedding gown tangling about her knees, she crawled toward the fireplace, and the broom leaning beside it.

Ram touched the blood on his face. He stared at the red smear on his fingers. A slow, menacing grin spread across his face.

"That's how you want it, Hattie?"

He stood up from the couch. Gazing down, he stalked her as she scrambled toward the broom. He halted her by slamming his dirty boot on her skirt. After a moment of smirking, he lifted his foot, laughing out loud while she continued to crawl for the only weapon in the room.

"Our marriage ought to be a lot more interesting from now on."

He was playing with her, enjoying this game of capture and release.

"There is no marriage between us. Not any longer."

"Says you and what—"

She lunged for his feet and yanked hard. Caught off guard, Ram toppled. His weight came down hard on top of her.

"Why don't you scream, wife?"

She punched him in the jaw. He shook his head but smiled all the wider. "Guess you know it won't do any good. Not with the whole town waiting in the church."

He ripped the lace bodice of her wedding gown, from collar to arm seam. He tore the veil off her head. The pin tinkled onto the floor and rolled beyond her grasp.

The broom handle was still a foot away. She dug her heels into the floor and pushed. It wasn't easy, not with Ram straddling her hips and taking great delight in ripping the shoulder of her dress while at the same time pawing up the ruffled hem.

"I'm going to put another baby in your belly, Hattie. You'll be the proud mama of an outlaw gang. Bring the Travers back good and proper."

The broom was only six inches from her flexing fingers but it might as well have been a mile. She had no choice but to keep reaching for it.

"You aimin' to sweep the floor?"

"I'm aimin' to be a widow again."

His deep, throaty laugh made her struggle not to cringe, to close her eyes and weep.

"We'll be married for a very long time. Might just as well relax and get used to it. No, never mind. I like you scared."

He snatched the broom and tossed it behind him.

"I'm not scared, Ram." Well, she was. She was terrified, but wasn't about to admit it. "I will fight you."

She grabbed his shirt and drew him down to her. To her surprise he lowered his bloodied face. She boxed both of his ears, smart and hard.

He bellowed. He balled his fist, then took a swing for her mouth. Abruptly, his eyes went blank and he pitched sideways.

Where her husband's face had leered at her a second before, James's face appeared. He brandished the broom handle in both of his fists while he kicked Ram off her.

Ram lay face up on the floor, unconscious with his eyes open.

James knelt to help her rise. She held tight to him.

A bloody welt swelled on Ram's temple, but he wasn't dead.

"Are you hurt, Melody?"

James backed her toward the door. He braced one hand about her waist. His other hand gripped the broom handle, white-knuckled.

Outside, warm rain pelted her head. It streaked down her cheeks and into the corners of her mouth. It washed away a smear of Ram's blood from her wrist.

"Who was that man? Do you know him, Melody?"

She nodded her head. She wanted to sob against her friend's shoulder, but she wouldn't give Ram those tears.

Reeve stood beside the preacher. A pinprick of worry tried to deflate his joy. His bride ought to be standing beside him by now, radiant and eager to finish the union they had begun last night.

The piano player finished a tune, then glanced at him, eyebrow arched. With a nod, he asked her to continue playing.

It was getting harder by the minute to shake the feeling that something wasn't right. Five minutes ago he and Hyrum had exchanged a glance, and he'd been uneasy ever since.

Evidently, Dixie had lied about some surprise so that she would be the one to walk Melody to church. As odd as that was, it didn't seem like a reason for Melody to be so late.

A while ago, James had volunteered to go out into the storm and have a look. By now he'd been gone long enough to have made it to the house and back twice.

Rain, driven by a sudden gust of wind, slammed against the tall church windows. Wedding guests seated on the pews turned their heads expectantly toward the double doors at the back of the sanctuary.

Over the past fifteen minutes, every slamming shutter or groaning piece of timber had brought the guests' glances toward the place where Melody should be making her appearance.

If she didn't step through those doors in another

minute, he would go himself and discover what the delay was.

He didn't reckon it was the weather keeping her from her vows. He didn't think it and neither did Libby or Mildred. By their account, his bride was dressed in his mother's gown, pretty as a flower and eager to be wed.

The girls had reported that Dixie appeared repentant of her past mistakes.

But lawmen had a sense about these things, a feeling when there was wrongness in the air. The fact that Hyrum's gaze returned to him for a second time, ripe with that suspicion, made him nervous.

He nodded and Hyrum stood up from his seat in the front pew. Reeve took a few steps toward the back doors, Hyrum at his side.

A second later the doors creaked, then swung wide-open. Heads turned.

The bride had come at last. She was soaked to the skin, her hair in disarray, and James stood behind her with his hand on her shoulder, holding the seams of her wedding gown together.

James glanced back over his shoulder. In his free hand he brandished a broom.

Reeve dashed down the aisle. He grabbed Melody and wrapped his arms tight around her.

"What's happened?" He cupped her face in his hands. With her skin pale, her eyes stood out like twin blue lakes in a field of snow.

She opened her mouth but closed it again. She swallowed hard, then shook her head, touching her throat as though trying to free the words trapped there.

A fine shiver moved through her body. He stroked

her hair and noted that her mother's veil was missing from what must have once been an elegant hairstyle. His mother's gown was ripped, as well. It sagged and bared the curve of Melody's shoulder.

The piano player stilled her fingers on the keys. Low whispers filled the sanctuary.

James pivoted, staring back out at the storm. The end of the broom was smeared with blood.

Dixie's? Not likely, but where was the woman?

"It's all right, Mellie," he whispered then drew her out of the sanctuary to a private corner of the vestibule.

He stroked her arms to try and soothe the trembling.

"I'm here. You're here. The preacher's here. Whatever has happened, we are going back through those doors and getting married."

She flung her arms about his neck, hanging on tight. She shook her head against his shoulder.

"Ram's alive."

"It won't make a difference," Reeve said, as soon as he knew she hadn't been injured. He said it not because it was true, but because it's what he wanted to be true. He knew that if he didn't pretend for a moment, he wouldn't be able to find his next breath.

"I'll get a divorce," she whispered. "We'll be together sooner than you think."

"It's just a little setback," he agreed.

She wouldn't get a divorce. She couldn't, not without running the risk of losing her children. Wicked men won custody of children over virtuous women all the time.

Joe and Hyrum stood at the doors of the vestibule,

keeping folks away. Even so, it wouldn't be long before the guests discovered that Melody was not a widow.

Already, they were crowding around James. As far as he could tell, James remained silent, indicating that they should go home.

"Mellie," he whispered in her ear, breathing in her scent, memorizing the shape of her in his arms.

In spite of what the two of them said at this moment, she must know as well as he did that things might never be the same. The life that they had dreamed of might never happen.

He wanted to find a corner and retch, but US Marshal Reeve Prentis had a job to do. Marshals always did what was required. He wondered if Mellie was right and this was who he was. Maybe it was not possible for him to find another line of work.

"I need to know what happened with Travers. I promise I'll arrest him, but you've got to tell me everything you know."

"I know that I was about to wed the most wonderful man and now..." A single sob shook her small frame. "It's the devil I'm married to."

"That doesn't mean you have to allow him back into your life."

"I doubt that Ram will care a fig about what I will or will not allow."

"Hear me, darlin'. I may not have the legal right to live with you, but that doesn't mean I will ever let Travers near you." Now that the shock was wearing off, his dander was rising. Now that the initial weakness in his bones had passed, he was ready to stand and fight. "I swear it on my badge and on my life, Mellie."

Whispers outside the vestibule grew louder. Too soon the respectability that Melody had worked so hard to achieve would be dragged, once more, through the dust of the Broken Brand.

With the wedding guests crowding closer, some wanting to offer comfort and some just wanting to know what had happened, there wasn't time to find out everything he needed to about her suddenly undead husband—the criminal.

All he could do in this moment was what needed doing. He had to let go. He had to step away from his woman and fight like hell to make sure that it wasn't forever.

She seemed to sense his thoughts because all of a sudden she clung tighter to him.

He took a long breath. "I love you, Mellie." Reluctantly, he pried her hands from about his ribs. "You know I always will."

He took a single step backward, but it felt like a long, cold mile. In a blink, Jillie was there to fill his place.

With their arms wrapped about each other, the women dashed out of the church and into the downpour. James, still gripping the broom, followed.

"Joe!" The boy hurried over. "Go along, will you? Watch for Travers?"

"Don't worry. I'll keep Mellie safe."

With that, the boy jogged out after them, his head swinging this way and that, watching for his uncle.

"It'll all come out right," Hyrum announced, coming to stand shoulder to shoulder with Reeve. "Won't take long between the two of us to bring that no-good in. Everything will come around the way it ought to, son."

The only thing to do was nod, but in this moment, it didn't seem as if anything would ever be right again.

Chapter Fourteen

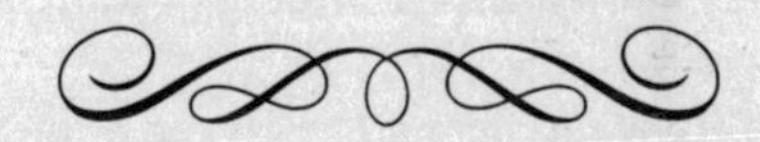

"It's been four days," Mildred declared, peering out the window at the bright summer morning. "I'd like to weed the garden."

Melody looked up from her task of scrubbing the floor. She supposed the blood from Ram's nose would fade with time, but it was an ugly stain on her house and she wanted it gone this moment.

"Until Reeve says my uncles are in jail, we'd best let the weeds be." Libby closed the book she was reading with a snap. "Doesn't matter that they seem to have gone, those Traverses are a sneaky bunch."

"Reeve has asked us to stay inside until it's safe," Melody agreed, listening to Pansy and Flynn playing upstairs. The children were beginning to show the effects of being housebound. Little ones needed fresh air and sunshine.

And didn't they all? The unknown was hard enough to deal with as it was. But to be confined, even in a home that she loved, meant there was nothing to do but think. Thoughts of "what if this" or "what if that" constantly nagged at her mind.

Mildred returned to staring out the window. "On occasion, I wish that I had been born a male. Joe is four years younger than I am, and there he is out walking in the sunshine with my brother."

For the tenth time that day, Melody resisted running to the front window. Sighing and mooning after Reeve would do her no good. She would only be reminded that she was not his happy bride, but Ram's involuntary and terribly unwilling wife.

Also, if Reeve happened to glance at the window at the same time she was looking out, and if their eyes met, well no doubt she'd run outside and launch her brokenhearted self into his arms.

Thanks to James, spinning her sorry tale in the most positive light to everyone, her hard-won reputation hadn't been ruined. Libby and Joe were not ostracized. Still, one inappropriate move on her part could change that.

At this moment, the folks of Cottonwood Grove saw her as a victim, pure and simple. Unfortunately, the line between a victim and a disgraced woman was a fine one.

Even though it killed her, she would put distance between herself and Reeve. Clearly, from the formal way he had been behaving, he understood the need as well as she did.

Sadly, knowing why they had to remain apart did nothing to ease the grief. All she wanted in the world was to fall into his arms and to hear him call her *Mellie.*

But she would behave as though Reeve was just a US marshal, like any other, doing his job and protecting a family from an outlaw gang.

For the sake of those who needed her she would not fall, either into his arms or into despair.

"There's that hateful Dixie woman, peeking out from behind her curtain," Mildred observed. "I wonder who she's more afraid of, my brother or the Traverses."

"According to Hyrum and Porter, Reeve laid into her severely while he searched her house for evidence," Libby reported. She rose from the divan, then crossed the room and leaned her elbows on the windowsill beside Mildred's. "I reckon it's my uncles she ought to be scared of. Dwayne is just dim, but Ram and Jack are mean."

Which is exactly what kept Melody confined to the house when she wanted to be out. She would leave the marshaling to Reeve. She knew about living with outlaws, but he knew how to fight them.

And as much as she wanted to be the one to banish Ram from her children's lives, how would she do it? Be stronger than he was, or more devious? While she had managed to fight him off for a moment, draw his blood even, what would have happened if James had not come when he had?

Scrubbing harder at the stain, she surprised herself by smiling. She couldn't help it. Jillie now looked at her beau in a new light. He was suddenly the hero she had dreamed of, and Jillie proudly wore his engagement ring on her finger. But, and her friend had made this quite clear, there would be no wedding until after Melody married Reeve.

Her smile sagged. That, it seemed, could only happen if she were willing to divorce Ram. Men usually got custody of children. Horrible fathers, criminal ones even, had more rights to their children than the best of mothers.

Besides that, how did one even go about getting a divorce from an outlaw on the run?

Not that it mattered. Ram had made it clear that it was not a divorce he intended, but the marriage renewed and her babies as part of his gang.

Divorce would not be a way out for her.

The spot on her floor seemed as bright as ever. She scrubbed at it until her fingers grew raw.

At midnight, Reeve walked the perimeter of Dixie's property, guided only by the light of the moon.

It was probably a waste of time. He doubted that the Travers cousins would sneak back to their old hideaway. Besides, he'd laid the fear of lady justice into Dixie a few nights earlier so he didn't think she would have the courage to take the outlaws back even if she had a mind to.

It was hard to tell whom she was more angry with: him, for threatening her with legal action, or Ramsey Travers, who had backed out on his promise to give her Melody's house.

He reckoned he wouldn't mind if they tried to come back and force themselves inside. He could arrest them and be done with it.

Life would be a mountain of a lot easier that way. But tonight, he didn't know where they were. They might be holing up in the woods, or miles away, biding their time.

His gut told him that the outlaw wasn't close by.

Watching the house for approaching shadows was, at this point, a waste of time.

He crossed the road and stood at Melody's gate. The scent of pipe tobacco wafted from the dark front porch.

"You ought to get some shut-eye, Hyrum." He crossed the yard and mounted the stairs.

"As far as I can tell, the only ones able to sleep are the babies."

Reeve sat down on the top step, watching Hyrum take a draw on his pipe.

"I don't believe our criminal is here," the retired marshal declared.

"Not Ramsey, but one of them could be. Makes sense that they would leave someone watching the house, waiting for me to give up here and go after them."

"That's a possibility." Hyrum nodded and extended the pipe.

Reeve waved it away. Crickets chirruped in the brush, but neither the pipe nor the cheerful night song could settle his nerves.

As far as apprehending Travers went, he'd be damned if he went after him and just as damned if he hung around here.

"My guess is that he won't be expecting me to follow."

"Mine, too, son. He'll figure on you guarding your lady here at home."

His lady? She never would be unless he took care of Travers.

Of the things he'd worried about before the wedding, Ramsey Travers had not been one. Not in the flesh, at any rate.

"His trail will be cold by now." Maybe he should have lit out after Travers first thing, but somehow it hadn't seemed right. Leaving Melody so soon would have been wrong.

"Deputize me. I may be retired—" Hyrum leaned forward, bracing his elbows on his knees "—but I can still out-scent a bloodhound."

"I appreciate the offer, but if we both go, that leaves Melody unprotected."

"There's a risk, whatever we do. And she does have Joe. He's young, but the kid's got heart. And don't forget Jillie's young man. We'll put him on the front porch with his broom."

"I reckon there's no choice, then." He stood up, silently gazing down at Hyrum. He wasn't positive that leaving was the right thing to do, but was damn sure that staying and doing nothing would be wrong. "Is everyone in the house asleep?"

"I don't reckon they are, but go say goodbye to your gal anyway."

The sounds of the summer night drifted in through her open bedroom window. They ought to have lulled Melody to sleep, but lately, slumber eluded her.

Sitting upright in her bed, she breathed in the sweet scent of Hyrum's pipe. It wasn't sensible to leave the window cracked open on the ground floor, but the room still held the stifling heat of the day.

She had to sleep in this room because it was close to the boys. At any rate, she could not bring herself to sleep in the top-floor bedroom that was to have been hers and Reeve's.

She pictured Hyrum in the chair on the front porch. Then she imagined Reeve patrolling the house, as he did every night. She ought to feel that her children were safe, but try as she might, she could not put down the baseball bat that James had loaned her. Her fingers closed about it, tight and sweaty.

No matter how safe the men tried to make her feel, it was a fact of life that no one could hear danger in the night the way a mother could. If Ram somehow got past Reeve and Hyrum, he would not get past her.

All of a sudden, a floorboard creaked outside of her room. It might be anyone living in the house, or it might be Ram.

She slid from her bed, hoping that her nightgown didn't rustle. Since Ram's unfortunate resurrection, she did not feel comfortable sleeping in the nude.

She crossed the room, her bare feet padding silently on the floor. Taking a place beside the closed door she forced her ragged breathing to slow down, but surely her heartbeat could be heard all the way in town.

To her unease, the doorknob turned. She lifted the bat over her head as the door swung slowly open.

"Mellie?" came the whisper in the dark.

"Reeve!" She dropped the bat. It clattered onto the floor.

She jumped into his open arms as though she had been floundering in the water and he was a raft floating by. Someone might come and investigate the noise, but just now she didn't care.

"I shouldn't be here, I know," he whispered, but instead of stepping away, he drew her in tighter. "It's not proper."

"It's late, and you're in my bedroom. If you go proper on me I'll whack you with that bat. Oh, Reeve, you smell like heaven. I've missed you so much."

"I've been here all along, love."

"No, you haven't. Marshal Prentis has been here, but you've been gone."

"That's the way it has to be for now. If there's any chance for us to be together, I've got to be the marshal. I've missed you, too."

His lips lingered near her ear, then her cheek. When his breath, still holding the scent of a recent cup of coffee, passed an inch from her lips, he drew back.

"When this is over, I'm going to kiss you. I'm going to lay you down on our bed upstairs and make you mine again. Do you understand me?"

She wanted that now, needed it badly.

But in the end, nothing changed the fact that she was still a married woman, just not married to Reeve.

He took a step away. She took two.

No matter what she did to make her life better, no matter how strong she tried to be, Ramsey Travers would always be there to crush her. Yes, he might end up in prison, but that didn't mean he would be there forever. Once he served his time, what then?

She nodded her head. "Catch him, Reeve. Catch all of them."

"I've got to go." He stooped, picked up the bat and set it in her hands. "Hyrum's coming with me. It's our best shot at catching Travers."

"I know you'll get him. You were born for this."

"I was born for you. For our family."

It hurt to see him close the door behind him, knowing that she was not even his wife. If the day came that they did marry, she would face this parting time and again. But if she had learned anything in the past few days it was that being with him would be worth any cost.

Imagining her life without seeing the lift of his crooked smile, or the spark of possession in his eyes decreeing that she was his woman, was too hard. She did not want that life.

Recently, life had taught her to stand strong on her own. She wasn't blind to the challenges she would face as a marshal's wife. Given the chance, she would take him and be grateful for the times he would be at home.

"I'll be waiting, Reeve," she murmured, looking out the window while he and Hyrum strode away from the house. "I'll always be waiting."

Once again, Ramsey Travers leaned over his wife's bed and watched her sleep. It was gratifying to see that this time there were shadows under her eyes.

Beyond the bedroom window an owl hooted. The noise didn't make Hattie stir. Ramsey bumped the bed gently with his knee. She did not react, not even by a twitch of her eyelash.

Evidently, she had taken to sleeping with a baseball bat. Very nice. It lay in her limp fingers across her chest.

Gingerly, he picked it up and glanced about. On tiptoe, he made his way to her vanity and set it down between her brush and her comb.

She'd be frightened, realizing that he had been close enough to hurt her, all without her being aware.

He, the master of deceit, had gotten to her again.

With cunning, he crossed to the door, feeling a well-deserved grin spread across his face.

If only there was someone here to congratulate him on his well-executed plan. He'd been brilliant in his patience. Waiting five days to make his move had kept everyone on edge, sleepless and fatigued.

The waiting had even exhausted him. He'd figured the marshal would set out on the false trail that his cousins had left much sooner than he had. And wasn't it a bit of luck that the old marshal had gone along with Prentis?

That made one less nosy lawman sniffing out things that were none of his concern.

It was enough to make a sinner laugh out loud. He couldn't just now, but he did grin, imagining the pair of them wandering in circles while he had collected what was his and was well away in the other direction.

"See you soon, Hattie," he whispered, then eased into the hall, closing her bedroom door behind him.

His sons' room, he'd learned, was just across the way. He slid in as easily as a fly through a rip in a screen door.

Flynn wouldn't fuss; he'd be pleased to see his pappy.

And the baby? Lots of times they cried and no one paid them any mind. But just in case, there was a rag in his pocket dipped in sugar water to act as a teat.

Bending over the bed, he scooped up Flynn. The boy lay in his arms, limp in slumber.

"Took you long enough to get here, Uncle Ram," came a voice from too close behind his shoulder. "Are you taking the babies?"

"You thinking to stop me, boy?"

Joe, by the looks of it, was just roused from sleep. He rubbed his eyes.

"No, uncle, I'm thinking to go with you. Respectable life is beginning to eat at me. They make me go to school. You won't believe this, but I can't even steal a peppermint stick from the general store without Hattie getting all in a snit."

"So you say. How do I know you won't turn on me?"

"I could have already, if I had a mind."

That was probably true.

"I'll take this one. You take the baby." If he found he couldn't trust his nephew, he'd deal with the problem later.

Between now and then, he'd have to take care turning his back on the boy.

Something hit the floor with a thud, but when he spun about, Joe held Seth in his arms with the kid wrapped in a frilly blue blanket.

"I just accidentally kicked the bedstead when I bent down."

"Maybe I ought to shoot you now, just to be sure you won't do it to me first."

"Check my pockets." His nephew shrugged, shushing the baby when it stirred. "Ain't got no weapon. Wouldn't use it on you even if I wanted to. It's not the Travers way and you know that, uncle."

As far as he was concerned, the Travers way went up in smoke along with the Broken Brand. In the future, the Travers gang would be run by Ramsey Travers's rules.

"Let's go, then, kid. Just see that you never cross me."

"No, sir, I wouldn't. I aim to grow up and be just like you."

Hell, there was something he could take pride in.

This little trap he was laying for Hattie was going to be even better than he expected. One of her own had turned tail on her.

That would break her faithless heart.

"Hard to believe they had the brains to send us off in the wrong direction," Hyrum admitted. "We might as well light a cook fire."

Reeve nodded, easing off his horse then stretching the saddle aches from his body. Warm beans and coffee would be welcome after spending a hot, sweaty day on the trail.

"Don't make it too big," Reeve said while he settled the horses for the night. "Air's still as sticky as glue."

"Could be we'll get some rain."

Reeve walked to the stream, carrying a bucket. He listened to the comforting clank of tin mugs hitting each other and Hyrum whistling as he went about the chore of setting up camp.

Rain might cool things off, but it would also distort the correct track once they found it.

When he returned, a small fire warmed a pot of beans. Hyrum scooped up a mugful and handed it to Reeve along with a fork.

"Best beans I ever tasted, Hyrum." When a man was famished, nothing beat a can of warm beans with a dash of cayenne whisked in.

Hyrum nodded, accepting the compliment and taking a spot on the far side of the simmering pot.

"We'll find the trail first thing in the morning," Hyrum said, pointing his fork in Reeve's direction.

"I trust your instincts, Marshal," Reeve answered.

"There's one thing troubling me, though." Hyrum shoved some beans into his mouth and chewed. "It's three criminals we're after. As far as I can tell, we're only trailing two of them. Reckon you noticed that, too."

Reeve nodded. He'd suspected it.

Rushing water from the stream filled up the silence while they chewed their supper.

"It's most likely they split up to try and confuse us," Hyrum grumbled. "They succeeded, too. Wasted the better part of the day."

"What if they didn't do it to confuse us? What if Jack and Dwayne went out, but Ramsey stayed in Cottonwood Grove?"

"Try not to dwell on that, son. All it will do is confuse the here and now. Don't you worry. Our little gal is well watched over. That boy, Joe, he's got good sense. Courage, too. I've got a good feeling about him. With him and Porter to hand, she's safe enough."

"I hope you're right."

Hope didn't keep his insides from knotting, though. When Hyrum rinsed the mugs and filled them with coffee, he had to refuse. He was too much on edge already.

For a long time, he wrestled silently with the things going on in his mind. The thought of Travers hurting Melody had him strung tighter than a coil.

With an effort, he quashed a vision of shooting Ramsey Travers for the simple reason that he wanted to. The world would be a safer place without him in it.

"You thinking about what I think you are?" Hyrum dashed the rest of his coffee in the fire.

"Don't want to think it, but can't seem to get it out of my mind."

"It's only natural. I've dealt with the urge a time or two. Sometimes, a dead outlaw is a hell of a lot easier to bring in than a troublemaking cuss is." Hyrum stared at the fire, quiet for a long time. "After a while, when you've thought on it a bit, the urge will pass."

Reeve nodded and picked up his mug. Maybe he did need something warm and solid to hold on to, after all.

"Guess that's the difference between us and them," the old man mused.

Listening to the gentle rustlings in the night, life sounded peaceful and easy, but nothing could be more deceiving.

"I reckon so, Hyrum."

Chapter Fifteen

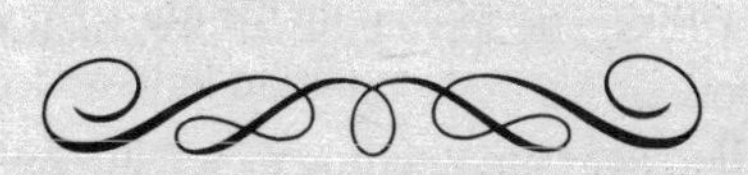

Even before she opened her eyes, Melody knew that the weather today would be as uncomfortable as it was yesterday.

She breathed in a lungful of warm, moist air and groaned. If only it would rain.

Since there was no help for it but to rise and shine, she opened her eyes.

To her surprise, dawn light streamed through the windows. *How strange.* She never overslept.

Where was Flynn? There hadn't been a morning recently when he hadn't dashed into her bedroom, scaled her tall bed then pried her eyelids open before he dashed off to do the same to the rest of the household.

Was he sick? Had he fallen, or choked on something? She sat up suddenly and swung her legs over the side of the bed.

It was then that she spotted the bat that she had fallen asleep clutching, lying between her brush and her comb.

Dread churned her stomach. It tightened her throat.

There was no time to scream or curse even if she could have.

She ran across the hall and flung open the boys' bedroom door.

Both small beds were empty.

She tore back Flynn's blankets. She felt for her son's warmth, but the bedding was cold. Turning over the cradle mattress, she gave a quiet cry, then her knees hit the floor.

She pulled her hair, needing to scream but not finding the voice. She gasped and grabbed her stomach as the awful truth settled in.

Ram had come in the night and stolen her children.

He had to have hovered over her, probably admiring himself and his gift of depravity. The bat was his message to her. No doubt he had been gloating over how close he had come, and how vulnerable she had been.

He wanted her to know he had taken the boys and that the only way she would get them back was to submit to being his wife.

And submission it would be. He would own her. She would be no more than a piece of property for him to use according to his whim. He would rule her with a heavy hand; that was the message behind the bat.

Ram's intention had been to paralyze her with fear. And she was afraid, more than she had ever been in her life.

But she wasn't paralyzed. She was furious.

Most of the time, when the Traverses kept a hostage, they sent a ransom note with details for the exchange.

No doubt, Ram would let her stew for a while before he demanded that she come to him.

"I'm on my way," she muttered, but what he wouldn't know is that she was coming after him, not to him.

She took a deep, steadying breath and willed her body to quit shaking.

She spotted something lying half under the bed. It glinted in a ray of sunshine stabbing through the window.

She leaned forward and picked it up.

It was Joe's knife. The one that Colt Travers had given him.

Wrapped loosely around the handle was a short string of yarn cut from Seth's knit blanket.

What on earth?

She nearly yelled for Joe, but didn't. The last thing she needed was to alert the rest of the house to trouble. No doubt, they would insist upon sending the law after her sons.

The law she trusted was already hunting Ram.

She trusted Reeve and Hyrum with all her heart, but they didn't even know Ram had taken the children.

Seth and Flynn needed their mother. They needed her now.

Quickly, she rose from the floor and dashed up the stairs to Joe's bedroom.

It, too, was empty. As far as she could tell, he'd left in a hurry without even wearing proper clothing. His belongings hung in his wardrobe, untouched.

That could only mean he'd gone with Ram. Had he been abducted, as well? No, she doubted that.

Clearly, he'd meant to give her a message by leaving the knife, otherwise he'd have taken it with him.

What was it he had said when he'd showed the knife

to her in the wagon coming away from the Broken Brand?

It was hard to think with so much racing through her mind at once. It seemed important to remember, though.

She stared at the knife, gripped it hard in her fist.

Oh, yes… Colt had given Joe the knife when he'd declined to leave the Broken Brand. As young as Joe was, he already had a grown man's sense of responsibility.

Joe would watch over her babies as best he could, but the truth was, he was still a child himself.

Panic urged her to run out the door, but good sense made her slow down. After all, Ram would not be expecting her to come until he sent a note and told her where to come.

Time would give her the advantage over him.

As calmly and as quietly as she could, she dressed in sensible clothing and tucked Joe's knife into her garter. She touched it underneath her skirt, checking to make sure it held secure and was within easy reach.

Next, she went to the kitchen and gathered a bit of food for when she found the boys. As soon as she borrowed Mildred's horse, she would be ready to go.

Except she didn't know where she was going.

She hoped that the blue yarn wrapped around the knife was Joe's way of telling her that he would be leaving a trail.

At last, with the horse in tow, she scanned the perimeter of the yard.

One last glance at the house reassured her that everyone remained asleep.

With her gaze on the windows, she stepped on a small stone and nearly lost her footing. When she glanced down she spotted another piece of yarn.

It was laid out straight, pointing east or west, depending upon how one saw it.

Reeve and Hyrum had gone west.

She mounted the horse.

"Come on, Junebug. We'll try east."

If he had to do it over again, Ram decided, batting at a fly that was determined to crawl up his nose, he'd have taken his wife and left the brats behind.

If he had done that, his butt wouldn't be taking abuse on a hot, jagged rock while he composed the threat to get her here. Which was all but impossible with a baby screeching and a toddler pestering him.

He jabbed the pencil between his hair and his ear when Flynn grabbed for it for the tenth time.

"Get away!" The glare that went with the command made no impression on the small grasping fingers.

Since he couldn't reach the pencil, Flynn snatched the paper lying across Ram's lap.

"If you want your mama to come, you'd better give that back, you little heathen!"

All of a sudden, the boy began to wail.

"Mama! Mama! I want my mama!" The boy opened his mouth wide but his breath seemed to be caught in his lungs. His face puckered and turned red. Still, he held on stubbornly to Ram's only sheet of paper. "Maaaaa-maaaaa!"

"Give me that or I'll make you cry about something

that hurts, boy." He raised his fist. It was high time the kid learned that some words were not idle threats.

All of sudden Joe rushed forward and scooped Flynn out of reach. Joe uncurled the paper from Flynn's fist and handed it back.

"He's only tired, uncle. He misses his mother. Little 'uns do."

Joe settled the pint-size hellion on his shoulder and patted his back. Gradually, the boy quieted from sobs to hiccups.

With any luck, the brat would fall asleep.

Not that things would be any more peaceful. The baby was still bawling its lungs out.

"Dwayne, shut the kid up!" Ram tried to refocus his attention on the threat he was composing.

"Uncle, those clouds on the horizon are getting closer. We'll need to find shelter by this afternoon."

"Shelter? Only sissies need shelter. You better toughen up if you want to be a proper Travers."

"I'm just saying so for the baby's sake."

"Maybe the shock of a good, cold downpour will finally shut it up."

"I say we dump it in the brush and go the rest of the way in peace." Jack glared at both little boys.

"You raise a hand to what's mine and I'll shoot you between the eyes."

"You just nearly hit Flynn yourself," Jack grumbled.

"That's because he's mine. I got the right to."

A man had just claim to do with his family as he saw fit. Other men did not.

"Dwayne, do something about that baby or I'll shoot you, too."

"The way I see it, Ramsey, is the little mite wouldn't be squealing if you'd thought about bringing him some food. Who kidnaps a nursing babe without bringing his mama along, or at least a goat? If your ears are ringing, it's your own fault."

"Sometimes, Dwayne, you wear at me. If I could have managed to get the mother away without a fuss, I wouldn't need the brats."

"Well, they is yours," Dwayne resettled the kid over his shoulder and stroked it along its spine. "We've passed a half a dozen goats along the way. Should have grabbed one."

"I'll fetch a goat, and even take the babies with me so they won't be a bother," Joe volunteered.

On a rock a few feet away, a lizard lay in the sun, stretched out and content-looking. All of a sudden its tongue lashed out and it caught a fly.

Joe's volunteering had been just that fast. The boy still made him uneasy. He had spent some time away from the ranch, under Hattie's questionable guidance.

For all he knew, Joe would come back with the marshal instead of a goat.

He'd tie Joe to a tree and leave him if he wasn't the only one keeping Flynn from one mischief or another.

Lightning scattered electric fingers in the distant clouds. When the storm hit it would be a big one.

Hell and damn. No matter what else went on, no matter how he tried to ignore it, the baby continued to caterwaul.

Apparently, he was going to have to send someone to steal a blamed goat.

"Dwayne, you and Jack take Sam and go fetch a goat."

"It's Seth." Joe's brows knitted in a frown. "Your son's name is Seth."

"He's a baby!" This was turning out to be the most difficult abduction he'd ever taken part in. "Who cares about his name?"

From the sour expression on his face, Joe had something to say about that, but he kept it to himself.

"Meet me and Joe at the bluffs up yonder. You recall the place?"

"We camped out there with the snakes and bugs too long to forget," Jack grumbled.

"Them cliffs make me nervous as a cat." Dwayne shivered. "Don't like those drop-offs. Ain't a bit safe for Flynn."

"Joe will see that no harm comes to him, won't you, boy?"

"Yes, sir, uncle."

Either Hattie or the goat had better get here soon. He'd bet a hard-robbed dollar that his eardrums would never recover from the day's abuse.

"What do you suppose two men, a baby and a goat are doing sitting beside the road with a soaker coming on?" Reeve arched a brow at Hyrum.

Grinning, Hyrum stood up in his stirrups, gazing down the hill at the road.

"I'd bet my retirement that's our Seth." Hyrum took off his Stetson, then wiped the sweat from his brow with his sleeve. "Wonder where the others are."

"We've got plenty of brush cover, and they won't

hear us with the baby crying. It shouldn't be hard to find something out before we arrest them."

Reeve dismounted his horse. Hyrum followed him, down on his knees and into the brush.

Fragrant leaves slapped Reeve's face. Scratchy twigs pulled at his hat so he took it off and crawled with it held between his teeth.

Overhead, thunder rumbled. He hoped there was still time to get Seth to shelter.

"Now that we went to the trouble to steal the goat, what good is the smelly thing?" Gazing through the brush, Reeve watched the rougher-looking of the men glare at the brown-and-white creature while it nibbled on his shoelace. "Still got to get the milk from the udders and into the baby."

"We need to look for a ranch that's got a baby. There's bound to be a feed bottle," said the outlaw who held Seth.

"That'll take time, Dwayne, given that you got careless and let the horses loose. If we don't get back to camp soon, Ramsey's going to have our heads."

"I reckon he's stewing already, but I don't cherish the idea of going back to those cliffs. It's a long fall down to the river."

"I say we put the kid on someone's porch and hightail it—leave Ramsey to handle his wife on his own."

"You're one coldhearted man, cousin. Look at that storm up yonder. Little fellow might drown before somebody finds him." Dwayne drew Seth closer, as though he didn't want Jack venturing too close. "Maybe if you was to cup some milk in your hand, you can drip it into the baby's mouth. Once he's fed we'll get him to his pappy. Eventually, he'll end up back with his mama, who will feed him proper."

"Then we can eat this cussed goat." Jack yanked the remainder of his shoelace out of the goat's mouth.

Reeve nodded at Hyrum, who nodded back. They stood up, guns drawn.

"Afternoon, gentlemen," Reeve said. "The pair of you are under arrest for kidnapping."

Reeve had expected some kind of resistance, but Dwayne looked at Jack and shrugged.

"Guess we's been caught, just like the rest of our kin."

"Ram's gonna be madder than a hot pistol," Jack said.

Dwayne stood up, then handed Seth over to Reeve, giving the baby a stroke on the head in passing.

"You reckon you can get us to a cell before it starts to rain, Marshal? I ain't partial to getting wet."

The wind came up suddenly, howling across the ground. To Reeve's relief, it hadn't yet begun to rain.

Gazing up at the bluffs, he suspected it was a different story there. Inky clouds with lightning bolts shivering inside them indicated that the storm was pounding down with a fury.

He knew that Hyrum would do his best to get Seth to shelter before the storm broke down here, but it would be slow going with a pair of outlaws tethered behind the horse.

For all the time they had wasted off course the day before, Cottonwood Grove was less than a day's ride away. With a bit of luck, Seth would be safe in his mother's arms not too long after dark.

Because Dwayne Travers had been eager to get out of the impending weather, he had been quick to give up his cousin's location as well as Ram's plan to lure Melody to the bluffs, where she would once again take up her duties as his wife.

That, Reeve vowed, would never happen.

After parting ways with Hyrum, it had taken only an hour of hard riding to come upon Ramsey Travers.

With thunder making a convenient hullabaloo, he was able to observe the hideout beside the streambed without the outlaw being the wiser.

According to the talkative Dwayne, Flynn and Joe were with Travers. He felt a little uneasy at not seeing them.

He drew his rifle from the saddle and pointed the muzzle toward the darkening sky. Listening hard for any echo of where the boys might be, he tied his horse to a tree limb. He walked down the steep bank, the crush of his boots muffled by the wind.

A twisting gust ripped the hat from his head and sent it tumbling toward the water where Travers knelt, scooping water to drink.

The Stetson slapped the outlaw's wrist. Startled, he fell backward, reaching for a gun that was not in his belt.

Reeve dismounted his horse. As yet he didn't feel the need to point the rifle at the outlaw, but he held it in the crook of his arm, ready.

"You Ramsey Travers?"

"Got the wrong fellow, Marshal." Clear water dripped from his fingers and dribbled down his chin.

"What have you done with the boys?" Reeve stopped beside the water, gazing down at the outlaw. It was easy to see how Melody had been deceived by him. An innocent young woman might well believe his well-formed face held only good intentions. Going by appearance alone, he looked like a man to be trusted.

"Don't know what—"

"Reeve!" Joe stepped out from behind a stand of trees, carrying Flynn asleep on his shoulder and leading a horse. "We're here, but my other uncles took Seth."

Joe tethered the horse, then carefully made his way down the bank. He had a gun tucked under his belt.

"You slimy little whelp! How'd you get my horse and my weapon?"

"You got so caught up in that threat you were writing that you weren't paying us any mind," Joe said, scowling at his uncle.

"Seth is safe with Hyrum, and your other uncles are on the way to jail."

Travers made a sound like a treed wildcat.

A blast of wind cracked a branch in a nearby tree. It crashed to the ground, bringing a few more with it.

"We were just about to ride away when I saw you, Reeve," Joe said.

"You're a damn disgrace to the Travers name, boy," Travers declared, rising slowly to his feet. His posture gave every indication that he intended to bolt.

"Guess that's why I'm going to change my name to something else."

"Prentis, if you have a mind to, Joe." Just now he couldn't think of anything that would make him more proud than adopting this boy.

"You'll still be a Travers, no matter what you call yourself," Ram sneered. He took two fast steps toward Joe and Flynn.

Reeve snagged his arm, handcuffed him then slammed him butt first beside the water.

"I ain't never been one of you," Joe declared, then he spat on the ground.

"You're under arrest, Travers," Reeve said. "Joe, I want you to ride for shelter as fast as you can. See if you can make it home to Melody."

"I don't know for sure if she'll be there," Joe said while he mounted the horse and settled Flynn between his legs. "I left her a clue, and some blue yarn to follow."

Reeve took a deep breath and sent a quick prayer that Melody hadn't found the clues. The thought of her being caught out in the storm made him nervous.

"Hurry on home, son," he said, liking the way the endearment settled into his heart. "I'll be along after I lock up this one in a jail cell."

Joe turned the horse's head and took off at a gallop.

"Get up," Reeve said, his rifle still snug in the crook of his arm. Thunder rolled across the treetops.

"Why, so you can shoot me in the back?"

"Don't tempt me."

"I reckon you're more than a little tempted."

He looked Travers hard in the eye. Behind the congenial face was an evil man, one who would take pleasure in hurting his wife. One who would sentence his sons to a life of crime.

Yes, he was more than a little tempted.

"Where's the letter you were writing?"

Travers clamped his mouth shut. He'd rather not hunt through the man's clothing for it, but it was evidence that would help convict him.

After a moment of struggle, Reeve ripped a folded sheet of paper from the outlaw's shirt pocket.

What he read made his fist shake. Suddenly he was no longer a marshal, bound by rules of law. He was a man whose woman was being threatened, a man who wanted justice of the most primitive sort.

"If you killed me you'd be free to have my wife." Travers's sneer was ugly, taunting.

"Shut your mouth, Travers," he growled before the truth of what the outlaw said had time to take root in his heart.

All at once, rain hit the tree canopy overhead, heavy and fierce. He welcomed the drenching distraction.

He forced himself to remember that he was a lawman, and therefore not allowed to make the judgment that the world would be better off without Travers in it. That everyone he loved would be safer.

"You'd be free to live the pretty life you counted on."

Water lapped at his boot toe.

"Anything could happen if you don't. I'll serve my time, then I'll come after them. I swear I will. Could be I'll escape and you'll never know when."

There was no one around. It would be his word against a dead criminal's.

"The problem is—" Travers was so caught up in

himself that he didn't appear to notice the stream growing muddy and that he was now sitting in a puddle "—you ain't like me. It would eat at you all your life, knowing you done someone in who you were honor-bound to deliver safely to a judge. Every time you took my wife you'd see my dead eyes looking up at you."

"Don't you think," he said, squatting down and staring Travers in the eye, "I'd be willing to pay that price?"

That seemed to shake the outlaw. His eyes widened and his mouth dropped open, frozen in silence.

After a few seconds, his face grew red. Anger clearly pulsed raw in his cheeks.

"You gonna shoot me in the back, Marshal—or between the eyes?"

"Don't need to do either one." He stood up. Roiling muddy water lapped his boots, ankle high. "Do you feel that rumbling in the ground?"

Travers scrambled to his knees, suddenly aware of the rising water. He glanced about, panic making his eyes bulge.

"All I have to do is walk away. The odds of you escaping a flash flood with those cuffs on aren't good."

Upstream, the sound of violent water and splitting trees grew louder.

"Unlock me, man!" Travers bolted up but his feet slipped. "It's your duty."

It was. As US Marshal Reeve Prentis, it was. But as the man who had vowed to protect Melody?

He took two strides up the bank. The water lapped up the shore behind him.

He turned and saw Travers scrambling for footing but slipping closer to the deep churning mess.

A fallen log rolled past, carried on a deadly current.

All of his problems would be solved if he simply ignored Travers's screeching and walked away.

He could do this. Take one more step to the top of the bank, mount his horse and ride away. He could do—

Hell! He raced back down the bank, sloshing through knee-deep water while he reached in his back pocket for the keys to the handcuffs. His feet stuck in the mud, and his badge felt as if it weighed a hundred pounds.

Travers, on his back now, was trying to push up the bank backward. His chin barely cleared the waves.

Reeve caught the bound wrists. He tried to insert the key, but he couldn't see beneath the muck.

Halfway up the bank a large rock jutted out of the water. With one arm looped behind the cuffs, Reeve dragged Travers up the slope toward it.

Roiling water hid the ground. He tripped over branches and turned his ankle on some unseen lump.

When he thought he was spent, that his heart and his lungs would burst, he reached the rock, wrapped his legs around it and held tight.

By luck, he got the key in the lock on the first try. The cuffs sprang open.

His prisoner flopped over and scrambled for a handhold on the rock. Slick, muddy water made it impossible.

With floodwater buffeting him side to side, Reeve

tightened his thighs around the rock. He grasped one of Travers's wrists and held on.

In the end, the slickness between their hands and the tug of the current became more of a force than either man could fight.

Travers's hand slid out of his grasp. Slipping away, he floundered, then went under. Reeve crawled up the bank, coughing out a lungful of water.

He glanced over his shoulder, saw Travers come up for air, but then get hit by a log. With all the debris riding the stream, he lost sight of him.

At last, far enough away from the flood to be safe, Reeve flopped over on his back, gasping for breath and staring up at the sky.

Lightning stabbed the top of a tree a hundred yards away. He felt the sizzle in the air.

To his right, not far away, his horse yanked on his tether.

"It's all right," he called out.

He turned over, making it to his knees, then after what seemed a very long time, his feet. He stumbled to the horse and leaned against him. "Steady now, good fella."

Had Travers survived? There was no way of knowing for certain.

Only when the storm had cleared and the casualties had been determined would he know for sure.

At the moment, he had only one person on his mind. Worry for her made him mount his horse when he wanted to sit and catch his breath.

There was a chance—more a certainty, really—that Melody had come looking for her children.

Would she have known to go to the bluffs?

He closed his eyes and prayed that she had not followed the stream.

Chapter Sixteen

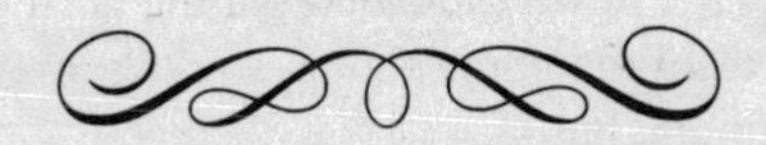

Melody felt a shiver run through the horse, but clearly Junebug had been well trained. Many horses would shy or bolt in this hazardous weather.

"Good girl. Hold steady."

Looking up at the bluffs, she watched lightning hit the earth, strike after strike.

Maybe she would be safer off the horse. She slid to the ground, feeling the weight of Joe's knife graze her thigh.

A lot of good it would do against Mother Nature in a fit of fury...

Perhaps it would be safer at the water's edge, where trees grew closer together. Given the choice between being hit by a falling tree limb or hit by lightning, she would choose the limb.

Fear shook her to the bone. Not fear of the elements, although they were terrifying, but fear for her children. She prayed that Joe had been able to convince Ram to get them to shelter.

Her husb— No! No matter his legal status, she

would never think of him that way again. But that man would know where every cave or hideout was located within a hundred miles. He'd probably used every one of them at one time or another.

Wind pummeled her skirt, ripped her hair out of its bun and lashed it in her face.

"Let's go, Junebug." She tugged on the mare's bridle to urge her down the bank, but the horse resisted.

She stroked the horse's long, smooth jaw. "I know it's frightening, but—

The ground trembled under her feet. From upstream came a crashing, roaring sound. While she watched, the pretty, clear stream turned into a muddy, violent river full of debris and destruction.

Pity anyone caught unaware, as she had nearly been.

Quickly, she mounted the mare, visualizing her babies safe with Joe in one of the caves. If she could imagine it, it could be true.

She turned the horse toward the bluffs. On the other side of the muddy torrent lightning hit a treetop.

Even from this side of the river, she saw splintered wood, actually on fire, flying through the air. She smelled it burning.

She followed the flood as it veered east.

Faintly, she heard a man's voice screaming. Standing tall in the stirrups, she looked upriver, then down.

The sound drifted closer but she didn't see anyone.

"Hello!" she called. Only the roar of rushing water answered back.

Junebug, her ears forward and alert, continued on, staying well back from the water.

Melody was sorry for the person in trouble, but the

reality was, there was nothing she could do for him. Besides, it would be foolhardy to risk her safety and therefore her children's well-being for the sake of someone she couldn't even locate.

After a moment, the voice became fainter, then she didn't hear it at all. She prayed for the poor soul's safety. It was all she could do.

She rode east for, what she guessed, a few miles, but time and distance were distorted by lashing rain.

Not far off, the land began to rise toward the cliffs. She scanned the big muddy expanse, looking for a safe place to cross.

What on earth? She pulled Junebug up short. Just ahead, a broken tree was stuck in the mud. A man lay over it, unmoving.

With any luck, she could reach him before the current sucked his teetering sanctuary back into the surge.

Twenty feet of craggy rock and broken branches lay between her and the newly tumbled shoreline. She dismounted and tied Junebug to a tree, well away from hidden debris.

Carefully, Melody picked her way over the carnage. She knelt beside the man but couldn't see his face. It was turned away from her, covered by strands of long, wet hair and a thick smear of mud.

He wasn't dead, at least. His chest rose and fell in a deep regular rhythm.

"Hello?" she said, giving his shoulder a gentle nudge. "Mister, how badly are you hurt?"

Not too gravely, she hoped. If he was, what could she do about it? Her medical knowledge was limited to kissing and bandaging Flynn's scrapes and bumps.

And she only had the one horse. How would she carry the children and an injured man to safety?

Still, she could hardly ride away and leave him. She shook his shoulder again.

"Mister?"

He whispered something, but it was difficult to hear what it was over the slap of rain on mud.

She bent her ear close to the hair hiding his mouth.

"Hattie Travers..."

He turned his face. The hair slid away, revealing an all too familiar sneer.

A striking rattler couldn't have made her jump up and away quicker.

She ought to run, fast and hard, but a creeping dread held her to the spot. If Ram had nearly drowned in the river, what had become of her babies?

He reached out and grabbed her ankle.

"Where are they?" She kicked against his grip, but for a man recently facing the grim reaper he held her with amazing tenacity. "What have you done with my sons?"

Hand over hand, he pulled himself up her leg. Only the fact that she was stone-cold furious kept her upright against the pull of his weight. Amazingly, he somehow missed touching the knife in her garter.

She shoved against him but he draped his arms over her shoulders, breathing hard against her neck.

"Where are my children?" she yelled in his ear, wriggling to be free.

"Take it easy, Hattie." He backed up a step, giving her the charming, false smile that had lured her away from home. "They're safe and sound in a cave just up yonder."

He pointed to the bluff a few hundred feet up from the water.

"Help me mount your horse and I'll take you to them."

There was a very good chance he was lying. It was what he did best, after all. She'd never know for sure, though, unless she went up there with him.

"For once in your life, you better be telling the truth." She let him pull her up behind the saddle, then she wiped her hand on her skirt. Even that brief contact of skin made her feel sullied. "How do you propose to get to the other side?"

"Simple as this." He kicked the horse hard, hollering and cursing until sweet Junebug plunged into the gullywasher.

By some miracle, the three of them emerged on the far bank uninjured.

"I hate you, Ram," she gasped, then heard him chuckle in the way that always turned her stomach.

Good sense told her to slip off the horse and run away.

But she was a mother, so she latched on to the back of Ram's shirt and resisted the urge to reach for her hidden knife.

But if she found her babies harmed, there would be no resisting.

Eternity passed, or so it seemed, before they reached the cave overlooking the river.

With two riders on her back, Junebug struggled. A time or two she nearly went down.

Ram, oblivious of the horse's valiant effort, cursed and kicked her. Melody felt deep shame that she had ever cared for him.

Finally on flat ground, Ram slid off the horse. He yanked her down after him. When she turned to race toward the cave mouth, he caught her arm.

Spinning about, she pinned him with a glare.

Nothing was quite as ugly to her as his grin. Most of the time, he did it while inflicting pain. He squeezed the tender skin of her wrist until it burned.

Her heart stuttered. "What have you done with them, Ram? Where are the boys?"

"Couldn't say for sure. Lost in the storm for all I know."

Only a truly evil person would be smiling while saying such a hideous thing about his children.

"You don't look like you even care."

He shrugged, tugging her toward him. She dug her heels into the mud.

"I got what I want right here, Hattie. But don't fret. I'll get some more brats in you."

"I hate you, Ramsey," she said again, and so coolly that it surprised her.

"That's neither here nor there, Mrs. Travers. You belong to me. Whether my property hates me or not makes no never mind to me."

He dragged her to the cave entrance and backed her up against the rock wall.

Grabbing her hair he yanked her face up. Hot, moist breath puffed at her.

"I won't kiss you," she murmured, trying to turn away.

"Sure as hell wasn't aiming for a kiss. Why would I waste such a tender sentiment on an adulteress?" He chuckled low in his chest. "You should have guessed I wasn't dead before you put on that pretty little wedding gown."

He slapped her face lightly, then he gripped her elbows, bruising them in his fingers.

"Who do you think you are, trying to live happily ever after? But then, you always did figure you were better than any of the rest of us."

"Let me go, Ram. We've got to find the children."

"What about your marshal? Don't you want to know about him?"

"You've seen Reeve?" Hope surged inside her, but she tried not to let Ram see it.

If Reeve had been near the children, he would have taken them to safety.

"Right up close. Close as we are now." His eyes narrowed and he pinched her chin between his fingers so that she had nowhere to look but into his cold glare. "Saw him drown, right before my eyes. He begged me to help him. I reckon I could have saved him, but why would I? I watched him slide away into the flood, crying and choking."

He watched her eyes closely, clearly waiting for them to well up with tears. In the past, that was something he had taken delight in.

Well, she would not cry today. This time, she would not let him lick the tears from her cheeks.

"Give 'em up to me, Hattie. I'll have them one way or another."

"I will not." It was astonishing that her voice sounded smooth, confident even, when her insides quaked.

"I drowned the baby. He was a bawler and not worth the trouble, and I made the marshal watch."

"Did you come out of your mama's womb telling lies, Ram?"

"Gimme one little salty trickle, honey. Just for old times' sake."

"I won't give you anything."

"You ain't the fun girl I married anymore. That's all right. I reckon I like you this way just fine." He let go of her chin and caressed her neck. His eyes moved to the pulse beating there, judging the degree of her fear, no doubt.

"Don't touch me." She stood still, barely breathing.

"Tell me that the marshal never did. Bet he had his paws all over you." The gentle strokes turned into scratches. She knew from experience the red marks that his fingernails would leave behind. "Can't look me in the eye, can you, wife?"

"I thought you were dead."

"Here I am in the flesh, ready to take up my husbandly duties."

"You are no longer my husband."

"Says what court of law?"

"I say so!" She kicked his shin, her facade of calmness slipping.

He grabbed her ears, bringing her nose to nose with him.

"Tell me you are sorry you tried to marry him," he growled. "Say it out loud."

"I'm not sorry. I'm only sorry you weren't dead so that I could have."

Now she'd pricked his pride. There'd be no more predatory grinning. Now his self-control would slip away.

Anger quickened his breathing. It made the tic in his jaw pulse. As so many times before, she saw her death reflected in his eyes.

This time she would not cower and beg for his mercy. This time she would fight.

He shoved her away, then paced in a circle around her. Did he notice the difference in her? Would it make him act differently?

All of a sudden, he grabbed her upper arm and dragged her to the edge of the cliff.

The ground was soggy. A clod of dirt and grass broke off and fell three hundred feet down.

"Say it or I'll shove you off."

"I'm not sorry. I'll marry Reeve one day."

"How you gonna marry a dead man, Hattie? One more chance to say it! One more!"

The soft earth shifted under them. Ram scuttled backward toward firmer ground.

She followed but he shoved her back toward the edge.

There would not be another chance for her. Whether he pushed her over the cliff right now, or he destroyed her little by little over the years, he meant to kill her.

"Say it!" he shouted. Spittle drooled from his mouth.

If this was to be her last moment, she had no intention of using it to please Ramsey Travers. Reaching under her skirt she withdrew Joe's knife.

Her hands were wet. The hilt lay slippery in her fist.

"Stand aside, Ram."

He laughed at her. He ducked his head and charged. She slashed at him but missed. In his attempt to avoid the blade he stepped wide.

This set him on soft ground again. It fell away under his feet. Not all of a sudden, but chunk by chunk, giving him the time to grasp for whatever was at hand.

The thing at hand was her skirt. He grabbed it in one fist.

Suddenly off balance, she slipped and fell belly down on the mud.

Panicked, Ram screamed. He kicked, flailing his legs in the air.

Slowly his weight dragged her backward. Digging her fingers into the earth, she scrambled for something to hold on to.

She stabbed the knife into the loose soil but it only slid with her.

Glancing back she saw Ram dangling free in the air, one fist desperately clinging to the ruffle of her skirt.

She dug her elbows in, pulling against the drag, but in the end, her strength would not be enough to keep them both from going over.

Her fingers scraped over something in the mud. It felt like a thick root. There was no tree nearby so it must be left over from one long dead.

She gripped it hard with one hand. She stabbed the knife in the earth beside it, holding on to both.

Still, it wouldn't be enough. It could only be seconds before the weight of a two-hundred-pound man dragged her completely over the cliff.

Already, her legs and hips hung over the edge.

Ram was not going to kill her this way.

Gripping the root with one hand, she plucked the knife out of the mud.

She leaned down, swiped at the fabric of her skirt. Pain seared her shoulder from the effort of holding on with one arm.

The first cut made a small rip. She cut again. Ram clawed at her skirt. He knocked the blade from her hand.

The ruffle that he clung to unraveled. Rending cotton shrieked. All at once, she was free of the drag of Ram's body.

She closed her eyes, tried to close her ears, but couldn't block Ram's screech as he descended. Suddenly there was silence.

With both hands, she clung to the root. She tried to swing her legs up to more stable ground, but the movement only caused more of the earth to crumble away.

It could only be a few moments before her strength gave out, or the root gave way with the dissolving turf.

In her last moments, she would not be like Ram, crying and wailing, kicking against the inevitable.

She closed her eyes, bringing images to her mind. Seth nursing at her breast, his quick baby smiles… Flynn laughing while she ruffled his hair… And Reeve…

Her fingers began to slip.

She thought of the sweet pressure of Reeve's lips when he kissed her, warm and full of love.

"I love you, Reeve." Let those be the last words out of her mouth. "I love you, I love you, I love—"

"Hold on to me, Mellie. Hold on tight."

All of a sudden strong hands gripped her forearms. Her chest slid across the mud. Then her thighs met solid ground.

"I love you, too." He gathered her into his arms and cradled her across his thighs. Pressing here and there, he checked her for injury. "I love you, too, Mellie."

Reeve tried to stop Melody from shivering by rubbing his hands briskly over her arms and back, but he figured the shaking was due to shock more than being wet.

Crouching, he curled over her, drawing her back against his belly in an attempt to keep the rain off.

"It's all right now. I'm here." He cupped her hands, one in each of his, to keep them still. "Breathe, steady… That's my girl."

"You aren't dead!" She wriggled about, gazing up at him. Freeing one of her hands, she touched his cheek, then his mouth.

"You aren't, either."

But it had been so close. When he'd seen her slipping and the cliff giving way, his heart had stopped, nearly fallen out of his chest. Thinking back, it had all happened in a blur. How he made it in time was something he would never figure out. He'd been sure he wouldn't.

"Ram is… I killed him."

"I know, love. I saw what happened. Don't you be

sorry over it. That was self-defense, in the eyes of the law and, I reckon, in the eyes of God."

"But I am sorry." He tried to shelter her from the storm but rain sluiced over her hair. It dripped off her nose. "Not for that, not for using the knife. What he did killed him. But I am sorry for a life gone so wrong."

"You only did what you had to do. He would have killed you."

Her quaking increased.

"He said… My babies…"

"They're safe. Seth is with Hyrum, getting close to Cottonwood Grove, I imagine. Joe has Flynn. They ought to be almost home, too."

All of a sudden she started to cry. He pressed her to his heart, rocking her back and forth.

"Let it all out." She clutched his shirt and buried her face, weeping. When she was ready, he said, "Now look at me."

She wiped her eyes on his sleeve then blinked up.

"We will have a good life," he told her. "Nothing will ever keep us apart again."

"We will be apart, sometimes. It can't be helped." She brushed her eyes again. "I'm ashamed to say so, but there were times I wondered if I could be the wife you needed. I wondered whether I had the courage for that life. But when I thought you could be dead I— I'll take whatever time I have with you and be grateful for it."

Mud streaked her left cheek and a scratch scraped her right. She was the most beautiful person he had ever seen.

"I've put away my last outlaw, Mellie." She drew

away from him with a frown. "When my term is up, I'm calling it quits."

"You can't, Reeve! You are an officer of the law. It's more than a job—it's who you are."

"It's who I have been. Who I am now is the man who is going to marry you. I'm the man who is going to raise our children."

"I won't let you do this because of me."

"I don't want that vagabond life any longer. And it is all because of you." He kissed her. "Now that I know how settling down feels, it's the life I want. When a man's got a family, his obligation and his joy is being with them."

"What if it's not enough? You've spent your whole life bringing law and order."

"How would you feel about being married to a judge?" She looked surprised. "I'd still be enforcing the law."

"I suppose you have the background for it. But would it make you happy?"

"Nearly as happy as it would make my mother and my sisters. They all agree that it's the only thing that makes sense."

"If that's what you want, I want it, too."

"Can you see me in my robe? Everyone standing up when I enter the courthouse?"

"I'll be so proud."

"I love you, Mellie."

"I love you, too."

He reached for her, wanting to carry her to the horses, but she shook her head.

"I need to walk away from here on my own. Please just walk beside me... And hold my hand."

He kissed her fingers.

"Let's go home, Mellie."

A half a mile from Cottonwood Grove, Melody spotted torches, the flames moving and shifting on the outskirts of town.

"What do you suppose is going on?" she asked, leaning against Reeve in the saddle. "Something to do with Dixie, maybe?"

"Or us," Reeve answered. The rumble of his voice rolled through her. There would never be a time when she took that for granted. After the events of today, she would live every moment fully and joyously.

She suspected that this night was shaping up to be one that would be spoken of for years to come.

The worst of the storm had passed, but a steady rain continued to fall. With a gentle patter it cleansed the mud from her hair and her clothing.

If there was one thing she needed, it was cleansing.

Thirty minutes before, they had crossed paths with Dixie on the road. What appeared to be all her worldly goods were piled high in a wagon driven by the widower Stephan Duclat.

"Everything all right here?" Reeve had asked.

Dixie told them she had taken all she could of quiet Cottonwood Grove and was on the move to somewhere more lively, with a new man.

"Right as...well, rain," Stephan had replied cheerfully.

As soon as the wagon had begun to roll away, Dixie turned on the bench.

"Just so you know, your little boys made it home safe."

Without another word, her stepmother faced the dark road ahead.

That, Melody reckoned, was her act of contrition.

"Thank you for telling me," Melody called after her. And that was her act of forgiveness.

Still, the truth was, they were relieved to be rid of each other.

"I've never seen anything like this," Melody murmured when they got close enough to town to make out a few blurry details.

James and Jillie led a crowd of folks, all wearing sleeping garments.

"They look like they've just been roused from bed." Reeve sounded surprised. "Must be the whole town by the looks of it."

Some carried torches; some shovels and rakes; and others, rifles. A few were mounted on horseback, but most were not.

The good folks of Cottonwood Grove were dead serious about something.

"Hold up there, riders!" It was Hyrum's voice. He stepped out in front with his rifle braced in the crook of his elbow. "State your business!"

"My business is to wake the preacher and marry my gal."

Murmurs spread through the crowd.

"Mellie!" Libby ran forward, dropping the broom she carried.

Joe outran her.

"Got to mean Uncle Ram is dead!" Joe looked hopefully up at her. "And you found Colt Wesson's knife?"

She slipped off the horse then hugged Joe to her. Was it her imagination or had he grown overnight?

"It saved my life."

"And cost Travers his," Reeve added.

"I'm relieved of it." Libby joined in the hug. "Now we'll all be safe."

"Looks like we aren't needed after all. Travers isn't coming back, and our Melody is home safe and sound. Let's get back to our beds."

She wasn't sure who said it, but she wanted to kiss him. Emotion welled in her chest, knowing that her town stood behind her, defying what could have been a scandal.

They had come out in the elements to make sure Ram did not come back. That must have been what had driven Dixie away, fear of Ram returning.

All at once, a big wind blew in and swept away the clouds. The town was washed in the light of a full moon and a dazzling show of stars.

"Hold up a minute. You are needed, every single one of you," Reeve declared. "You're all invited, just as you are, to a wedding."

Cheers and hurrahs rippled through the crowd.

"I'd like to marry Mellie right now if she'll have me, and if we can rouse the preacher."

"I'll have you."

No matter that she was wearing a wet, ripped dress and that her hair hung in tangles about her face. There was nothing she needed more than to have her husband hold her through the night. To turn on the mattress and have him fold her in his big, strong embrace, and to live in it forever.

"No need to rouse the preacher," the preacher exclaimed, hoisting his rake in the air. "The missus and I have been up since the call to aid went out."

Melody glanced about at everyone, feeling the reassuring weight of Reeve's hands on her shoulders. But there was still something she urgently needed to do.

"My babies," Melody said. "I need to see my babies." She was aching to hug Flynn, and knew Seth would be desperate for milk. The wedding would have to wait until she had held her babies again.

Melody turned on her heel and dashed for home.

By the time the clock in Town Circle had struck midnight, every home was empty. Residents gathered in front of the church, torches burning, the bright moon shining and the stars twinkling extra bright.

Standing with Reeve and the preacher at the top of the steps, she gazed down at folks dressed in robes, nightshirts and long johns. There had never been a more wonderful congregation.

Reeve grasped her hands. He pledged his love and his life.

In turn, Melody promised the devotion of a lifetime.

When they were finally proclaimed husband and wife, he kissed her long and fervently to the applause of all.

He gathered her up in his arms. This time she let him. Then he sprinted home, holding her close.

Gradually, the cheers of the crowd faded. Reeve's

boots hit the stairs, running up two at a time. He swept her into the bedroom then kicked the door solidly closed behind them.

Epilogue

On her first Christmas Eve as Mrs. Reeve Prentis, Melody stood at the parlor window, her nose pressed against the cold glass, watching the snow fly by. The flakes were carried by a vicious, bitter wind. Drifts piled three feet high against the sides of the homes up and down the street.

Beside her, the Christmas tree was aglow with candles. The scent of gingerbread wafted from the kitchen.

All was calm, inasmuch as a house full of people could be calm, and all was bright.

But where was Reeve? He could be anywhere within three states.

It had not been his plan to continue chasing down criminals after their marriage, but there was one particularly heartless outlaw on the loose, a killer who preyed on the young in particular.

When the assignment came, he could do nothing but accept, and she could do nothing but encourage him to go.

Her husband had promised to be home by Christmas, but considering the weather, she hoped that he had the good sense not to try.

Even though she was worried to the bone, she would not show it, not on this special day. She had taken Reeve as her husband knowing that there would sometimes be days of concern and uncertainty.

So now here she was, staring out at a blizzard as if imagining him plowing toward the house through impossible elements would actually make him appear.

Squaring her shoulders, she made herself smile. And really, there was so much to be grateful for. There was something she wanted to tell him; she was nearly bursting with the good news.

Please, God, she thought, watching the storm toss snow this way then that, *bring him home to us, safe and hale.*

She closed her eyes, listening to the busy hum of activity behind her.

Flynn laughed at something that caused Pansy to screech.

“Give that back to Pansy, you little wild man!” she heard Mildred scold, but with laughter in her voice. “Boys don’t wear bows in their hair.”

“I do wear bows in my hair!” Flynn declared. These days her little boy had a quick mind and an even quicker tongue.

“All right, then,” Mildred said. “Let’s see how pretty you look.”

Melody opened her eyes and spun away from the window. This was something she had to see.

Flynn held the frilly red satin bow against his ear, flashing Pansy a triumphant grin.

Pansy snatched it back.

"Want to bounce on the couch?" he asked her, apparently forgetting the bow entirely.

All of a sudden, Joe caught Flynn and tossed him in the air.

In a heartbeat there were more children reaching up to Joe, wanting a turn to fly. Pansy tugged on Joe's pant leg. Sarah's little girls screeched in anticipation.

Reeve's sisters now lived in Dixie's old house. He had purchased it in the fall and given it to his mother, Sarah and Delilah.

Having them here had been a greater blessing than Melody could have imagined. Not only did Reeve feel relieved to have his family under his protection, but her father had blossomed in their company.

To be precise, he had blossomed in Reeve's mother's company. She was not sure if it was the simple companionship of a female his age, or if the relationship went deeper. Whatever the case, he stood straighter and laughed more often. Truly, he looked ten years younger than he had last December.

Turning once more to the window, she gazed out. As much as she wanted Reeve here with her, she hoped that he did not risk his safety to fulfill his promise to be home for Christmas.

The front door across the road opened. Light spilled across the snow, making it glitter.

She grinned wide watching her father, shovel in hand, clearing a path toward her front door. Oh, yes, he was becoming stronger in body and spirit. No matter what, this would be a merry Christmas.

Delilah stepped outside, dressed in bright red. Mrs.

Cooper, the housekeeper, wearing holiday green, pushed Reeve's mother's chair onto the front porch. Together, they pushed her over the path that her father had cleared.

Delilah's arrival in Cottonwood Grove had been ideally timed. The schoolteacher was about to marry and leave her job, so Delilah took the position. From everything Melody had heard, the students adored her.

There was a tug on her skirt, down low.

"Mama." She glanced down.

"There's my baby." She scooped Seth up in her arms and had no sooner nuzzled his neck and cooed into his soft ear that she loved him, than Libby snatched him from her arms and twirled him away. Libby tickled him, told him that Santa Claus was coming tonight.

There was only one thing that Melody wanted from Santa. Ah well, if only Reeve's way home was as easy as hitching a ride in a magical sled.

The front door opened. Papa, Reeve's mother and Delilah blew inside along with a gust of snow.

"Our piano player is here at last!" Jillie clapped her hands.

She and James had been married for four months, and already Jillie's pregnancy was beginning to show. James could not seem to keep from proudly patting the small bulge.

Papa helped Reeve's mother get from her chair to the piano bench. She flexed her fingers, clapped her hands and then began to play.

The strains of "Hark! The Herald Angels Sing" filled the house. Everyone sang along. Hyrum's deep baritone voice and James's tenor rose in beautiful harmony.

Melody scanned the happy group gathered about the piano. For one flash of a second, she saw her own mother sitting next to Reeve's on the piano bench. She heard her mother's voice raised in joy and praise.

And why would she not? This was Mama's home, the way she had always hoped it would be, filled with laughter and love and family.

"Merry Christmas, Mama," she murmured with more joy than sadness.

The house was toasty warm because of the huge fire in the hearth and the happiness of the people gathered before it. Christmas joy wrapped them in its arms; it washed them all in rejoicing.

All except Reeve, the very man who had brought them together and made this celebration possible.

Even though she tried not to, she did worry. Was he cold, or maybe hungry? Was he sitting alone in a hotel room, thinking of them all?

She spun toward the window once again so that no one would see the sneaky tear streaking down her cheek.

Something, a shadow perhaps, shifted in the snow at the corner of the yard. She strained to see it while she dashed the tear from her cheek.

Her family sang "Silent Night." Her heart swelled with the beauty of the song and their voices while she stared hard out the window.

One second the image was there, coming slowly forward, then the next it was gone, lost in the swirling snow.

Her heart began to pump hard. She felt it thud against her ribs.

Second by second a form materialized out of the white curtain. It looked like a snowman.

A tall, broad-shouldered snowman!

She dashed out of the front door, closing it behind her. Caught up in the carol, no one inside seemed to notice.

She ran toward the front gate. The snow-covered figure came toward her at a run.

Reeve caught her up in a hug but lost his balance. They tumbled down into a snowdrift, a tangle of arms and legs locked tight about each other.

"You made it home!"

"I promised I would."

"Yes, but the storm… I thought you'd stay someplace safe."

"I didn't want you to worry."

She brushed snow from his face to better see his wonderful green eyes.

"Did you put that awful man away? If you did, it was worth the worry."

He nodded. Then he kissed her long and hard. It was funny that one could be lying in a snowbank and feel so hot. It was a wonder the snow did not melt beneath them.

"That was my last outlaw, Mellie. No more wandering from home." He kissed her again; his gloved hands skimmed her chest, then squeezed her waist. "I'll be out of a job next month."

"I have some good news." She had been holding on

to this secret for so long she thought she might burst with it.

"Is it what I hope it is?"

"Yes! It's exactly what we've been waiting for."

His hand slid from her waist to her belly.

"When?"

"They want you right away. You're going to be a judge, Reeve!"

Disappointment dimmed his smile. Melody suddenly understood. Oh, dear, his judgeship wasn't the only thing they'd been hoping for.

"That is fine news." His hand pressed her belly. "What do you say," he murmured in her ear, then kissed the ticklish spot behind it, "we sneak around to the back door, go upstairs and work on making a special Christmas blessing."

"It will happen tonight." It easily could; the timing was right. "I feel a Christmas miracle coming our way."

She brushed a dusting of white from his shoulders. "But first there's a houseful of people mad with the hope you'd come home in time."

He took her hands then lifted her from the snow. Huddled together, they leaned into the wind and walked toward the front door.

Pausing at the window, he hugged her close while they gazed at the family gathered inside.

Hyrum spotted them looking in, and all of a sudden there was a blur of bodies rushing for the front door.

"Welcome home, Reeve" was all she had time to say before he was swept inside the house on a tide of love.

* * * * *

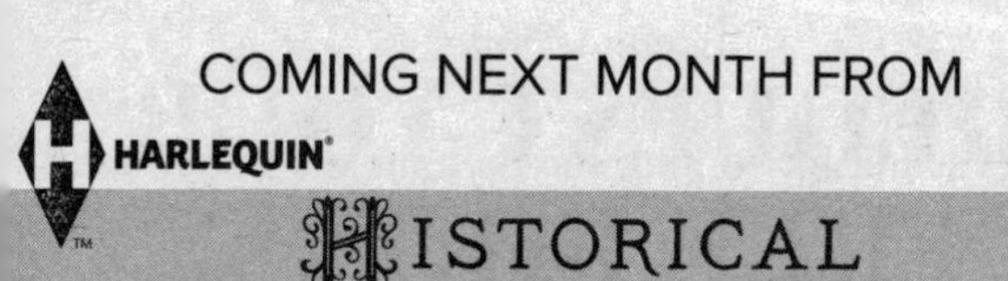
COMING NEXT MONTH FROM
HARLEQUIN®
HISTORICAL

Available December 16, 2014

THE GUNSLINGER AND THE HEIRESS
by Kathryn Albright
(Western)

Caleb Houston is shocked when heiress Hannah Lansing arrives in San Diego desperately seeking his help. Can Caleb finally convince Hannah to put her own happiness first?

PLAYING THE RAKE'S GAME
Rakes of the Caribbean
by Bronwyn Scott
(1830s)

When the devilishly handsome part-owner of Emma Ward's beloved sugar plantation arrives, she knows she's in trouble. But maybe there's a way to get Ren Dryden onside...

MARRIAGE MADE IN MONEY
The Penniless Lords
by Sophia James
(Regency)

Lord Montcliffe must marry into money to save his debt-ridden estate, but he doesn't expect to like it—or his bewitching future bride, wealthy heiress Amethyst Cameron!

BRIDE FOR A KNIGHT
The Knights' Prizes
by Margaret Moore
(Medieval)

Mavis of DeLac knows there's a softer side to her stern new husband, Sir Roland of Dunborough. Could she be the one to unlock this noble knight's buried compassion?

YOU CAN FIND MORE INFORMATION ON UPCOMING HARLEQUIN® TITLES, FREE EXCERPTS AND MORE AT WWW.HARLEQUIN.COM.

HHCNM1214

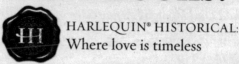

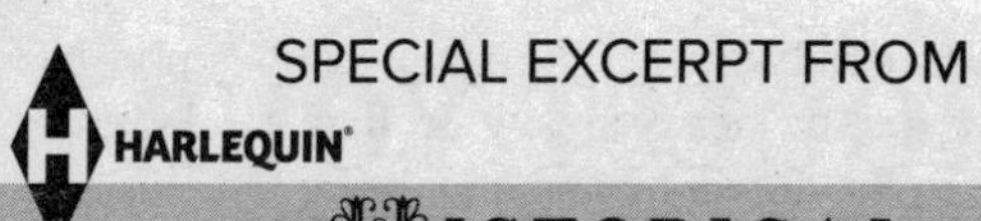
SPECIAL EXCERPT FROM
HARLEQUIN
HISTORICAL

Could Lord Montcliffe's marriage of convenience to heiress Miss Amethyst Cameron be the start of something truly precious?

Read on for a sneak preview of MARRIAGE MADE IN MONEY, the first book in Sophia James's stunning new quartet ***THE PENNILESS LORDS.***

Daniel had the sudden impression that he might have been agreeing to far more than he knew he was, but she soon went on to another topic altogether.

"Papa's insistence on a harmonious union should not be too onerous either, my lord. Nowhere in the marriage document is there any mention of how many days a year we would need to reside together. It need not be a trap."

"Are you always this forthright, Miss Cameron?"

"Yes." No qualification. She looked at him as if he had just given her the biggest compliment in the world.

"Clinical."

"Pragmatic," she returned and blushed to almost the same shade as a scarlet rug thrown across a nearby sofa.

Such vulnerability lurking among brave endeavor was strangely endearing and although he meant not to Daniel caught at her hand. He wanted to protect her from a world that would not quite know what to make of her; his world, where the cut of a cloth was as important as the name of the family and the consideration of others less fortunate in means was best left to the worry of others or to nobody at all.

HHEXP1214-1

As he had already noted, she smelled of lemon an flowers, none of the heady heavy aromas the ladies court seemed to be drawn toward and desire ignited with in him, as unexpected as it was unwanted. Abruptly h let her go.

"You must know that it is not done for a lady to vis a gentleman alone, Miss Cameron, under any circum stances."

"Oh, I am not a lady, my lord."

"You soon will be."

Again she shook her head. "I do not wish to chang Lord Montcliffe. There is just simply too much for m to do. This is why I have come to make certain that yo know…" She stopped, and he got the impression she wa trying to work out exactly how she might give him he truths.

"Know what?"

"I will marry you, my lord, and my father will in tur nullify the debts of your family. But in exchange I wis for two things."

She waited as he nodded.

"I want you to make certain no one will ever bothe my father again and I want you to promise that whe Papa leaves this world…" her voice caught "…you wi let me go."

Don't miss
MARRIAGE MADE IN MONEY by Sophia James,
available January 2015 wherever
Harlequin® Historical books and ebooks are sold.

HHEXP1214

HARLEQUIN®
A Romance FOR EVERY MOOD™

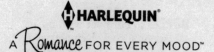